Something moved again in the bushes. The gardener's too-large hand thrust out at waist level and a red funnel poured from the snout of the blaster. Time seemed to slow, the blaster flame to jerk across the frames of a sprung movie reel. The first nerve itch of response began in Kane's arms and legs, but it could not hit the muscles in time. He could only watch. The Imperator started to turn toward the weapon. Chuddath lunged a first step on the top hinged insect legs as Pendrake's white ponytail straightened and his head jerked forward. A strong slender hand pushed against Kane's chest. He was down and rolling as the air above him zipped into the wake of the blast. He came up on all fours. Chuddath grabbed the assassin as Beth and the Imperator fell in flames.

THE IMPERATOR PLOT

THE IMPERATOR PLOT

STEVEN SPRUILL

A TOM DOHERTY ASSOCIATES BOOK

THE IMPERATOR PLOT

Copyright © 1983 by Steven G. Spruill

All rights reserved, including the right to reproduce this book or portions thereof in any form.

Reprinted by arrangement with Doubleday & Company, Inc.

A TOR Book

Published by Tom Doherty Associates
8-10 West 36 Street
New York, N.Y. 10018

Cover art by Tom Kidd

First TOR printing: June 1985

ISBN: 0-812-55488-4
CAN. ED.: 0-812-55489-2

Printed in the United States of America

To Dad with Love,
A Gift for the Giver

CHAPTER 1

Kane stood outside and listened, knowing that if he came in she would stop. He had known Tyson for almost three years now, and all he had heard of her playing were occasional snatches when he showed up unannounced. She would always stop as soon as she heard him come in or sensed him nearby. He stood very quietly now, breathing softly, balancing on the hard soles of his dress boots, afraid even to lean against the doorjamb. She had an uncannily sharp ear, which was partly why she was so good at her work, but with him it was something more. She knew when he was there. A tingling at her spine, she called it, and he would smile at the subtle flattery, the sexual connotation, but still, somehow she always knew.

She was playing Rachmaninoff, he thought. It sounded like the recording she put on occasionally, the Prelude in G Minor. She had got to the middle part, and Kane realized that this was different from the recording. He was not a musician, not even an amateur, but he could carry a tune, and he liked listening to records on the exquisite digital laser system at Tyson's Long Island estate. Now, even through the door of the practice room, he realized that Beth Tyson's technical skill was brilliant, better than the recorded version. She played the music with sensitivity bordering on pain. As he listened, she crossed that threshold, and he began to feel the music closing in, invading him, altering him. The left hand runs reached wistfully for the tolling minor chords of the right hand, reached and fell back, reached and fell back, the cycles obsessive and mournful. Kane knew that this was what Rachmaninoff had meant by the music, that Tyson had raised the composer's ghost from the grave, only that it could once again see its own end.

She was good, almost unbearably good, and Kane found that he did not want to go on listening. An image came to him through the closed door of Tyson bent over the piano, her fingers snared among the keys, pulling almost free only to be jerked back, whiteness of bone and ivory locked together in agonized pirouettes. He stepped back, wanting to escape. He had come to the door happy in a shallow, almost witless way. Happy at his walk to the concert hall through the sparkling winter night of Cerulyx. Happy though the sun would never rise during the two weeks he accompanied Tyson on her tour through the northern hemisphere of the planet. Dauntlessly happy to be with her and Pendrake, to be idle, to be living in the placid valley of now, with its womblike horizons. The sounds she was making, the perturbations of air shattered his crystal cocoon of contentment with a terrible secret. The piano bled it from her fingers with slashing teeth, the knowledge of death.

He withdrew another step, swallowing against a tumorous lump in his throat. She stopped in mid-chord. Kane pressed a thumb and forefinger against his eyelids; stars showered his darkened retinas and then relief swept him. He was glad she had not finished, as though by refusing to play it out she had gained some kind of victory over the music. When the door opened, he was the composed and dapper Elias Kane. Still, the look on her face shook him.

Her black hair stood out from her face as if blown in the stillness of the room by some spirit wind. Her face was pale and still a little stricken, and he was glad he had not walked in on her while she was playing.

She smiled wanly at him. "Sneak."

He wanted to reach for her and feel her alive and hungry against him, but the spell of her music was still too close, a shadow slipping over the formal columns as it receded down the hallway. So he put on a look of offense, drawing himself up. "I just got here."

"Liar."

"Then why didn't you stop?"

Her face grew solemn. "I should have. Sooner."

"No."

"Yes."

They stood in tableau, uncomfortable, eyes averted. It was she who reached for him. Her mouth was warm, wet and cinnamon with her gloss. He felt his own leanness, hard muscle and rib under her fingers. He pulled away first, afraid that someone would come down the hall and see them, afraid together.

He looked at his watch. "Van Kuiper is on in ten minutes."

She leaned against the doorjamb. "You look wonderful, Elias. So dashing. You ought to wear the navy whites more often."

"I feel like a birch tree."

"You look like admiral of the fleet." She cocked her head. "No, you look like a young Roman senator, tall and haughty. If you drew that cape around you like a toga . . ."

Kane held the sides of the cape out, arms spread. Tyson clapped in delight. "An eagle, a white eagle. You've got the right nose for it."

"If you're through insulting me."

"Where's Pendrake?"

"He's already in the box."

"Would you and he mind if I just stayed right here?"

"You'll miss your man's debut."

She smiled, not letting him slip the jibe past her. "You're my only man, poor dear jealous Elias."

Kane snorted.

"And I'll not miss it." She turned and reentered the practice room. Reluctantly, he followed. The piano sat in one corner, a small polished grand with the top leering open on a short prop. There were two elegant drawing room chairs, looking too rich against the chalky whiteness of the wall, the bare wood of the floor. They did not belong in the room, he realized. She'd had them brought in.

"See?" She pointed to a corner of the ceiling. A small holoscreen and a pair of speakers had been mounted on a metal shelf. A few flakes of plaster dotted the floor beneath, and Kane realized she'd had the equipment installed for her use tonight, knowing she'd not want to sit in the concert hall. It was not a new quirk, her need to escape the opening night crowds when one of her people performed.

"The director must have been pleased," Kane said.

"He pouted, but what could he do?"

"Okay." Kane slipped gratefully out of the cape, laying it across the mouth of the piano. He sat on one of the chairs.

"Hadn't you better tell Pendrake?" she said.

"He already knows, I think."

"Am I that predictable?"

Kane gave her an indulgent smile. She sat down beside him and flipped on the monitor. There was an instant change in her, a stiffening, an intake of breath as she stared at the tiny static image of stage and piano. She had blocked it out until now, he knew—her nerves, her dread of all the calamities that could befall her performer tonight. In only a few minutes Van Kuiper would enter that picture, seat himself and begin his first concert as a professional pianist. The crowd was at its last ebullient peak before the

house lights would go down. It was a sound that defied
analysis, five thousand voices at all pitches, murmuring,
laughing, chattering in a blend, a torrent of sound churning
through the gilded canyon of the great hall.

Then the house lights did fade, and spotlights reached
down, gleaming off the concert grand. The crowd noise
drained away. Van Kuiper appeared at the edge of the
stage and strode to the piano, bowed once to the applause
and sat. Beth Tyson's nails dug into Kane's arm. Well
practiced by now, Kane did not respond. She sat forward
in her chair, still clenching his wrist. Her lips were a vivid
red against the whiteness of her face. Kane eyed her
covertly. Several times she had thrown up at this moment,
this interval between the applause and the first note. There
was nothing to do then but help her forward, hold her so
that her dress stayed clean for the parties afterward. Van
Kuiper hit the keyboard, and it was on, and Beth's grip
eased on his wrist. He recognized the opening chords of
the Prelude in G Minor, the same piece Tyson had been
playing in the practice room. But not the same. It crashed
and rolled and soared, and it was as Kane remembered
from the recording. When it was over, Van Kuiper drew
enthusiastic applause. He stood and bowed several times,
his tanned handsome face composed and confident.

Beth sighed and sat back. "That's it. They love him.
He's going to be fine." Van Kuiper began to play again
and she turned the volume down to zero. Kane was not
surprised. She often tuned her performers out after the first
piece. If she said Van Kuiper was going to be fine, then he
would be fine. It would be a rich tour, a million for Van
Kuiper, 200,000 for Tyson. The booming economy of
Cerulyx would channel a tiny portion of its wealth into ten
more nights of the pianist. Another success for Elizabeth
Tyson, impresario and socialite, millionaire, confidante of
princes and viceroys, finder and shaper of talent. A woman
who, quite apart from all of that, he thought he loved, and
whom he now realized he didn't know.

"You were much better," he said.

She eyed him blankly for a moment before realizing what he meant. "You know that?"

Kane was not offended, but he was surprised. He'd expected another answer. *Oh, no, Elias. Not better than Van Kuiper. I'm just a dabbler.* Then he would try to argue her out of it. "Yes, I know that now, tonight," he replied. "I could have known it three years ago, if you'd let me."

"I'm sorry, Elias." She patted his arm, a fretful gesture, seeking more comfort than it gave. She got up and he watched her pace to the piano, smooth his cape, touching him at a safe distance. The gesture was disturbing, making him a voyeur at his own window.

"I always assumed you were embarrassed by your playing," he said. "That you didn't want me to hear you because you weren't as good as the musicians you manage. Not good enough to please yourself."

She kept her gaze on the cape. "Not embarrassed, no."

"So what is it? You don't want to cast your pearls before swine?"

She smiled, mystified. "What?"

"An old expression."

"What would pigs want with pearls?"

"Exactly."

"Oh, no, Elias. It was never that." She came back and sat next to him. He put his arm on the back of her chair before she could reach for his hand, knowing he was being perverse. Why? Because she had shut him away from a piece of herself? On the monitor, Van Kuiper was pounding through some piece, blond hair flying with jerks of his head and shoulders. Even in the silence of the dead speakers, he was entertaining.

"He is a good pianist, isn't he," Kane said.

"Yes."

"And he's also a vain fool."

"Yes, he is."

"So why is he sitting out there while you're sitting in here?"

"I'm where I want to be."

"You know what I mean. Damn it, Beth, I'm not putting him down out of jealousy or you on a pedestal out of blind devotion. You're good. You admit it. You're crazy about music. You have twice the style and flair of Van Kuiper, and the crowds would adore you."

"I don't think so."

Kane sighed. "I want to understand you."

"So it won't be blind, your . . . devotion?"

"You know that I love you."

She touched his mouth, as if rewarding it, and he caught her hand in both of his, taken aback by his own words. Had he really never said them before, not in three years? The words had power, perhaps more over him than over her. Was that why he hadn't voiced them? *I love you.*

"Yes, I do know," Beth said. He gazed at her over their three hands held up between them, and they were closer than they had ever been, even in bed.

"I love you," he said again, and grinned.

She laughed. "I know, I know."

"Even if you're not a concert pianist."

She sobered. "Elias, what did you hear out in that hall?"

"I heard Rachmaninoff."

She waited.

"And I heard you."

"What did we say together?"

Kane didn't answer. He remembered the way he'd felt, hearing her play, seeing in his mind the piano, the music devouring her.

Tyson motioned to the screen. "Van Kuiper plays the piano. He's good. It never beats him, never climbs on top. He's got it under control. When people hear him, they'll feel good afterward. They may get a stirring in their hearts, a small lump in their throats, from time to time.

But only a small lump. Mostly they'll feel good. They'll tap their feet or, if they think they're too sophisticated, they'll just hump their toes inside their shoes. They'll beat their palms together and go out into the night knowing that they took part in something fine. I look for that in all of the entertainments I manage. That's what I want for my audiences. Fun, pleasure, joy.''

"It sounds . . ."

"Banal?"

"Don't we sometimes need to be reminded of the pain, realize that we're mortal?"

"Why? Elias, *why?*"

He gazed at her and could not answer. She went over to the piano and sat down, pushed gingerly at the keys, drawing out soft, random tones. "I wish I could find something else in it," she said. "I wish I could *play* it. It brings things out of me that I want to forget. And yet I can't seem to leave it alone, not altogether. But they don't need it." She gestured at the holoscreen. "They need Van Kuiper. And I want them to have him. I want him for myself, too."

"That's why you turn the volume down."

It was her turn not to answer.

"There is other music you could play. Music without the sadness."

"Have you ever heard *Die Kunst der fuge?*" she asked. "The Art of the Fugue. Most people would say that Bach wrote happy flowing music." Tyson began to play. The music was different from the Rachmaninoff, more tightly structured, centered in the middle of the keyboard, four voices, four melodies played together in measured, interlocking cadences. Kane listened, trying to hear only the notes, the rhythms. She stopped in the middle of a phrase.

"You can go on," he said, hoping she would not.

"No, I can't. Bach was old and sick and blind. The phrase ends there. We'll never know how he would have finished it because he died, after that note and before he could write the next."

"You're only proving my point," Kane said. "You didn't have to play that. You could have done something else he wrote, something happy."

Tyson stayed bent over the keyboard, her hands fallen now to her lap. A veil of black hair hung forward, hiding her face. When she spoke, her voice sounded flat, drained, and Kane thought again of the piano bleeding her. "Yes, I could play happy music. You could put it in front of me and I could play it. If I was a performer, an entertainer like Van Kuiper, I could do it well. What I wish even more is that I could feel it, your happy music."

"You're saying you need the agony."

She turned and the hair flew angrily from her face. "No, Elias. I'm saying I need to *feel*."

And Kane saw. She had to take what music gave her, to give what it demanded from her. He'd seen an exhibit once of the art of Edvard Munch—ghastly, stark render-ings of humans in despair. Could Munch have drawn children playing in the park?

Kane walked over to her, put his hands on her shoulders. She covered his fingers with hers. "I want to be happy. Elias, will you make me happy tonight?" She said it with such appeal, such desperation, that he found himself pull-ing her up. He held her and let her hands grope up and down his back, pulling at him, as if she wanted to crawl inside.

"I'll make you happy tonight," he said, wishing too late that he had left off the last word.

But she pushed back from him, her face bright and smiling. "Good. Let's go."

"Where?"

"I don't care. Let's get something to eat at some little out-of-the-way place. I'm famished."

"The concert isn't over."

"So what?"

"The director will have apoplexy. I'm sure he wants to show you off at the party afterward. Elizabeth Tyson, most famous living impresario."

"Bleah." She stuck her tongue out and crossed her eyes and still looked beautiful to him.

He laughed. "Fine."

She jumped up from the bench and grabbed his cape, and whirled gaily out of the practice room. He paused to put the piano lid down flat. When he glanced back, the closed mouth smirked cruelly, knowingly at him.

They slipped out a back entrance of the concert hall. Snow crunched under their boots and the still air stung their nostrils. Some trick of the atmosphere pooled the city lights, neon estuaries flowing into the night. Stars winked through like lights at the bottom of a sea. Dizzied by the illusion, Kane planted each step squarely, a fly creeping along a white ceiling, with the world yawning overhead. They walked to the edge of the city, kissed among the glimmering titans of a marble quarry. They found a restaurant on the outskirts of town. It was a plain bar and grill, a walkdown leading to a long narrow room full of smoke and sizzling sounds and the smell of spiced meats. The bar ran the first half, and then a few square tables without cloths were crowded corner to corner. Brawny men and women in overalls stained red with Cerulean iron ore stared at them as they wormed past. Kane felt conspicuous in his spotless whites, but Beth swept through in front of him, nodding at the people who turned, and greeting them with such chirpy good humor that several of the patrons had to smile back at her. What could have been a stony silence broke back into the comfortable babble of people hiding out together from their troubles.

Beth seated herself in the position Kane always chose, with her back to the kitchen so she could watch everyone. Kane settled in facing her, only a little uncomfortable at having a score of rough colonists at his back. An outdoor flush lingered at the tops of Beth's cheeks though the atmosphere of the bar was almost tropical with heat and sweat. "That meat smells terrific," she said. "I wonder if it's real or tank-cloned."

"Don't ask," Kane advised, knowing it was the artful spicing she was really smelling.

"That's a good motto," she said. "Don't ask."

He leaned across and kissed her, amazed at his own impulsiveness.

"Elias!" Her knees found his under the table, one on either side, a wanton squeeze of soft flesh, and he was glad there was a table over his lap.

A squat man with one arm missing bellied up to the table. "What'll it be?"

They ordered while the man wrote laboriously on his plastic apron with a stubby grease pencil, using one thigh as his desk. Kane caught the somber look on Beth's face as the man moved off, but she smiled at him, a warning, and he bit back what he'd been about to say about how being a one-armed waiter might be better than working the mines. She was right. It seemed so clear that he wondered what streak of puritan masochism had kept him from seeing it. If man's lot was misery and death, then solace was his noblest aim. He had, he realized, always thought of Beth Tyson in the back of his mind as dealing in frivolity, playing in a world of work, a charming but sheltered woman, passionate and loving because she could afford to be. He had responded to that passion, had trailed along on her tours feeling half guilty, because there had been no work for his fledgling detective agency, no work since the plague. But he'd held a part of himself in reserve, aloof, thinking himself superior to her in his seriousness, his ascetic side trips into loneliness and pain. Now he saw that she was out on the line with her troupe of performers, her actors, her comedians, her musicians, in the capital of Imperial Earth, the great colony cities and a dozen grim backwaters every year. It took nothing to feel the night, no special sensitivity to wallow in pain, but it took something

few people had to fight back. And she paid a price. He had
felt her agony through a wall.

She was gazing at him. "I love you too," she said.

"I know." He felt the urge to say it, then, to say let's
get married, one of the old contracts with a ceremony
where we pledge to love each other forever and stay
together always. Let's wear the rings and put it out front
and promise each other. We haven't gotten tired of each
other for the first time yet, and when we do I want us to
have a promise to remember, a contract to uphold. He felt
raised high above his life. He could look down the length
of it and see that they would always be better off together,
he and Elizabeth Tyson, even at the worst of times. But
there were two weeks left on the tour, plenty of time to
think it through. There was no pressure from her, he
knew. In fact, she might say no. Who was he to think he
could have a woman like this to himself forever? Fog
closed over his clairvoyance, leaving him once again in the
single blind moment of now. It could wait. He could think
it through.

And then the bar went quiet and Beth was looking over
his shoulder. He turned and looked up into the faces of
two men. They were dressed in the tight-fitting black
uniforms of Imperial praetorians. One was about fifty,
gray haired, and the other young and obscenely muscular.
The low light of the room caught and circled the silver
embellishments of rank on the sleeve of the older man.
The patrons had turned behind the two Imperial guards and
were staring at them sullenly. A single navy lieutenant
with a beautiful woman was one thing, two troopers from
the Imperial palace on Earth quite another. Praetorians
were the Imperator's elite guard, charged with protecting
his person. They were sorely out of place on this colony
planet light years from Earth. Nevertheless, the two men
wore the habitual cool arrogance of their kind.

"Are you Elias Kane?" asked the older praetorian in a
voice not quite bored. Kane nodded, knowing that they

knew it already, that they must have followed him here. Perhaps they had watched him and Beth kissing among the slabs of marble. "We have a message for you . . . sir."

Kane accepted the cream-colored envelope and broke the crimson Imperial seal, wondering why the major had called him sir. The note was short.

To Elias Kane:

Greetings, Elias.

I would be most grateful if you and Pendrake would come to the palace at your earliest convenience. My pleasure would be redoubled at a chance to see the beautiful Elizabeth Tyson once again. These praetorians stand ready to command an Imperial ship at your bidding.

> Respectfully
>
> Gregory Amerdath
> Imperator

Beth reached across and put a hand on his wrist, and he thought fleetingly of his promise. *I will make you happy tonight.* He looked up at the major. "We just ordered dinner." The praetorian gazed down at him and said nothing. The note had said it all in a phrase no less imperative for its politeness: *at your earliest convenience.*

CHAPTER 2

"Someone wants to kill me, Elias."

They were in the garden when the Imperator said it:
Kane, Pendrake and Beth Tyson, strolling with Gregory
Amerdath and his Ornyl bodyguard. On the sides of the
path, golden shrubs pruned into the shape of lions faced
them with eyeless discretion. The animal motif was ram-
pant through the five terraced acres of garden. Blue and
copper vines brought from Centauri IV fleshed out steel
armatures fashioned in the shape of archaeopteryx. The
great effigies sat atop granite monoliths, brooding symbols
of the permanence of the palace. The mists of four water-
falls pooled in the garden's low spots and rolled glittering
against the sun-struck western wall.

Kane looked above the mists to the garden ramparts.
Eight praetorians—twice the usual number—stared down.
They paced like leashed hunt dogs, arrogant in their black
and silver hides. Only the ramparts fit with Amerdath's
words. Death did not belong in a morning perfumed in
mint and hyacinth. The sun was still soft; the palace rose
in tiers above the Garden of the Nine planets, glowing

20

where later it would pain the eye. Gregory Amerdath was lord of the palace, master of the city below, of the desert around, of Terra and the eight worlds beyond Earth's solar system. And someone wanted to kill him.

Kane glanced at Beth. She was walking a few feet away from the rest of them, her hands in the pockets of her skirt. She was looking at Amerdath, and her face had that relaxed, faraway look, as though she were planning a concert tour. But Kane could see that her hands had bunched into fists within her pockets.

"Someone besides the usual?" he said.

The Imperator gave a short mirthless laugh. "Elias, I get twenty threats a week. A drunk in New Orleans blames me for his divorce. A rich tax rebel on Beta Tenoris thinks he can jitter me for the price of a snipped-up newspaper and a postage stamp. This is different." Amerdath extracted a folded piece of stationery from his tunic. Kane accepted it by the bottom corners, where people seldom touch their writing paper. It was habit only—any fingerprints would already have been recorded by Amerdath's security people. The message was typed:

AMERDATH, THOU ART SATAN'S SWINE. I BE THE SWORD OF GOD, FORGED TO STRIKE THEE DOWN IN HIS JUDGEMENT. THE DAY IS AT HAND. *Mene Mene Tekel Upharsin.*

Tyson turned Kane's hand so that she could read the note too. Her touch gave him a moment of prescience, a sharp sense of things slipping away. He'd had so little time alone with her since the Imperial summons. Two hours after the praetorians found them, they had lifted off from the military sector of the Cerulean spaceport in a navy corvette. They'd had time to pack only a few necessities. The praetorian major had made no secret of his disapproval of even that much delay, but Kane had insisted. It had not been the clothes he would not leave without, but the suitcase itself, with its set of special tools and its false bottom. The thought that he might soon be using the tools brought a stirring of excitement. As for the false bottom, he hoped, at least in the more civilized, conscious part of his mind, that it would remain closed forever. The corvette was built for speed, with a very high drive to ship mass ratio. It was a newer version of the type Kane had piloted during his navy service. There were no private quarters. They passed the sixteen-hour trip in webfoam recliners, napping and watching the auroras of paradoxical space glow and twirl. They made planetfall outside Chronos in the Nevada desert, took the short ride to the palace, and were shown to their suite by one of Amerdath's secretaries. Then it had been Beth's hands on his shoulders, smooth forearms on his chest, her face above him, seen through the dark tunnel of her hair. He loved her, an ache in his hands and his stomach. But in this garden now there was something dark, a cold breath on his neck.

"What are those last words?" Tyson asked.

" *'Mene Mene Tekel Upharsin,'* " Kane quoted. "A phrase from the Old Testament. Belshazzar, king of Babylon around the sixth century, B.C., was throwing a party in his palace. He got drunk and started making fun of the Israelites, who'd been in captivity since they were subjugated by the Medes almost fifty years earlier. The Israelites' sacred temple vessels had been taken as part of the loot. Belshazzar committed deliberate sacrilege by showing off the vessels and drinking wine out of them. He sobered up fast when a hand appeared in the air and began writing those words on the wall."

Beth stared intently at him, waiting. Kane glanced at the unsmiling Imperator, not wanting to translate the message Amerdath must have found so offensive. "The words mean—*meant* this: 'God hath numbered thy kingdom and finished it. Thou art weighed in the balances and art found wanting. This day is thy kingdom given to another.' "

Tyson ignored the slight warning shake of his head. "Did the prophecy come true?"

"Within months the city was conquered by the Persians. Belshazzar was Babylon's last king."

Amerdath stared up at one of the monoliths, at the perched ghost of an epoch gone. He did not seem angry, but the Ornyl bodyguard stirred behind him, his bright insect head turning accusingly toward Kane. Kane sensed Pendrake drifting closer behind him. He turned and the pumpkin-colored head with its crest of white hair inclined in serene reassurance. The Cephantine's hands were clasped loosely at his back. The obsidian eyes were steady on the warrior's face. When Chuddath made no further move, Kane turned back to the Imperator. "Sir, what makes this different from the nut mail? If it wasn't too much trouble, you could probably trace the typewriter to a church basement in Oklahoma."

"It's been traced," Amerdath said.

Kane nodded as he thought it through. "So it's from here in the palace," he mused, "but not anybody's private typewriter. Probably one of those shiny new machines on display in one of the emporium-level stores. The kind window shoppers type about quick brown foxes on."

Amerdath clapped, whether sardonically or with sincere delight Kane could not tell. "You've lost none of your edge, Elias."

The praetorians on the wall, who had turned at the sound of the clapping, went back to their pacing. Kane thought about the implications. Amerdath was right to take this note seriously. It would have been bad enough had the threat come from the Imperial city of Chronos, sprawled around the perimeter of the palace mesa three hundred meters below. But the palace housed the people closest to Amerdath, his friends and those who served him. Here were quartered the elite praetorian guard, the bureaus of ImpSec and the Special Branch, the top level governmental administrators and appointees of Amerdath, the Imperial family, and the hand-picked engineers, cooks, servants and merchants who kept the palace running. Of course, the threat did not necessarily come from one of these people. Outsiders did have access to the palace. Kane considered this possibility. Most visitors were intermediate-level civil servants who lived and worked in Chronos, or the ubiquitous delegations that sought audiences with Amerdath or his chief administrators. But outsiders had to face tight security routines. Anyone who ascended the column of rock to the palace did so in one of six exposed elevators of clear plastite. All visitors were vetted in anterooms at the elevator termini. No one was admitted without official business, which was always double-checked by Amerdath's security forces. Still, the reality must be faced. Someone, whether a palace regular or an authorized visitor, had threatened the Imperator's life from within his own house.

Poised on the edge of the problem, Kane felt an embryonic stirring in his stomach, excitement tainted by guilt. He tried to suppress the feeling: It was macabre to see in the threatening note a chance for his own amusement. And there had been that other feeling, gone now, the warning twinge from the hindbrain. This situation could work itself out in a thousand ugly ways, ways short on amusement. "What steps have you taken?" he asked.

"The guard is doubled," Amerdath replied. "I saw you pick that up the minute we stepped into the garden. Commander Sabin is also putting some praetorians on plainclothes duty."

"Sabin doesn't trust the Special Branch?" Tyson asked.

Amerdath grunted sourly. "The cobra and the mongoose. There's always been bad blood between the Special Branch and the praetorians. Always will be. Each thinks itself superior in protecting me."

"What's left for the Special Branch to do, then?"

"Fowler Giacomin is fielding his own plainclothes agents," Amerdath said. "He'd never let Sabin steal his game. Special Branch is around us right now, probably stumbling over Alvar's people. Giacomin's also working his compusayer, sifting the memory files for every reli-

gious fanatic who's come to the attention of security for
any reason."

"The note is written in the colonist style of speaking,"
Tyson said. "Is that being taken into account?"

"That doesn't really tell us much," Kane said. "A lot
of religious people slip into King James English when
they're in church, or praying or talking about the Bible. It
wouldn't be unusual for a religious fanatic who's never
been off Terra to write a note like that—or someone who
wants to deflect suspicion onto the colonists."

The Imperator bent to inspect the leaves of an Alyone
wreath plant. The leaves glittered like thinly hammered
gold as a breeze sent currents through the garden. Amerdath's tunic stretched as he bent, tightening across planes
of back muscle only slightly eroded by his eighty years.
When he straightened again, his face was fatalistic. "I
have my own compusayer," he said. "It loves to compute
odds. It's got data on every assassination attempt in recorded history. At breakfast yesterday it informed me that
if Fowler Giacomin and Alvar Sabin pull out all the stops,
they'll reduce the chance of this assassin getting to me by
seventeen plus or minus ten percent. Might as well spit
into a blaster beam. Whoever typed that note knew we'd
trace it to the palace. He *wanted* me to know. He's not
going to be put off by four hundred agents and five
thousand praetorians. Chuddath, here, is probably worth
more than the lot of them put together."

Kane looked beyond Amerdath at the Ornyl bodyguard.
Up to now he'd shied away from really looking at the
alien. Realizing it made him look all the closer now.
Chuddath was a biological engine of war. The sight of him
was designed by nature to bypass reason, to intimidate the
hindbrain. The alien appeared to be a grotesque crossbreed
of man and giant insect. The carapace, the hunched and
massive upper shoulders, the second, grublike pair of vocal limbs at mid-thorax, the blank faceted eyes that saw
without looking, were all sociobiologic red flags for one of

man's most instinctive loathings. Even the normally socia-
ble Pendrake had avoided the other alien, barely acknowl-
edging his presence. The Ornyl was a born killer, but
whatever his combat skills might be, his appearance was
his greatest asset. Amerdath was correct. Chuddath was a
more potent weapon against a would-be assassin than an
army of men.

But there was one thing that Kane could not reconcile
with the alien's fierce image. It was said in the palace that
Amerdath had grown very close to Chuddath in the six
months since the warrior had been brought from his home
planet of Emprymis. The rumors had it that no human was
as close to the Imperator as Chuddath, that the two com-
muned often and at great length. Now, in the presence of
Chuddath, Kane decided that the rumors were absurd—the
alien was too repellent in speech as well as appearance.
Only once had Kane heard him speak. The pale vocal
limbs had snaked along the abdominal chitin to produce an
eerie cellolike parody of a human voice. It was not a voice
to draw Gregory Amerdath or any sane person into
conversation.

"Does he meet with your approval?" Amerdath asked
dryly. Kane realized that Amerdath was watching him,
that his reaction to Chuddath had crept into the small
muscles around his mouth. Movement behind a nearby
hedge caught Kane's eye and caused Chuddath's head to
rotate sharply and tilt, mantislike, but it was only a gardener pruning the waxy plum-colored leaves of a hedge.

"Of course," Amerdath mused, "if Chuddath is not
enough, I have the best physicians anywhere. I've set my
chief physician, Martha Reik, to work. She's developing
techniques with lab animals for treating wounds you couldn't
imagine a man surviving."

Kane was struck by the Imperator's descent into mor-
bidity. It was as if Amerdath *knew* that whoever typed the
note would try to carry out the threat and that nothing
could stop it. Kane's palms began to sweat. The air tasted

of metal, and he thought of seconds ticking down. It was absurd, a glandular misfire, tainting more rational thought.

Amerdath stopped abruptly in the path and turned to Kane. "I want you and Pendrake on this," he said. "Elias Kane, Investigations. I'll give you official police standing in the palace and Chronos. I . . . uhm . . . know about your run of bad luck at the casinos after I paid you off the last time. I thought 500,000 credits might sound good."

Kane laughed. "Run of bad luck" was a charitable way of putting it. Most of the million credit Imperial reward for solving the psychopath plague, blown away in a two-month binge. And he had deliberately avoided the games of skill, like GalTac, where he could have doubled his money. He'd thrown it away on the roulette wheels, the dice tables and the unguessable whirlings of the Kadaxed carousels. *Five hundred thousand credits? He'd do it for room and board.*

Something moved again in the bushes. The gardener's too-large hand thrust out at waist level and a red funnel poured from the snout of the blaster. Time seemed to slow, the blaster flame to jerk across the frames of a sprung movie reel. The first nerve itch of response began in Kane's arms and legs, but it could not hit the muscles in time. He could only watch. The Imperator started to turn toward the weapon. Chuddath lunged a first step on the top hinged insect legs as Pendrake's white ponytail straightened and his head jerked forward. A strong slender hand pushed against Kane's chest. He was down and rolling as the air above him zipped into the wake of the blast. He came up on all fours. Chuddath grabbed the assassin as Beth and the Imperator fell in flames. Pendrake rolled them along the ground and Kane slapped at Beth's hair until the fire was smothered. Sirens screamed on the garden ramparts. The odor of cooked meat struck Kane's solar plexus, blocking his will to breathe. Pendrake's hand steadied him at the neck as he vomited. When he'd got the spasms under control, he heard the odd snapping sound.

The Ornyl had grasped the gardener around the throat and knees and was stretching the man's body almost gently, popping the joints of spine, leg and ankle. Kane yelled and Chuddath got control of himself, easing back so that the man hung suspended by wrists and ankles like a slain deer. One of Beth's knees lay outflung on Kane's lap. He straightened it.

A woman's voice cut through the siren and the shouts of the praetorians. "Chuddath, give that man to the guard and carry the Imperator. You! Cephantine! Bring the woman."

Kane got up. The two aliens hurried to obey the woman, a tall redhead who carried a med-kit she'd not bothered to open. Pendrake lifted Beth and went after the woman, and Kane followed, weaving. He concentrated on the chore of coordinating his legs, watching his feet slap down behind the moccasined heels of the Cephantine. They crowded into the terminus of the elevator. It dropped fast, sucking Kane's stomach against his diaphragm, and he was nearly sick again. As they entered the med-section emergency room, the uninjured side of Beth's head was toward Kane, pale but whole. He began to doubt that he had seen half of her skull sliced away. Pendrake lowered her onto a biotable. Beyond her, Chuddath had already deposited the Imperator. The blackened meat of Amerdath's arms and legs sloughed in places from the bone. The chest had been caved in, the internal organs pulped. Kane remembered the shape of the weapon in the gardener's hand. It had been a shattergun—a vicious weapon that fired a percussive wave within the cone of its blast.

Amerdath's doctor pulled down spiraling tubes already infused with blood from life-support equipment above the dying Imperator's head as another physician hurried to Beth. The doctor bent over her, straightened without looking at Kane. "I'm sorry," he said. "Her brain."

Kane concentrated on the doctor's words. *Her brain her brain*. At some unheard moment Beth had stopped, had stopped playing, and the song would always be unfinished. The lines of the room wriggled and blurred. Kane walked away from the biotable and back again, his feet lost and numb below him. A circular saw descended from the ceiling over Amerdath's biotable, guided by the red-haired physician. The saw whirled into motion. It made no sound, even as it dropped through the Imperator's neck.

CHAPTER 3

There is a period when the condemned man sits strapped into the hard chair. He hears the pellet of cyanide drop into the bucket of acid. He hears it sizzling and knows the room is full of death. He holds his breath. He is still alive for those few seconds. Perhaps more alive than he has ever been.

Kane felt himself vividly to be in this room of ice-blue walls, masked and gowned mimes, stalactites of medical hardware. Beth was dead. The Imperator had just been surgically decapitated. It had happened, it was happening, it would happen forever. He would have to let it in. But not yet.

The Imperator's body was beyond reclamation. It was a blackened and oozing sack that could only poison whatever life might remain in Amerdath's head. The neck stump bled only slightly as the chief physician carefully separated head from body, and Kane realized that the saw blade must have been coated with a coagulant. The physician joined catheters dangling from the lowered equipment to the exposed veins and arteries, inserting color-coded tubes into the jugulars. Kane backed away until he was again standing beside Beth's biotable. Light glanced off the partially retracted saw, red and silver, into his eyes. An astringent smell scoured his nostrils.

"I'm sorry, but you'll have to leave now. All of you will have to leave."

Kane stared at Beth's doctor. "Not me," he said. It seemed to him that he said it right away, but the doctor had already turned from him and was making shooing motions at the Ornyl warrior.

"Get back from the table," the doctor commanded.

Chuddath's vocal arms uncoiled across his abdomen. "I will stay."

"Impossible."

Without turning from her work, the woman said, "Never mind about them. Come and help."

"I'll have to scrub."

"There's no time for that. We'll block sepsis with an antibaxin spectrum. I've got to catch these vagus and spinal nerve trunks or they'll desiccate and shrink into the neck. You finish connecting the carotid arteries. The catheters are tagged."

From somewhere Kane dredged up the woman's name: Martha Reik. Swing doors opened to admit a team of O.R. nurses and technicians. Kane became aware of Pendrake's hand on his arm. He bent to look at Beth's face, but the Cephantine pulled him back and gently turned her head to the side. The suction system of the biotable hissed to life, draining off the blood that spilled from the open skull through the grid of the table. Kane took Beth's hand, pressed it between his palms.

"Get the body out and pack it in ice," Dr. Reik said to the entering medical team. "We may need skin grafts for the neck stump, so look for unburned patches." Two men in surgical greens threw a sheet over the Imperator's body and flipped it onto its stomach, grabbing the edges of the sheet to form a sling, and carrying the body from the

room. Then it became more real, what Reik was trying to
do, because the body was gone and the head remained.
Kane felt the shock, the visual rip of it. The head was such
a familiar thing, until it no longer had a body under it.

"Doctor, if you've finished with those carotids, I need
an EEG," Reik said.

The male doctor stepped back from the table and Kane
saw that his forehead was slick. "I don't know, Martha."

Reik did not look at the other doctor, but continued with
her work. A technician lowered a light behind the lens
Reik was using to enlarge her view of the nerve cross-
sections. "More dye and more cauterol," Reik said. A
nurse drew a dangling nozzle close to the neck. Through
the lens, pinpoints stood out in greens and yellows as the
dye reacted with the stumps of severed capillaries and
nerves. "Just a bit closer with the light. Doctor, I want
you to hook up that EEG. Now."

The other doctor stared at Reik, his eyes blinking rapidly.
"No. No, I'm not going to do it. I object to this whole
procedure. If you save Amerdath, you'll be condemning
him to horrors no man has ever faced. You'll be damning
him to hell. If he keeps even a shred of sanity, he'll curse
you for making him live."

Several of the nurses and technicians straightened around
the table and eyed each other over their masks. The other
doctor waited nervously for Reik to respond. When she
said nothing, he started up again, his voice almost hysterical.
"We're physicians, not Frankensteins. I say we quit this
right now. I say . . ."

"I order you to set up the EEG," Reik said.

"And I refuse. You *were* his chief physician, but he's
dead. I say he's dead. Damn it, I *pronounce* him dead.
There's no pulse, no blood pressure. . . ."

"Have you forgotten brain death . . . *Doctor?*" Reik's
voice remained calm, heavily patient, as though she expected nothing but his ultimate obedience. She continued
threading filaments from the unit over Amerdath's head

into the open neck. Chuddath, who had remained near the head of the biotable, stepped toward the doctor. "Imperator is not dead," the alien said. "You will obey Dr. Reik."

"I'll not be dictated to by a . . . ."

"You will obey Dr. Reik." One of the massive upper arms lashed out at the doctor's head, slowing only at the last second so that the long fingers could close precisely around the man's forehead. It was a movement too fast to see, like the tensing of a grasshopper's legs in the instant before it jumps. The doctor gasped and began to claw at the armored joints of the arm.

Pendrake moved close to the other alien. "Force is not required. I am sure this man can cooperate better if he is not terrified."

Chuddath released the doctor.

"It would be best if you obey quickly," Pendrake murmured to the man. The doctor swung an EEG unit into position at the head of the table. The leads were attached and the green scope lit with a pentad of erratically dancing lines. Reik's hands stopped as she glanced up at the monitor.

"The Ornyl is right," she said.

"It's weak. It may stop at any moment, and even if it doesn't, we don't know the quality of the cortical activity. He could be a vegetable."

"He's alive."

The operation continued in silence. Kane stared at a crumb on Beth's skirt. It was from the breakfast rolls they'd eaten only hours ago, after they'd showered together and dressed. He raised the white arm to his face and smelled the scent of her, lilac soap, and his throat felt like a hot poker was being forced down it. He wanted to scream, to smash things, but he merely stood, straitjacketed by a lifetime of sanity.

"Perhaps it would be best if we leave now, Elias," Pendrake said.

Kane nodded, but Pendrake had to pull his fingers away from Beth's hand and lead him out into a waiting room.

The lounge was done in mild pastels and furnished with oversized nurturant chairs. Shunning them, Kane sat on the floor, his back against the wall. Pendrake took a chair next to Kane. The alien's eyes grew glassy and unblinking as the minutes passed. Looking at the stoic face, Kane remembered something Pendrake had said just after they had first met Elizabeth Tyson at the gambling casino in the Atlantic. *She is known as a beautiful woman, Elias, though I find her too small and entirely too skinny.* It had been funny then, but now it spoke through three years of growing friendship, unbiased by sexuality. Perhaps the alien's love had in some ways surpassed his own romantic love. Yes, and if he could pity Pendrake, perhaps the loss would be for at least a moment someone else's. Repelled by his own unblinking self-perception, Kane tried to make his mind blank. Time began to slide by in meaningless gaps. As Kane stared at the soothing blue of the opposite wall, focus began to slip away, the hard planes of wall and floor to melt into numbness. Finally the door to the waiting room opened and Dr. Reik entered. She collapsed into the chair across from Pendrake and rubbed her eyes. Kane noticed a surgical monitor bracelet, studded by indicator lights, that had not been on her wrist before.

"Mr. Kane, I am truly sorry about Elizabeth Tyson." Reik's voice was low and hoarse, as though she'd been shouting.

"You knew her?"

"Not personally. But everyone with any cultural interests must know her name. I knew of both of you. No one has forgotten what you did. I was among the Imperator's crew of medical researchers. We worked on the psychopath plague for months, as you know, without success. When you solved it, I . . . ." Her voice became a drone. Kane realized after a few minutes that she'd stopped, that she'd asked him a question.

"I'm sorry?"

"Don't be. I always babble after surgery. Can't seem

to . . ." She trailed off and for a long time she stared directly into his eyes.

"The Imperator?" Kane asked.

"Alive."

"Do you think he will recover?" Pendrake asked.

"I don't know. In the usual case, if the heart keeps pumping, if the kidneys do not fail, if there's no internal hemorrhage . . . But Amerdath's body is gone. His organs have been replaced by a set of machines. The stump of the neck is sealed with cauterol except where I tied in artificial blood vessels. The ends of the major nerves that extend through the neck have been capped and packed in anesthetic. There'll be some blood pooling where I missed capillaries, but we can drain that off. The esophagus and trachea are temporarily sealed over too, and infused with antinecrotics and amino glycoside derivatives that should combat infection. That's our biggeset worry: infection. His only immediate vital sign is the brain activity. We'll oxygenate and nutrify the blood and look after the tissues, but he's sustained a horrible shock. Physically, he can bounce back very quickly, since the only part of him that remains is uninjured. But mentally there may be nothing coherent left."

"How can such a thing be possible," Pendrake asked, "to sustain a man's head?"

"It's not been done successfully that I'm aware," Reik said, "though it has theoretically been considered possible since the late twentieth century. Cases where it might be indicated—complete body destruction in which the head is undamaged—are rare. But during the last month I've been trying to prepare for the rarer type of emergencies—the ones I couldn't handle without special preparation. I guess you know about that."

Kane focused on Reik's face. She knew why the Imperator had summoned them. Was she such a confidante of Amerdath's? He let the spark of curiosity die. Wondering was too much work. He didn't care.

"Anyway," Reik went on, "with recent medical advances in noncryogenic tissue stasis, I realized that it should be possible to sustain the Imperator's head apart from the body, and I did appropriate research with laboratory animals in case it should become necessary. . . .''

Pendrake's normal orange color turned dusky and Reik looked closely at him. "You're a Cephantine. This must be very difficult for you."

"I would prefer that we not speak about it now," the alien said softly.

"Of course. Mr. Kane, would you like something?"

Kane looked at her a moment before understanding. "Yes, I would," he said.

She rose. "Wait here. I'll get medication to help you sleep for a while."

Before she reached the door, it slid open and the Imperator's Ornyl bodyguard ducked through. For a moment he merely stood, the blank eyes staring at everything and at nothing. Martha Reik hugged her elbows as if chilled. Kane got up. The bodyguard's vocal arms began to circle, making several passes over the abdomen before bringing forth a sound like moaning wind. "Elias Kane. You will come with me."

CHAPTER 4

The palace of Gregory Amerdath was built like an immense hive. The Imperator's private chambers were in the bottom center, surrounded to the sides and above by three levels of praetorian billets. Beneath the Imperator's quarters and the rest of the palace was a two-tiered column of solid rock. Before the palace, there had been a monolith of natural stone in the desert. The engineers and laborers and machines had come and sheared this formation off at two hundred and thirty meters, making a surface so flat and smooth and level that a marble could be rolled straight across the half kilometer of it. Then they had quarried huge blocks of granite and shaped and smoothed them. These blocks had been raised on mass inversion sleds up the sides of the rock formation and fitted together like thick jigsaw puzzles stacked one upon the next. As the blocks were assembled, sound sensors were planted through the seams of each massive puzzle and across the interfaces between layers. Once the palace was built, these sensors would take up their duty as electronic sentries, warning of any attempt to dig tunnels up through the granite. When

the engineers were done shaping and stacking the rock
pieces, they had a cylinder of granite seventy meters high
on top of the sheared monolith. Then they shaved away the
slopes of natural rock below, leaving a hybrid column of
rock, perfectly round and slightly flared toward its base.
On the top of this, they built Amerdath's palace.

Twenty-five levels reached out and up from the central
Imperial chambers. The walls were dressed in polished
stone and precious metals—silver, chromium, hammered
gold, copper, onyx, marble—each sector according to its
own theme. The artists of the nine worlds crafted their
dreams and visions through every room, every hallway—
bas-reliefs, carvings, statuary, murals, dazzling chandeliers,
rich tapestries, a splendor that a year's walking through the
chambers could not discover. Even once the whole had
been seen by anyone so determined as to make the full
circuit of the palace, it could not have been comprehended.

Beneath the golds, the silvers, the paintings and the
tapestries, every wall was constructed of beta-steel alloys,
developed from colony ores in a process known only to the
Imperial engineers. The atmospheric air routes to the palace were patrolled around the clock by computer-controlled
fighter planes kept permanently aloft by mass-inversion
units. Likewise, the changing trajectories of entry from
space were continually guarded by dreadnaughts of the
Imperial navy. In the extremely unlikely event that these
defenses were breached, a direct nuclear strike could destroy the palace. It could not be taken, not from the
outside. And yet, a single shattergun had done what a
legion of attackers could not.

This thought spun in the emptiness of Kane's mind as he
followed Chuddath. He worked hard to keep up as the
alien led him down the palace's curving corridors. The
Ornyl warrior seemed to be expending little energy, walking with a smooth swinging gait dictated by his oddly-
jointed legs. Kane tried to remember where he had seen
such a manner of walking before. Part of an animated film

documentary on dinosaurs played across the screen of memory—the part showing the tyrannosaurus hunting its prey.

As he alternately walked and trotted, Kane thought of Martha Reik. She had tried to stop him from going with Chuddath. She had been too protective, behaving as Beth would have behaved, and for that it was hard to forgive her. Kane knew his anger at her was irrational, a spillage of his real rage. Only what Chuddath had said in summoning him mattered.

"You have lost your female," the Ornyl had said, pausing at syntactically awkward points, apparently to rest the delicate arms. "You are entitled to . . . see the assassin."

Reik had caught his arm. "You want to get at the killer. I understand that, but it will only make things harder." The memory of her fingers clutching, pulling open as he jerked his arm away, tingled in his wrist.

Chuddath stopped in front of an elevator. Kane and the alien descended in silence through the heart of the palace. When the platform settled, they stepped into a chrome-plated corridor displaying the number three and a black painted leopard's head opposite the elevator doors. Kane reached out to stop the alien, but his grip was pulled open easily by the casual swing of Chuddath's arm. The alien halted anyway and turned to face him.

"I thought we were going to interrogate the assassin."

Chuddath waited patiently, as though Kane had said something extraneous and would eventually get to the point.

"This is a praetorian level. The Special Branch would be in charge of the prisoner, not the praetorians."

"No." Chuddath turned away from Kane again as booted steps approached around the curve of the corridor. There were two praetorians. One carried the silver baton of a captain. They stopped and stepped apart to keep Chuddath or Kane from passing them.

"Ornyl. What brings you here?" The captain's voice carried the expected tone of praetorian hauteur and something more, a cold contempt.

Kane said, "We've come to see the assassin."

The captain inspected him. "You're Elias Kane, aren't you? You should not have let this bug bring you here. As it should know, the assassin is in the sole control of the guard. No one else sees him."

Chuddath drew his vocal limbs into a protected position behind the upper arms. The two praetorians tensed.

"What the hell is this?" Kane demanded. "Aren't we all on the same side?"

"Turn around and get on the elevator," the captain said. Kane did not move, even when the captain began to walk toward him, striking the baton against his open palm. In his forearms and fists Kane felt the knowledge that he wanted the captain to try to stop him. He wanted something in the way, something of meat and bone to smash aside. He forced his fists open, keeping his hands at his sides.

"I find it odd," he said, "that the Imperator's personal bodyguard would be denied access to any part of the palace."

The captain stopped an arm's length from Kane. "Too bad the bug can't talk for himself."

Chuddath stepped toward the two men and their hands moved for their blasters. The rest of it happened too fast to see without the added takes of memory. The warrior's arms blurred, plucking the blasters before they had begun to angle up. Flipping the weapons down the corridor behind him, Chuddath scooped up the two praetorians, tucking one under each arm. Things slowed again; the praetorians thrashed like gaffed fish. Finally they stopped and dangled, red-faced, in the alien's grip.

"Maybe you should take us to the assassin now," Kane said.

The praetorians led them to an anteroom with doors on

either side. One of the doors was guarded by two more praetorians. Chuddath dropped a hand onto the nape of each captive's neck in a comradely gesture. "I will see Sabin," the alien said.

One of the guards raised his blaster, but the other, an old noncom with the sloping shoulders of a spacer who'd spent too much time on heavy-G planets, pushed the weapon down again. "Don't be stupid," he said. "This is an *Ornyl,* boy. He can crush their necks before you can twitch." Kane noticed a monitor lens above the guarded door. The door slid open and a short, powerfully built man with white hair stepped out. The man was wearing praetorian blacks, plain except for the usual silver trim and the stylized leopard of the corps on the belt. Adornments of rank were unnecessary: none of the five-thousand-man guard nor anyone else familiar with the unification war forty years past would fail to recognize Alvar Sabin, the man who had fought at the side of then Admiral of the Fleet Gregory Amerdath.

Sabin looked stonily at the embarrassed faces of the disarmed praetorians. "Release them," he ordered Chuddath. His voice was below normal speaking volume, empty of expression.

"We will talk?"

The commander nodded and Chuddath's hands dropped from the two necks. The men stepped toward Sabin, both attempting to speak at once, but the commander silenced them with a flick of two fingers. "Confine yourselves to quarters." He turned to Kane. "Since the creature you are with is no more eager to talk than I am to listen to it, perhaps you can explain why you and it have intruded here."

"I'm Elias Kane . . ."

"I know who you are, Mr. Kane. Please accept my regret over the death of Elizabeth Tyson." Despite the toneless way he said it, Sabin seemed sincere.

"Chuddath and I are here for the same reason," Kane

said. "I want to see the man who . . ." He stopped, unable to finish the sentence. Sabin gazed at him, waiting. "I have a stake," Kane said.

"Nevertheless, this is no place for you." Sabin hesitated. "You've just come from the Imperator?"

"He's alive. That's what Dr. Reik said. Unconscious but alive. Perhaps you should bear that in mind when dealing with his personal bodyguard."

Sabin's expression did not change. "This alien has failed in its duty."

"As have you."

"I will forgive that because of your former service to the Imperator and because you're distraught."

"Keep your forgiveness. Amerdath will recover. When he does, he'll hold you responsible if you've thwarted the investigation of the attack." Kane delivered the threat with a sense of detachment, as though he were listening along with Sabin. He knew he was provoking an important man, that Sabin would not forget it. If the Imperator died, his threat would then become an insult to be avenged without fear of reprisal. It did not matter. Only getting through the door behind the praetorian commander mattered.

"I thwart nothing," Sabin said. "Your threats mean nothing to me. I stood with Gregory Amerdath on the torpedoed bridge of the Scaramouche when your worst problem was acne and this insect was eating its mother's body. Your standing to investigate depends on the Imperator's recovery, as I'm sure you know. But I'm going to let you observe. You're to keep your mouths shut. If either of you attempts to say anything in the assassin's presence I'll have you both thrown out."

The Ornyl brushed his abdomen, producing a low wordless sound that might have been derision. Kane and the alien followed Sabin into the chamber. It was a boxlike room. The walls, ceiling and floor had been mirror polarized. In the center, pinned on a forcechair, sat the man from the garden. He was naked. The stink of feces filled the room.

Kane stopped just inside the door. The man was sitting three meters away, trapped, forced to see himself in every wall. Kane knew that in two steps he could be at the man's throat. Every muscle strained to be let loose, and yet Kane could not move. There was nothing he could do. He was in his own forcechair, as surely as the killer, and on every wall of his mind he saw only the one truth. Beth was gone. The minutes, hours, days and years would flow in only one direction, away from her.

The assassin did not look up. He sat with a meditative air, staring at the place where the wall opposite him met the floor. When Sabin walked in front of the forcechair, the prisoner transferred his attention to the praetorian's leopard emblem belt buckle. Kane noticed that the killer was well-muscled. His body had undergone rigorous training. The man's calm was infuriating. He should have been cringing, terrified of what was to come. Kane wondered if he had been drugged into a pliant state. There were no visible injection marks, but none could be expected—the needles were sunk in the back and arms of the forcechair and would emerge at a touch on the console Sabin held now in one hand.

"You were telling us your name," the commander said.

"Mark Clemis." The man replied quickly, as though eager to please.

"Good. Now tell us why you wanted to kill the Imperator."

"I am but the sword of God. It is His will I have done."

Disgust showed on Sabin's face. "And what makes you think it is God's will that your Imperator should die?"

"He's a degenerate."

"What does that mean, 'a degenerate'?"

"He has debased the high position given to him by God."

"Explain."

"He sleeps with the young women of the court. He

surrounds himself with decadence. He consorts with
infidels.'' The man moved his head the few degrees toward Chuddath permitted by the chair's force field. ''That
one. An instrument of the devil.''

Sabin glanced at the alien, who remained still. ''You
tried to kill the Imperator because he debases his position?''

''Yes.''

''You're lying.''

''No, I swear!'' The man's forehead wrinkled and his
eyelids drew back, exposing crescents of white. A buzzer
sounded and Sabin turned with an irritated expression to
stare at the monitor of the outside corridor. Kane looked
too and cursed under his breath when he saw Pendrake on
the screen, flanked by two nervous-looking praetorians.

''He says he must join Elias Kane,'' explained a guard,
speaking into an intercom pick-up.

Sabin glared at Kane. ''This is no place for a Cephantine.
He'll interfere.''

''I give my word that I will not,'' said Pendrake.

''Go away,'' Kane said.

''I am sorry, Elias. I cannot.''

Sabin started to shake his head, then looked speculatively
at the Ornyl warrior. ''All right. Let him in.''

As Pendrake entered, Kane wondered why Sabin had
given in so abruptly. Perhaps he knew of the Cephantine's
dislike for Chuddath and thought that Pendrake would help
control the Ornyl if he became violent. Or perhaps he
wanted to exploit the intimidating effects of the two aliens
on the assassin, who clearly despised Chuddath. For a
moment Sabin's motives engaged Kane's mind, but only
for a moment. He could not really pretend that it mattered.
Why did he even stay here? There was nothing to be done,
and the sight of the assassin only aggravated his despair.
Even his anger was gone—his last protection. He felt
Pendrake move close behind him. ''How'd you find me?''
he whispered.

"I followed at a distance. Do not be angry with me, Elias. I could not leave you to this alone."

Sabin had turned back to his prisoner. "Who were your accomplices?"

"I have none."

"Who helped you plan this?"

"No one."

"Stop lying. Who helped you? Answer me!" Sabin's hand moved over the console to a button controlling the chair's electrodes. The assassin turned rigid. His face purpled and his mouth worked soundlessly before he sagged again.

"N-no one," he stammered. "I had no help. I swear it."

"Why do you not . . . ask him how . . . he became the Imperator's gardener?" Chuddath asked.

Sabin turned on the warrior. "I warned you about talking. Get out. Now!"

And then Kane knew why Sabin had warned them to silence. He understood what it was that Sabin wanted to hide. He stepped in front of the prisoner before the praetorian could react.

"How did you become the Imperator's gardener?" he asked.

Clemis drew himself up in the chair. "I'm no sod-grubbing gardener," he said. "I am a praetorian."

CHAPTER 5

Before the prisoner finished speaking Alvar Sabin had his slug gun pointed at the Ornyl warrior. Chuddath hesitated in mid-turn and then stopped. For a second there seemed a glow, a distortion of air around the warrior's head, like heat shimmering off pavement. The alien's rage was incandescent, filling the room, invading everyone around him like a physical current. Kane felt fury, as though a switch had been thrown, and then weakness, disorientation. Pendrake groaned, the prisoner squirmed in the forcechair; Sabin took a step backward as though he'd been pushed.

"You knew," Kane said to the commander.

"That this man is a praetorian? Of course. I know all of my men."

"If Clemis is your man, and you didn't know what he was planning, how did he, out of five thousand praetorians, happen to pull plainclothes duty in the garden this morning?"

"I'm not accountable to you," Sabin said. The door to the interrogation chamber opened and four more praetorians entered, weapons drawn. Pendrake edged between Kane and the newcomers.

46

"The Imperator may recover," Kane said. "If he does, how will you explain our deaths?"

Sabin sighed wearily. "I've no intention of killing you. This was bound to come out."

"Then why try to keep it from us?"

"Time. If it becomes known too soon that Clemis was a praetorian, I'll get no chance to find who planned this. They'll make me the scapegoat. Clemis is a praetorian; I'm the commander of praetorians. The palace is hysterical. Whoever in the royal family takes charge will be tempted to throw me to the wolves. I'll accept any blame that's due me, Mr. Kane, but I'll not be stopped before I've found who's behind this."

"Sabin lies," Chuddath said.

The praetorian flushed. "I should shoot you down where you stand. No one would blame me. You were *there*, and you didn't stop it."

Chuddath made a screeching sound and Kane again felt the heat of the alien's rage. Sabin spoke without taking his eyes off Chuddath. "You'll have to be detained. I'll make you as comfortable as possible. It shouldn't be more than a few hours before everyone involved in the attempt is exposed."

Chuddath's vocal arms moved. "I will not be . . . put aside. I demand to hear this . . . man's confessions myself, not . . . the lies you will . . . invent after you have killed him."

Sabin made a motion with the slug gun. The four praetorians stepped into position around Chuddath. The alien easily held his position as the praetorians tried to steer him toward the door. One vocal arm twisted, giving the single word the inflection of a sneer. "Shoot."

Sabin's teeth showed; his finger tightened on the trigger. Pendrake stepped in front of the gun. "Commander, I beg you to consider . . ."

Screened from Sabin's weapon, Chuddath flicked the men surrounding him to the floor. He rushed Sabin.

Pendrake took the force of the charge against his back,
tottering forward a step and throwing out his arms to
contain the other alien behind him. Kane slapped the
commander's arm, deflecting the gun. It discharged into
the floor with a smacking sound. Kane wrestled with
Sabin, trying to pin the short powerful arms.

"Enough."

The voice was not loud, but it had the timbre of a
cracking whip. The combatants stopped struggling. Kane
released Sabin and stared at the woman in the doorway.
She was beautiful, and his first impression was that she
was somehow not real, but a stunning laser-sharp projec-
tion of some powerful machine. Her hair was a dazzling
premature white, full around the face, falling to such
fullness in front that the long throat was hidden in shadow.
She looked athletic and strong. She wore a short dress of
iridescent scales that rippled in the light with the smallest
movement. Sandle straps of the same material twined to
mid-thigh like the twin serpents of a caduceus. Her irises
were a shocking deep green, the color of Archepellan jade.

The praetorians Chuddath had thrown down got up and
stood rigidly at attention. Chuddath's arms dangled in
sudden docility.

Sabin cleared his throat. "Princess, I . . ."

She silenced him with a hard glance. "My father fights
for his life while his protectors scratch at each other's
eyes." Kane stared at her. It was his first encounter with
Briana, daughter of the Imperator, twin of Prince Lucian.
The press photos of her had conveyed various views of her
face often enough. In them she was merely beautiful. No
photo could have prepared him for her presence, for the
force of her personality, for the ravening energy trapped
behind her eyes. Was this how Gregory Amerdath had
been at thirty?

"Outside," the princess commanded. "All of you."

The men and the two aliens filed into the hall and Kane
realized that his face burned, as though he were a mischie-

vous child, caught and scolded. The princess set herself in front of them. At either elbow were two additional praetorians with the stylized white tree emblem of the family guard at their belts. Briana glared at Sabin. "Why are you holding the assassin here? He should be Giacomin's."

"Princess, it is my duty . . ."

"Internal security. You know that, Alvar. Your men are the muscle, and it's a little late for that now. Fowler Giacomin has techniques."

"As do I."

"Don't challenge me, Commander. Until my father dies or recovers, you will put yourself under the command of his heirs."

"And in cases where you and your brother disagree?"

She smiled. "In those cases, should they arise, you will have a dilemma to resolve. I'm sure you will make the safest choice."

Sabin frowned, but did not reply. As the initial visceral shock of her began to subside, Kane studied her with more objectivity. She did not seem to be the grieving daughter. Or perhaps she had learned the strict self-control of her father who, as a junior naval officer, had quelled a mutiny by coolly informing one of the sailors pointing a blaster at his face that the weapon's safety catch was on.

The princess listened as Sabin briefed her on the interrogation. When he told her that Clemis was a renegade praetorian, Sabin's face was expressionless as a death's head. Before Briana could say anything, Chuddath interrupted. "Will the princess ask . . . why Sabin's man approached . . . her father in disguise?"

Briana's face started to distort with irritation, and then it smoothed again. She stepped close and took the soft chubby hands of the alien's vocal arms in hers. Chuddath's head tilted back until he was looking at the ceiling. Kane sensed a fusion of emotions in the contact between warrior and woman, like opposite magnetic poles snapping together.

"Poor Chuddath," Briana said softly. "This has been so

hard on you, hasn't it? So hard on you and Alvar both.
You want it to be Alvar, you need it to be Alvar's fault,
because then those grinding wheels in your head could
stop.'' The princess dropped Chuddath's hands and stepped
back, and Kane saw a tremor pass along the gray-green
carapace. ''You will transfer the prisoner to the Imperial
Security division,'' Briana told Sabin. ''There, you will
assist in his interrogation. As will you, Chuddath, and
you, Mr. Kane.''

''Princess,'' Sabin said, ''with all due respect for Mr.
Kane's abilities, having so many people at the interrogation can only complicate our work. As for the Ornyl, it
hardly has the sophistication for this sort of thing.''

''Chuddath is still my father's chief bodyguard. This
gives *him* the same rights as you. If I exclude *him—him*,
Alvar—I must also exclude you. As for Mr. Kane . . .''
Briana stopped. She seemed to be listening, though there
was no sound. Kane realized that she had undergone an
otic implant. She attended the receiver in her head for a
moment, then turned to Sabin. ''See that my commands
are carried out. Giacomin is waiting for you in his office.
I'll be in touch.''

The two praetorians followed her down a corridor and
out of sight. ''I'll call you when we're ready to proceed,''
Sabin said without looking at Kane. He went back into the
interrogation chamber, ignoring Chuddath, who followed
him in. Pendrake began to steer Kane back the way he had
come with Chuddath.

''Dr. Reik is waiting with medication,'' he said.

Kane held back, looking down the hallway where Briana
had departed.

''She is a forceful woman, the princess,'' Pendrake
observed.

''Forceful with Sabin. Gentle with Chuddath.''

Pendrake looked at him oddly.

''When she took his hands,'' Kane explained, ''and
tried to soothe him with all that 'poor Chuddath' stuff.''

They stopped in front of the elevator and Kane saw that Pendrake was staring into the polished chrome doors with a bemused expression. "I fear you did not understand, Elias. The vocal hands of an Ornyl warrior are exceedingly sensitive, as they must be to perform the intricate manipulations that mimic our diaphragmatic speech. The tissue beneath the surface of those hands contains thousands of delicate nerves."

Kane remembered how Chuddath had tucked the vocal arms into a protected position when confronted by the two praetorians. "Then, when she gripped his hands . . ."

"She was inflicting almost unbearable pain upon the Ornyl," Pendrake said. "Apparently she was irritated that Chuddath had presumed to interrupt her. Or perhaps it was because he failed to protect her father. In any case, she was punishing him. The Ornyl could not, of course, retaliate because of his loyalty to Briana's father. The sensory aftermath of what she did is almost as cruel as the initial pain itself. The agony will persist for several days in Chuddath's nervous system."

Kane thought of the princess' half-smile, of the soft voice as she had gripped Chuddath's hands, of the way Chuddath's head had arched back to stare at the ceiling. It had been gratuitous cruelty. It had happened to a being so alien that empathy should have been impossible, and yet it pierced Kane, reaching past the barriers he'd thrown up to protect himself from his own pain. It was too much. It was all too much. He would not be able to hold it away. The doors to the elevator opened. Pendrake took him by the arm and led him in.

CHAPTER 6

The people in the pharmaceutical labs meant well, and the doctors they hawked their drugs to meant well, and it was worth a try, so Kane took the injection. For what seemed like days, he bobbed up and down in a stuporous sea. Occasionally he would see Pendrake sitting in the chair by the bed, staring, or stretched out on the floor, eyes always open, always staring at inner visions. Once, Kane thought he remembered telling the alien to go to his own room and sleep, but he could not be sure. It ended with Dr. Reik straightening above him, a spent hypocapsule in her hand. Kane blinked as energy flowed into his body from a tingling place on his left arm.

"How long?" he asked.

"Just overnight," Reik said.

Kane digested that, looking for Pendrake. The Cephantine was visible through the bedroom door. He had dialed a vista of formal gardens on the parlor wall. The smells of dirt and green plants issued from the olfacunit and a bird, taped long ago, winked forward in time to warble for Kane. Pendrake saw he was awake and came to the bedside.

52

"How do you feel, Elias?"

"Okay. Fine." Kane smoothed his matted hair back. Reik sat down on the edge of the bed and he envisioned her hand on his knee where it stuck up under the covers. The thought was so natural, so automatic, that it jarred his sense of reality. He searched her face, but she was not Beth.

"How do you feel, actually?" Reik asked.

"Like I've been eating my mattress."

She nodded. "That will pass as soon as you get some water. Otherwise?"

Kane watched Pendrake disappear into the bathroom and return with a crystal tumbler of water. "I feel like I'm supposed to feel," he said. He drained the glass. "Why did you just give me a stimulant?"

"Because the Imperator wants to see you."

"Wait." Kane massaged his face, trying to relieve the feeling of skin stretched like drumheads over the bones. He studied the clock, a sculpted sunburst on the wall beyond his feet. "If I only slept overnight, the Imperator was wounded less than a day ago. Twenty hours ago, you took his head off, and you say he wants to see me?"

Reik nodded. "Given that Gregory Amerdath's brain survived the shock of what happened, his present state of alertness is not medically surprising. Remember that his head was physically uninjured. The body, where all the damage was, can cause him no symptoms. The recovery, in strictly physical terms, should be fairly rapid and straightforward from here on out. We've got pure nutrified blood, free of fatigue poisons, circulating through his brain at the pace that would be appropriate for a healthy twenty-year-old heart. All of the severed nerve endings at the base of his neck are packed in anesthetic. He is feeling no physical distress, other than occasional phantom pains."

"Phantom pains?" Pendrake said. "I do not understand."

"It's a phenomenon sometimes observed in amputees,"

Reik explained. "The nerve centers in the brain falsely record sensations from the missing limb. For that instant, the patient has feelings in the limb as though it were still attached. The sensations can be disturbing, but they won't interfere with Amerdath's physical recovery."

Kane let her go on while he stared at the cream-colored satin of his pajamas, trying to remember whether he'd put the night clothes on himself. Had he let them dress him? Had he let them put him to bed like a child? He sat up abruptly.

"Easy," Reik said.

"I'm all right," Kane snapped. "I'll get dressed now." Warned by the moment of dizziness, Kane moved more slowly. The room, the figures of Pendrake and Reik seemed flat and two-dimensional, while the scene on the holowall stood out in supernatural clarity.

"I'll wait outside," Reik said.

After she was gone, Pendrake turned to Kane. "Are you certain you are able to accept the Imperator's summons?"

Kane grunted.

"Let me help you with your clothes. . . ."

"Damn it, stop hovering!"

The Cephantine stood back.

"I'm sorry," Kane muttered. He dressed and brushed some of the cowlicks out of his hair. He felt greasy and slow-witted despite the stimulant. If he could just get into the shower for a few minutes. But Amerdath had summoned him, and the Imperator had never been a man to keep waiting.

A double row of praetorians formed a gauntlet in the anteroom of the Imperator's hospital quarters. Kane began to feel anxious. He should have prepared himself on the way over. Now there was nothing to do but go on in. The Imperator's head sat atop a life-support cart. Kane struggled to swallow, to loosen the clamped hinges of his jaw. Pendrake gripped his elbow. The alien's fingers trembled as they closed and Kane realized that Pendrake needed the contact for himself too. Kane looked away from Amerdath, then back again, and realized that he would be able to stand it. Praetorians were everywhere, backed up against the walls out of the way. Physicians hovered around the Imperator, checking equipment and making notes. The Empress Eunice, a plump woman of about sixty with hair the color of slate, sat in a corner of the room between two praetorians. Her half-lidded eyes surveyed Kane's party, settling on Dr. Reik. Chuddath towered behind the Imperator, watching everything with the compound eyes. There was an edge of vaporous sweetness in the air, probably from the anesthetic. The Imperator's head was held in place by padded supports that formed a horseshoe at the base of the skull and extended up with curving fingers behind the ears and at the midline of the skull almost to the top of the forehead. A silvery cannister occupied the shelf below Amerdath's head. A tube extended from the cannister to disappear into Amerdath's throat. On the lowest shelf of the cart and on either side of the cannister were clear plastic tubes. The blood in one set was bright red and in the other, darker.

The Imperator opened his mouth and one of the doctors bent instantly to flip a switch on the cannister. Incredibly, the head of Gregory Amerdath began to speak. "Come closer." Forced air from the bellows beneath continued to hiss from his partly opened mouth after the words were spoken. Amerdath's voice sounded hoarse. Kane forced himself to walk to within a few meters of the head. The Imperator's face was pink and healthy looking, but the white hair looked damp and there was a dappling of sweat on the upper lip.

"It's all right, Elias. I know how you must feel. I imagine I'm quite a sight, even though they forbid me a mirror—me, the Imperator of the Terran Empire." Amerdath's voice was tonally correct despite its hoarseness, and yet it was an unnerving sound, jarring in its continuous

hiss, in the lack of breath stops. "I won't be so hard to
look at next time," Amerdath said. "There are cosmetic
plans, but there hasn't been time yet. By the way, thank
you for not asking me how I feel. I'm so sorry for what
happened to Beth."

"She saved me," Kane heard himself say. "She pushed
me out of the way." His throat pulled tight as though the
muscles of his own neck wished to strangle him. He had
put away the memory of her hands pushing him down at
the moment of attack. And now Amerdath had pulled it
out with a sentence.

"I wanted to put my hand on your shoulder just now,"
Amerdath said. "I could feel myself reaching."

Kane longed to break eye contact with Amerdath, but he
did not. The Imperator's expression firmed. "I asked you
to come here now, so soon, because I want to waste no
time in establishing you as head of the investigation."

"Your daughter already commanded me to take part in
the interrogation," Kane said.

The white eyebrows arched. "Really? Well, she was
right to ask." Kane wondered if Amerdath had deliberately softened the verb or had merely misunderstood. The
Imperator's eyes moved to the side and he winced. "Damn
it, Eunice, do you have to sit at the edge of my vision like
that? Every time I try to look at you my head almost
splits."

The old woman stood and gestured with a veined hand.
The praetorians shifted her chair until she motioned a
second time. The chair was only marginally closer to
Amerdath's line of sight. Eunice sat down again, her eyes
unreadable.

"Thank you, my dear," Amerdath said, his voice carrying a hiss on top of that from the bellows. He looked at
Kane again. "Briana is strong-willed, but I am Imperator,
still Imperator. I will not command you. But I ask you to
find who did this to me—those behind Clemis. I assure

you, there are others. I was getting to that part of it in the garden, before I was . . . shot. Clemis was only the tool of an organized conspiracy against the throne. I need you, Elias, to uncover that conspiracy.''

Kane stared at the Imperator. Amerdath talked in even, reasonable tones, but he should have been shrieking out his madness. Winter had come to the man. His body was ash, scattered like fallen leaves. Words were futile.

''I'm sorry.'' Kane felt only indifference at the dead sound of his own voice. He had one need left, to escape this room.

''Don't refuse me,'' Amerdath said. ''I know what you're going through, but you've got to master it. We both must.''

Kane said nothing.

Amerdath took his bowed head for assent. ''Good. Now get me one of those doctors.'' Martha Reik was conferring quietly with one of the other physicians. She hurried over. ''Hook up the mike,'' Amerdath said. Reik angled a microphone up out of the cart to within a few centimeters of the Imperator's mouth. Amerdath's voice thundered into the room. The medical people jumped and even several of the praetorians flinched. ''I have charged this man, Elias Kane, with investigating the conspiracy to assassinate me,'' Amerdath said. ''You are each and all my witnesses to this. He is to be given the full cooperation of the guard and of anyone else on whom he calls. Anyone.'' Amerdath looked expectantly at Reik, and the seconds passed, and finally he was forced to say, ''Well, turn it off, turn the damned thing off.''

People turned decorously away as Reik switched off the mike, the self-conscious impassivity of their faces shouting what was in their minds: *The man was still Imperator, but how long could it last when everything he did, and all the things he could no longer do, trumpeted his weakness?*

Amerdath's eyes closed. The lashes squirmed together. ''That's all, Kane. I'm depending on you.''

Pendrake followed Kane into the outside corridor. "You have taken on a heavy responsibility, Elias."

Kane felt drained, too weary even to look up. "No, I haven't," he said. "I can't do it."

CHAPTER 7

Two days after the murder and assassination attempt a short funeral service was held for Elizabeth Tyson. The Imperator made his private amphitheater, on the top level of the palace, available for the service. The room was octagonal with tiers of white marble descending to the edges of a dais in the center. The walls were unadorned white stone. The ceiling was depolarized to the sky, which stayed an uncaring azure throughout the funeral. Gregory Amerdath sent his son, Lucian, a tall man with an underfleshed face and disturbing eyes, to serve as Imperial representative. Speaking in a diffident baritone, Lucian conveyed the deep regrets of his father and of the royal family and sat down. Several people talked about Beth, trying to resurrect her in their memories. Kane said nothing. He did not weep or acknowledge the pitying looks, or even look around him, but sat next to Pendrake, gazing at the silver capsule of ash in the middle of the dais and trying to think what roll of the genetic dice could have caused the left eye of Prince Lucian to be half brown and half green. At one point he stifled an urge to laugh, which came upon him with terrifying suddenness. He wondered if it was the first sign of madness.

Then it was over and he and Pendrake were back in the suite he had shared with Beth. Kane blanked the garden scene on the holowall, dialed the lights to dim and sat down by the autobar. He accepted a double Levian green label whiskey from the autobar, drained half of it and looked at Pendrake, who stood just inside the door, arms at his sides, as though the will to move had drained out of him between one step and the next.

"Can I order you an iced tea?" Kane asked.

Pendrake walked over and settled cross-legged on the floor, facing Kane. "What is that you are having?"

"A double Levian green."

The alien nodded. "That is the drink I bought for you at the casino, right after you threw the brass collar that was around my neck into the flashunit."

"You gave me no choice. You offered to buy me that drink, knowing full well that servants are not allowed to drink with their masters. It was either give up a servant or a free drink. Fortunately for you, I was thirsty."

Pendrake smiled, his herbivore teeth a soft gleam in the near darkness. "That is not the way I remember it, Elias."

Kane grunted. "A tea, then?"

"I believe I will drink what you are drinking."

Kane suppressed a paternal frown. If the alien chose to drink after a lifetime of abstinence it was not his place to object. He handed Pendrake the straight booze and watched the alien sip stoically, the long upper lip wrinkling only slightly in distaste.

"What will you do now?" Pendrake asked after a comradely interval of drinking.

"I don't know. I have a place in Arizona. Used to go there from time to time before the psychopath plague."

"Is that not the dwelling you have referred to as a shanty?"

"It's not so bad. There's a lot of life out there on the

desert. Quiet life. The nights are clear. Blackest sky you ever saw, but luminous too. You see the galaxies against that sky like a big snow waiting to fall. Here, the palace throws so much light up you can hardly see the moon. Days out there are hot. You sweat but it doesn't matter. You just sit on the porch and doze and let the sun crawl up and roll down the other side.''

''And what of Elias Kane, detective?''

''He doesn't exist anymore.''

''I see. He is dead too.''

''Why don't you just come right out and say you disapprove?''

Pendrake shrugged and drank more of his whiskey. ''If you feel you must run away.''

Kane gave a short sour laugh.

''I am not very subtle, am I, Elias?''

''You want to help. I understand that.''

''I am the faithful manservant, is that it?''

''Yeah, and I'm B'wana. Another drink?''

''If you please.''

They tipped fresh glasses at each other.

''Perhaps you are right,'' Pendrake mused. ''Perhaps we should go to the desert. After all, the Imperator's request that you head the investigation is not altogether a wise one.''

''True,'' Kane said. He let it ride a minute, knowing the alien was baiting him. So what. A game was a game. ''What's not wise?''

''Gregory Amerdath is extremely vulnerable now. Everyone is asking whether he can still be Imperator. In truth, his present plight has merely focused attention on what is always true. One person can rule only with the cooperation and allegiance of other figures around him. It is vital now that people such as Alvar Sabin not come to believe the essential strength of Amerdath, the man, to be lost. Such judgments are never untainted by politics, and it is bad

politics for the Imperator to appoint an outsider to lead the
investigation of his attempted assassination."

The twelve-year-old whiskey burned Kane's throat as he
rolled back a punishing gulp. *All right. So the alien was
way ahead of him, thinking the thoughts he was too addled
to think. Good for him. What difference did it make?
Pendrake was right—too right to be provocative. It was
just one more reason he could not take over the investigation.
A real reason—one Amerdath would have to accept.* Kane
nodded to himself. Alvar Sabin and Fowler Giacomin
could only interpret his appointment as chief investigator
as lack of Imperial confidence in them. It was good that he
would not accept. He would be saving Amerdath from the
resentment of vital subordinates, and a gamble that a
drifter and dilettante could find what Giacomin and Sabin
could not. *But was it really such a gamble? The dilettante
was good. Better, perhaps, than anyone.* Kane smiled
bitterly as he realized that Pendrake had steered him,
despite himself, to this last thought. "It's no good," he
said.

"Ah." Pendrake hid his expression by tipping his head
back as he drained his glass. "Did you love her very
much?"

"What the devil kind of a question is that?" When
Pendrake did not answer, Kane ordered another whiskey,
jabbing the autobar buttons. "Of course I loved her. We
would have been married."

Pendrake looked surprised. "I did not know you had
asked her, Elias."

"I hadn't. But I was going to. I was thinking about it in
the garden when she wash—*was;* was, was, was, when
she was killed." Kane watched the whiskey glass vibrate
in his hand. He *would* have asked her. Why was Pendrake
looking so surprised? He loved her. All he'd needed was a
few weeks to think it through.

"What do you feel, Elias?"

"The trick is not to feel."

"She had no right to leave you like this."

Kane glared at the alien. "That's insane."

"If it is what you feel, what good can come from calling it insane?"

"It is *not* how I feel."

"On Cephan," the alien said, "things are not so different when it comes to death. We go through phases of mourning such as humans experience. Denial, anger, depression . . ."

"Yeah, let's give it names," Kane said. "I'll just slog through the good old phases: Two days for denial, another week for anger. Depression, that ought to be good for, say, half a year, and then out into the sunshine, oh yes, sweet acceptance. Happens to all of us; natural as rain. Dust to dust, ashes to ashes, the Lord giveth and the Lord taketh away, blessed be the name of the Lord, only I'm not going to be able to accept it. Not now, not ever. She's dead. There's no reason for it. I can't bring her back and I can't accept it."

As the next double shot glass slid from the bar, Kane slapped his hand around it, spilling half over his hand and wrist. "May I have another of those?" Pendrake asked. Kane handed one across, trying to focus on the Cephantine's face; to see what effect, if any, the whiskey was having. Aside from a liquid look around the rims of the eyes, and a quirk at the corner of the thin-lipped mouth, Pendrake looked as he usually looked, calm, unflappable. The alien held the drink between massive thumb and forefinger and knocked it back. "Then you will go on being angry for as long as you live. That will require much dedication, Elias, but if it is what you want . . ."

"I'm not inna mood to talk about the rest of my life."

Pendrake nodded companionably. "It seems to be getting darker in here," he observed.

"'S the alcohol."

Time grew hazy, flowing in peculiar rhythms.

"Well, I will tell you something, Elias," Pendrake said. "This alcohol tastes very bad."

Kane peered at the alien. "You're drunk. I don't believe it. You got yourself drunk. Why did you do it?"

The simpering twist to Pendrake's mouth slowly evened out as Kane stared at him. Kane felt an intense surge of affection for the Cephantine. "No investigation can bring her back," he said.

"That is certainly true, Elias. I accept that you know it, and that you are not foolish or ruled by unreasonable emotions."

Kane tried to read the alien's expression. "You think I'm refusing to run the investigation to prove I can't be manipulated by death. You think I'm scared to play out a pitiable stereotype, the anguished lover, waving the rubber sword of revenge."

"What I or others think does not matter, Elias."

Kane struggled up with the care of a man erecting a toothpick house. He got to the bed with precise steps and fell face down. He grimaced at the thump Pendrake's head made on the floor as the alien rolled out full length into his customary sleep posture. The grimace lingered as though Kane's face had lost its elasticity. Pendrake had said that it didn't matter what others thought. It didn't matter what he thought either, or what he said. He was like Amerdath, severed, but there were phantom pains. They could not be suppressed. They were all he had left. They would goad and flay him and he would run on the missing legs, through the palace, around and around its concentric rings, down to the city, out to the stars if necessary, lost heart pumping, until he found out who and why.

CHAPTER 8

Kane's head was a crypt, his tongue a corpse rotting in the casket of his mouth. It was a misery he had earned, and it left little room for anything else, so he groaned a salute to it as he sat up. Pendrake was still lying on the floor beside his bed. In the dim light, Kane saw that there was something wrong, an unnatural stillness in the way the alien lay. He got up too quickly and had to lean for a second against the wall. He winced as he dialed the light around full. Kneeling beside Pendrake, he probed the cool waxy skin for a pulse. There was none. He groped vaguely in the air, as if it held the answer to the alien's stillness. Pendrake dead? He could not allow it. But the alien had drunk, and Cephantines, so far as he knew, never drank. Was alcohol more poisonous to them? Kane pressed his ear against the alien's chest. *For God's sake, where was the heart in a Cephantine?*

"Elias, I would prefer that you not touch me just now."

Kane jumped back, squatted, tottering on his toes. He stared at the pumpkin-colored face. The eyelids fluttered open just long enough to reveal fully extended nictitating membranes. A surge of relief made Kane's voice unnaturally loud. "Just lie still. I'll get help."

"That will not be necessary, Elias. I will recover without aid. Nevertheless, at this moment my entire body is experiencing a condition similar to your foot going to sleep."

Kane grinned so broadly that pain stabbed at his temples. Pendrake was hung over, in his own peculiar way. Just hung over. But the alien had never drunk before; he couldn't be sure that his symptoms weren't dangerous. Kane said, "I'm calling someone—Martha Reik."

"Do not trouble Dr. Reik. I know my own body better than any human, even a human physician." Pendrake's voice sounded testy.

"I'm sorry," Kane said. "Really sorry. I should have stopped you last night. Is there anything I can do?"

"Do not apologize, and do not disturb me for the next four hours."

Kane nodded and stood, backing away from Pendrake with exaggerated care. The sink in the suite's bathroom was crafted of a single piece of violet marble imported from Cerulyx. Kane filled the basin with cold water and plunged his head into it. The icy shock of it added only a little to the pain in his head. He stayed under for fifteen seconds, staring at the gold drain stopper. When he lifted his head, his misery had resumed its proper perspective. His head ached and someone had poured sand around his eyeballs while he slept. The cold water had not been such a good idea. However, as self-punishment it had succeeded. He towelled off gingerly, put on a fresh change of clothes, and only then permitted himself the deliverance of an alcolase tablet.

As Kane tiptoed around the alien, Pendrake spoke without opening his eyes. "Are you going now to tell the Imperator that you cannot head the investigation?"

"I'm going now to find a taxidermist for you," Kane

growled. He glanced back as he left and caught Pendrake's lips twitching in a brief smile.

Three hours later Kane walked through the broad curving corridors, back to his room. He could have taken a battery-powered chariot at any of the stations spaced every half-kilometer, but he needed time to think. His headache was gone, resorbed by the alcolase tab. In its place was a Brownian storm of thoughts and pieces of thoughts jittering around his efforts to concentrate. He'd walked in unannounced on Fowler Giacomin, chief of security for Gregory Amerdath, and afterimages of the confrontation would not seem to fade. There was nothing else to do but attend to them, to ride the rhythm of his legs and to turn the inner eye to the edges of the encounter, the things Giacomin had not meant him to see. First there was the man himself, Fowler Giacomin. His greeting had been polite and he had shown no surprise. He'd glided around his desk with the grace of a dancer and offered his hand. Kane sorted the frames of that all-important first contact. A tall man elegantly dressed in a tailored short-coat of ruby-colored satin, black breeches and boots. Cobweb wrinkling around patrician eyes and mouth, signs of a good plastician, visible only up close. A spidery handclasp, impossibly long fingers that later pressed lightly together and aimed across the desk at him. Only now, outside his well-mannered presence, did Kane get the sense that Giacomin's hands were weapons, that they had curled around throats, that the fingers loved and longed to kill.

Other things, too, became clear only now. The most important was that Giacomin had lied to him, with a sincerity so flawless that the security chief must, for the moment, have believed himself. The lie was important and, from Giacomin's viewpoint, essential. Three days had passed since the assassination attempt, three days during which Kane had made no move to carry out the investigation. And during all that time, the assassin had been in custody. And yet, Giacomin had claimed that he had not interrogated Clemis. Kane was in charge, the security chief had insisted—at the Imperator's order, Kane and only Kane was in charge. Giacomin had awaited Kane's wishes. He had done nothing. Impossible. Of course Giacomin must have proceeded. To have let Clemis sit idly in his cell while accomplices may have been escaping, trails growing cold, alibis growing hard, would have been criminal. But Giacomin would not admit he had grilled Clemis on his own initiative, while Kane had sat idly in another part of the palace, deluding himself that he would not lead the investigation. That meant that Giacomin was determined to keep full responsibility on Kane. Nothing would be done without his order, *nothing official*. It was the product of Giacomin's resentment, Kane knew, an anger at being passed over which was the more certain for Giacomin's refusal to show the slightest sign of it. If there was failure, it would be Kane's. And there was failure. Clemis had been interrogated for three days, and he had not cracked.

That was the last part of it, the part that haunted Kane most as he walked unseeing through the halls of the palace. Today he had gone to Clemis' cell with Giacomin, had presided over what was ostensibly the first interrogation of Clemis since Amerdath had placed him in charge of the investigation. Whether there had been earlier sessions hardly mattered. One of Giacomin's medical "specialists" had tortured Clemis and he had watched, and Clemis had given away nothing. *And he had watched. And he had enjoyed it*.

Kane stopped and leaned his head against the wall, let the cool corrugations of a silver bas-relief press against his forehead.

"Are you all right?"

Kane turned to find a man in engineer blues staring at him. He waved the man off and watched him hurry away, wondering what the engineer had seen on his face to make him leave with such haste. Was there a mark now? Some red core at the back of his eyes? *Drugs that brought nausea, drugs that brought searing chest pains like those of a heart attack, drugs that brought and sustained the agony of a kick to the groin. Oozing up from the arms of the forcechair into Clemis' pinioned wrists as the fat doctor's fingers played over the console. Beth had been gone in a second, but Clemis would die for weeks. No real damage, the fat doctor had said. Just peripheral nerve illusions. But life was all illusion, and death could sit between a man's ears and ride him while his heart went on beating and his lungs swelled and shrank and his feet beat crazily against the floor.*

Kane resumed walking. He had enjoyed it. Guilt and shame now could not erase that. But it would stop today. If Clemis had not broken under three days of truth drugs and torture, then he would not break. The decision to eliminate the torture gave Kane no relief. He wanted to kill Clemis, and he could not. He wanted Beth back. Relief was not possible.

Kane entered his suite. Pendrake was sitting cross-legged in front of the holowall, watching the silvery patterns of a waterfall.

"How's the hangover?"

Pendrake turned. "I do not have a hangover. Only human beings have hangovers."

"Whatever you say. Just remember, I offered you iced tea."

Pendrake smiled ruefully. "Next time I shall accept."

"Ready to do a little sleuthing?"

"By all means." Pendrake stood in a fluid motion of massive unwinding legs, not bothering to use his hand to help push up, and Kane realized with relief that the alien was fully recovered. "Where are we going?"

"To pay a visit to Dr. Reik," Kane said.

"Surely you do not suspect her of having anything to do with the assassination."

"Fowler Giacomin was full of juicy gossip about her. Seems her father was a colonist, and Giacomin hates colonists."

"That hardly seems . . ."

"Also," Kane said, "she's the one who does routine psychological screenings on all applicants to the praetorian guard."

"Then she tested Clemis." Pendrake frowned. "But Clemis appears to be deranged—a religious fanatic."

"And Reik passed him with flying colors," Kane finished.

Martha Reik was not at the medical suite that had been set up for Amerdath in the guard hospital near the heart of the praetorian section. She was not in her personal quarters either. Kane and Pendrake finally found her in the research labs, near the top level emergency room to which the Imperator had first been taken. She was at the far end of the lab, standing at a workbench, her back to them. The blaze of a ceiling spotlight gave her hair the richness of spun copper. When the transparent iris-type door to the labs cycled open a humid pungent smell met them. Pendrake halted. "Elias, that odor. . . ."

Kane paused and looked at the alien, alerted by the stress in his voice. He gestured at the banks of cages along either wall leading back to the work area. "It's only the animals."

Pendrake peered at the cages. Martha Reik remained bent over the workbench, apparently unaware of them. "These are the Terran life form called monkeys?"

"That's right," Kane said. "Rhesus monkeys."

"But why should a zoo be located in this place? And the cages are so small. Would not these creatures prefer to be on islands?"

Kane smiled. "This is not a zoo, Pendrake. Not like the zoological gardens we went to last year. These are research animals. They . . ." Kane hesitated, seeing the direction the conversation must take.

Pendrake edged into the lab and approached the cages, peering at one of the monkeys. The animal jumped back from the bars and bared its teeth, and the other monkeys began to screech and clamor, banging around their cages in exaggerated alarm. Kane glanced at Reik and saw with surprise that she still had not reacted to their presence. Her shoulders were hunched and her head was down. Her elbows pressed into her sides, as though the hands out of sight in front of her were engaged in a delicate task.

"I do not understand," Pendrake persisted. "How may these creatures assist in research? Surely they do not have the inclination or the intelligence . . ."

"Later," Kane said. "I'll explain it to you. When we're back in our quarters tonight." He felt exasperated, obscurely guilty. *No, friend, these creatures do not have the inclination or the intelligence to take our risks for us, to live in these small cages and die on the shiny tables.*

Kane led the way between the cages before the alien could say more. Perhaps by evening Pendrake would forget about the monkeys. Kane touched Martha Reik on the shoulder. Her hands froze and then retreated safely from the tangle of hair-fine wires that Kane could see on the circuit board in front of her.

"Elias!" She pinched her eyes shut for a second then glared at him. "You scared me!"

"Sorry. I assumed you'd heard us come in. The monkeys made such a racket." He watched her, only half believing. Could she really have shut it all out—the sounds of their entry, of the monkeys screeching and banging against their cages, entering her ears, but somewhere en route to the brain meeting an impenetrable wall of concentration and control? It was possible. Already he had watched her face down another doctor while working over Amerdath's neck. She had never even raised her voice. If she was capable of such control, he would learn now only what she wanted him to learn. If she had nothing to hide, it would be enough.

Reik nodded at Pendrake, then turned back to Kane. "How are you, Elias?"

"Fine. Everything's coming up clover."

She continued to look at him, arms crossed, fingering the wrinkles of sleeve around her elbows, and he saw that she understood and that she would not ask him again. He felt embarrassed, knowing that she was not taken aback by his sarcasm, that she had simply catalogued it and adjusted: *This man doesn't know how to suffer.*

"What's that you're working on?" he asked.

"The shoulder nexus of the Imperator's new left arm."

"New left arm?"

"I forgot. You don't know. I—me and my assistants— will be working in the next few days on the interior of a new body for Amerdath. Servomotors, myelon nerves, aluminum-alloy bones. It'll all be put inside a cosmetic shell. It's highly experimental, of course. Total prosthesis has never been tried before, and the nerve/myelon interface will present problems, but . . ." She stopped and rubbed gingerly at the corners of her eyes. "Why did you want to see me?"

"We've disturbed your work. We can come back later. . . ."

"You have questions. Ask."

Kane smiled faintly. "You don't believe in preliminaries."

"Not in conversation." She did not smile back at him, but there was something in her expression, soft and yet remote. He wondered why she'd subtly introduced the intimation of sex? To put him off balance from the start, perhaps. Or had it been there from their first contact, even with Beth lying on the table, a flesh and nerve awareness of each other. The thought made him angry. Gruffly he said, "You tested the assassin, Clemis."

"That. Yes, I tested him, and he seemed normal, so I passed him along to Alvar Sabin."

"And yet, he tried to kill Amerdath."

She nodded.

"Are you a psychologist, too?"

"My specialty is neurosurgery."

"Then why do you screen applicants to the praetorian guard?"

Reik was looking over Kane's shoulder at Pendrake. Kane turned and saw that the alien was standing immobile in front of the nearest monkey cage. The Rhesus had moved up close to the bars and was gazing at Pendrake, its head wagging back and forth and its brow wrinkled into an almost human look of perplexity. The other monkeys had grown quiet. All of them had come to the fronts of their cages and were staring somberly at the alien. Without looking at the two humans Pendrake said, "There is death here, Elias, is there not? These creatures will be killed."

"Perhaps we should go someplace more comfortable," Reik said, looking meaningfully at Kane. "I have an office just down the hall."

Pendrake followed Kane and the physician without further comment. The office was small and neat: two straight-backed chairs, a desk with a holographically projected model of the human brain, a few neatly stacked journals and an old-fashioned two-dimensional photograph of the head and shoulders of a man. The man had dark hair, and his face had an asymmetric handsomeness, a masculine variant of Reik's face. The doctor sat on the desk and indicated the two chairs. Pendrake nodded acknowledgment but remained standing.

"To get back to your question," Reik said, "I screen would-be praetorians because I have special training in computer-assisted psychometrics, a new field I got interested in after I finished my medical training. We've got a special compusayer programmed with the normative data for all the major projective and objective tests. Personality traits, states, intrapsychic functioning, needs, drives, inclinations, perversions, you name it. The machine is very eclectic. It culls from a dozen different theories, and uses factor analysis, among other techniques. All I do, really, is make sure the administration of the test occurs under standardized conditions. The compusayer has the combined knowledge of a hundred universities full of clinical psychologists, and it never gets sucked in by a pretty face.''

"So Clemis is sane."

Reik held up an admonishing finger. "He *was* sane at the time of the testing. On the day he shot the Imperator he might have been floridly psychotic."

"But surely there was some prediction of his emotional stability. He must have been more stable than average, or you wouldn't have passed him."

"Of course. But there are unpluggable holes in that. The limitations of the psychological screening procedure are inherent and well-documented."

"I'm listening."

"All right. High intelligence and cunning can defeat the procedure. Very smart people who are also socially shrewd can fool just about any test you want to throw at them— especially if they've gotten ahold of the psychological literature ahead of time and know how the various responses are scored. The bright sociopath is usually able to thwart psychometric detection, if that's what suits his purpose. Most diagnoses of sociopathy are made *after* the offending party has done something so obviously sociopathic that the diagnosis is redundant."

"Would you describe Clemis as bright and cunning?"

"I would now—now that he's done what he's done. Unfortunately it's an *a posteriori* judgment. Before, I would have said he was an intelligent, sensitive man with a history of normal behavior."

"So before he was intelligent and after he was cunning and shrewd."

"I'm afraid that's how we all tend to look at things— even psychologists."

"Have you seen Clemis in the last few days?" Kane asked.

"No, but I've heard about Sabin's interrogation—the one you broke in on right after they'd caught him. He was raving, spouting religious fanaticism. He could have been a fanatic all along. Fanaticism, after all, is a form of stability, and if he intended all along to get close to Amerdath and kill him for crazy mixed-up religious reasons, he's certainly smart enough to conceal the extent of his religiosity. Religious systems are, in a sense, inherently nonrational, a form of insanity that is normative and therefore cannot be considered insane. Lots of people believe in God and engage in practices that would be considered crazy in any other context. Like getting down on one's knees and talking to an invisible entity and asking this entity for a sunny day for one's personal picnic while the farmer down the road is praying for rain. But the key word is 'normative.' If it's a well-established norm, it ain't crazy, no matter how crazy it is."

"Did Clemis show religiosity?"

"Yes. He was fairly strong on it as I recall. But, by and large, such people make excellent employees. They tend to be trustworthy and dependable, and they usually have moralistic inhibitions that make them conformist and obedient. These can be desirable qualities so long as they're not excessive. They weren't in Clemis at the time of testing, or I wouldn't have passed him." Reik sounded annoyed, defensive, and Kane wondered if her control was beginning to slip. Or was she merely aware that he'd be looking for some normal signs of resentment? He remembered something Giacomin had said in his office after the interrogation of Clemis. Giacomin had hinted that Gregory Amerdath had propositioned his personal physician a number of times, and that Martha Reik was known, at least at first, to have refused his advances. Over the years, Kane knew that several women had been banished from court for rejecting Amerdath. But Martha Reik had stayed, had retained her powerful position as the caretaker of the Imperator's health. Giacomin had no evidence that she had ever given in, only that she had refused. If his information was accurate, then Reik had found some of the most elusive words in any language—those that would let a man of Amerdath's power and ego down gently. She had found the words, and the way of saying them, and it wasn't much good trying to guess now whether she was deliberately letting him see her irritation.

Kane realized he was tuned in to her too intensely, striving for a close view of her instead of concentrating on the larger, more objective view. There was something compelling about her. He did not want to admit it, but she attracted him. She was not beautiful, at least not until the eye had adjusted to the slight lopsidedness of her face, the adolescent leanness of her, the illusion of awkwardness. But as he spent time with her she seemed to gather glamour and force, and he found that he wanted to look at her; that he wanted to do more than look. He'd been searching for guilt in her because he felt so guilty himself; guilty about wanting her. He had seen her as powerful and devious, because he could not control or understand his own feelings about her. It was, he saw, useless to question her further.

He realized that he'd said nothing for a minute. Reik's expression had softened, and Pendrake was discreetly studying him. "So you're fixing Amerdath a new body," he said to Reik. "How are you at new heads?"

No one smiled.

CHAPTER 9

The ultraviolet eye of the compusayer blinked twice in strobelike succession, and Kane experienced a psychosomatic tingling at the backs of his eyeballs. During a delay that was leisurely by electronic standards and instantaneous to human senses, the compusayer checked and cleared their retinal patterns. In a melodious voice the machine introduced itself as "Morulius, the Imperator's personal compusayer," and invited them to enter the conference chamber. Amerdath was in a corner opposite the door. The medical cart on which his head was supported had been enclosed to hide the blood filtration and vocal air pressure equipment. Kane nodded at Amerdath and glanced around the room. It was large and, by the opulent standards of the palace, Spartan. The bulk of the compusayer was invisible, buried in the cream-colored walls, except for another ultraviolet eye centered in the ceiling. The floor was composed of cushioned tiles the color of wheat. The tiles were patterned with concentric black squares, nested to give the illusion of inverted pyramidal pits dropping below the grid formed by the tile borders. Kane found himself unconsciously centering his feet on the borders as he entered. A few straight-backed chairs were the only furnishings of the room besides Amerdath's cart. Kane guessed that there had once been a large desk against one wall, but that Amerdath had, after his injury, had it removed. One full wall of the room was a holoscreen, keyed to transmit in three-dimensional exactness whatever live or taped view was selected from cameras on the perimeter walls of the palace.

Alvar Sabin was standing in front of the holowall. He did not acknowledge Kane or Pendrake, but gazed out the wall, with his back to Chuddath and the Imperator. The Ornyl bodyguard stood behind Amerdath, upper arms crossed. There was one other person in the room, a thin man in a smock, who was working on an armature and some plastiflesh with the hot molding tools of his trade.

Amerdath was so absorbed in the plastician's activities that at first he did not seem to notice Kane and Pendrake. Then his head turned slowly atop the cart and he smiled at them. "Elias, Pendrake, sit down, sit down. I can't get Alvar to stop pacing the deck, but at least you'll have a seat." Kane took one of the chairs about two meters from Amerdath, and Pendrake sat next to him. The Imperator smiled knowingly. "You're wondering how I turned my head just now. They've implanted some electrodes in the muscles of my forehead above either eye. One controls this collar." Amerdath illustrated by wagging his head back and forth. They'd made the rotating support noiseless, and Amerdath's forehead wrinkled only a little as he contracted the muscle that sent signals to the collar. "The other muscle controls the bellows for speech, so I don't have to have someone standing by to turn my wind on and off. Fantastic, isn't it?"

"Yes, sir." Kane wondered if Amerdath was being sardonic, or if his booming joviality truly reflected his mood. The Imperator's complexion was ruddy and his eyes seemed bright, animated.

"I've been practicing, and it's quite simple. You've got no idea what a relief it is not to be straining to look at things out of the corner of my eye. Next thing you know, I'll—o-rrr-gh-h." The sound burst from Amerdath's throat and then there was a harsh sigh as the bellows began to subside. Kane fought an urge to laugh, the same terrifying impulse that had struck him at Beth's funeral. It frightened him, a finger of madness poking through a wall of his brain. He began to sweat. Amerdath did not try to finish his sentence. His head turned away toward the plastician, and Kane looked at the man too, desperate for any distraction.

The plastician was working mounds of soft pinkish-tan prep mixture onto the mesh of an armature that was shaped like a torso. The man was sweating and working quickly, with deft nervous dartings of his bony hands. He kept his attention entirely on the worktable, never looking up at the Imperator. Each time he swallowed, his Adam's apple strained at his thin neck as if trying to burst free. The man's anxiety spread around him into the room, making Kane want to get up, to give in to the muscles of his legs, the sensorimotor urge to flee. He understood why Sabin paced up and down in front of the holowall, hands clasped behind his back, delivered by long comradeship from his old admiral's command to sit. Only the two aliens seemed, each in his own way, immune from the charged atmosphere of the room. Chuddath's stillness was the ancient calm of the insect who, lacking a purpose, does not move. The compound eyes seemed directed at the plastician, but it was impossible to be sure. Pendrake watched the frightened plastician with compassion. The alien's hands rested loosely on his knees, the three fingers still and relaxed, as if he hoped to will his own composure into the sweating jerking man.

"Imperator." The voice, low and calm, issued from the ceiling.

"Yes, Morulius?"

"The human in the center of the room has entered an extremely agitated state. His pulse has reached one hundred and his respiration is rapid, and his skin conductance . . ."

"All right," Amerdath snapped. "That's enough."

The compusayer silenced itself.

"Mr. Courant," the Imperator said.

The plastician dropped the blob of plastiflesh he'd been working and turned to face Amerdath, his head lowered. "Your majesty, I beg your forgiveness. . . ."

"Don't . . ." One of Amerdath's eyebrows lowered slightly and his voice softened. "Don't grovel. I don't need anyone licking my boots, not anymore." Amerdath gave a macabre grin, but the plastician only bowed further, then caught himself and forced his head up. His face had turned the color of ash. The Imperator's smile grew cool.

"Sir," the man said desperately, "I . . . I wish no offense, but, your bodyguard, sir . . . I mean, really, your Highness, it's a compliment to him in view of his duties, but . . . he . . . frightens me."

The Imperator's smile became genuine again. "Chuddath? My dear fellow, you should have said something earlier. Sometimes he frightens me too. Well, get your things together then, and continue in the gold room. It's not far from here. I'll have some praetorians assist you. Morulius?"

"Yes, Imperator, I'll attend to it."

Kane watched the plastician fumble his tools together from a side table and push his work cart toward the door, knowing that it had not been Chuddath who had frightened the man. Credit him with quick wits, though. The Imperator had been eager to accept the excuse. Two praetorians, summoned from the company of guards and medical personnel in the chamber's anteroom, came to escort the man out. Amerdath said, "You understand, Mr. Courant, that I'll still want to keep track of your work. I'll look in on you in a couple of hours. You can stand Chuddath for a few minutes at a time can't you? After all, it is my brawny chest you're building there.''

The plastician forced a smile. "Of course, your Highness. Thank you, sir. I'm sorry." He pushed his cart through the door and was gone. Amerdath gazed at the closed door. His face sagged and Kane realized that he was not fooled after all. Amerdath knew that he was a monster in the eyes of the man who had just left, that he seemed more hideous even than the dreaded Ornyl warrior.

"Alvar, what *are* you staring at?"

Sabin turned at last from the holowall. "Only the people. They're still gathered outside the city wall at the foot of the palace mesa, several thousand of them. Keeping a watch for you, Admiral." Sabin's use of the old title seemed to soothe the Imperator. The slackness of his face firmed up, replaced by the inward look of memory.

"Yes, the vigil," Amerdath said after a moment. "Are they waiting for me to die, Alvar?"

"A few of them, no doubt."

"Damn it, couldn't you lie just this once?"

"You rule, sir, and ruling always makes enemies."

"I'll remember that," Amerdath said dryly. He looked past Sabin at the window. "I suppose soon I should go out on the east balcony in the morning sun and make a spectacle of myself for them. Tell them that their devotion has pulled me through."

Sabin turned. "That's an excellent idea, sir. When you get . . . the new body, go out and speak to them. We'll use the viewscreens at the base of the mesa, and the people with binoculars and telescopes will see you in the flesh. It'd calm down the press and ease things back toward normal."

"In the flesh," Amerdath mused. "Perhaps I will. As soon as they've got the flesh ready. I'll raise my arm, by God, and give them my blessing. What do you say to that?"

"I'd say blessing them would be going a bit far, sir." It was the first time Kane had seen Sabin grin.

"Fowler Giacomin is approaching, Imperator," the compusayer said.

"Send him in."

Giacomin entered, bowed to the Imperator and nodded at Kane and Pendrake.

"All right," Amerdath said. "Elias, I believe this is your circus."

"Alvar and Fowler have done most of the legwork," Kane replied. "I'll let them give you their impressions first, starting with what we think about the interrogation results." He hoped the evasion was not too obvious. In the end he'd have to say something of substance, but there was little to say. After finishing with Martha Reik, he'd merely gone through the motions, interviewing praetorian bunkmates of Clemis, and piecing together as much as possible of the weeks before the assassination attempt. It had all come to nothing. There were no real leads.

Giacomin said nothing. After an uncomfortable interval, Sabin cleared his throat. "We've grilled Mark Clemis exhaustively. At first we used drugs, pain and deprivation." Sabin glanced at Kane. "More recently we've tried the soft approach—persuasion, hints of leniency, every tactic we can think of. He hasn't bent, much less broken. At first I was convinced he was part of a conspiracy, but now I don't think so."

Giacomin's mouth quirked but he said nothing.

"I no longer think there is anything to break in that man," Sabin continued. "He is what he says he is— a self-styled avenger who thinks God commanded him to . . ." Sabin reddened slightly.

"To punish me for my debaucheries," Amerdath supplied. He looked at Giacomin. "What do *you* think?"

The security chief hesitated just long enough to create the impression that he did not want to contradict Sabin. "Clemis was smart enough to fool your personal physician at the screening, sir. He's tough, too, and he comes across like a fanatic, just as Alvar says. But one must dig deeper to get at the core of this.''

"Explain.''

"Mark Clemis has been preconditioned, sir. I'm quite sure of it. Whoever used him to get at you implanted a deep persona of religious fanaticism by a combination of hypnotic techniques and other methods of which we are not aware. He's been preconditioned to resist our methods. And he has no idea that it was done to him, which is why we can't positively confirm it.''

"Are you saying he's been brainwashed by some new undetectable method?''

"Essentially.''

Sabin grunted. "No preconditioned state could hold up under what your sweaty sadist friend was doing to Clemis. . . .''

"May I remind you,'' Giacomin interrupted coldly, "of the examples of history. Rome, where the Christians were fed to lions, made into human torches. Later, the Inquisition. It's the best defense possible. Utter fanaticism. Religious fanaticism is already a form of brainwashing in its natural state, brainwashing by the self or by others. It should be possible to do it more quickly and scientifically to suit a specific purpose. The resistance Clemis is giving us now was in no way indicated by the screening tests that cleared him for praetorian duty.''

"That's not exactly correct,'' Kane said. "Dr. Reik reports that there was some evidence of excessive religiosity in those tests . . .''

"But not to the point of fanaticism. That could only have been done to him after he was recruited, unless Dr. Reik herself falsified the test results.''

"There's no way for such tests to be definitive about the extent or genuineness of Clemis' religious orientation.''

Giacomin gave a tolerant smile. "Perhaps, Mr. Kane, you were taken in by Dr. Reik's brains and . . . charm.''

Kane frowned, knowing that things were slipping out of control, but unsure how to stop it. He could either bicker with Giacomin in front of Amerdath, or accept the innuendos in silence. Neither seemed a good course. "When you questioned her," Giacomin went on, "she may have deliberately equivocated. After all, it was her responsibility to keep people like Clemis away from the Imperator."

"Hers and yours and mine," Sabin said. "Don't forget that, Fowler."

"It doesn't seem that we can resolve this," Amerdath said.

"But there's something else, sir," Giacomin said. "The colonists . . ."

"Not that again," Sabin said. "If a mosquito bites you, you think it was sent by the colonists."

"Alvar, you are out of your depth here," Giacomin said, "so don't presume to challenge me. My agents intercepted a coded tight beam message from the Centauran frigate *Sentinel,* which, as we all know, has been for several days on its way to Earth bearing none other than the Imperial viceroy, Richard DuMorgan. The message is in a new code, which we have so far been unable to break. This message arrived on the morning, Imperator, *the same morning* that Clemis almost succeeded in killing you."

Kane felt the shock of Giacomin's words in the frozen silence. *A covert message from a ship carrying the chief colonist viceroy?* Sabin stared at the security chief, and Kane saw that he was equally taken by surprise. "Your agents on Alpha Centauri IV couldn't have intercepted a tight-beamed message," Sabin said, "from a frigate in space directed at a secret locus on Earth, and neither, except by the sheerest dumb luck of stumbling onto the right place at the right time with a mobile tracking unit, could any of your monitoring posts here on Earth."

Kane's shock began to turn into anger, but it was a bleak, impotent anger, turned inward by mortification. Giacomin was making both him and Alvar look incompetent.

When the three of them had met earlier to pool information for the briefing, the security chief had acted like he knew nothing more than they did.

Sabin's eyes narrowed with understanding. "You had a man aboard their ship."

Giacomin said nothing.

"There are no Terrans aboard the *Sentinel*," Sabin went on, "except for those in the praetorian honor guard. That means you corrupted one of my men to do your spying."

"Corrupted is hardly the word . . ."

"How many others have you turned?" Sabin's back was straight and rigid. A vein pulsed above the tight ring of his uniform collar. A hint of smugness turned the corners of Giacomin's mouth. "Perhaps Clemis was one of your agents," Sabin said.

Giacomin's smugness vanished. "Clemis was your man, Alvar. And if he were not, you should know it."

"I demand the names of any praetorians who you have made into your agents," Sabin said. "Now or in the past."

"That need not concern you—as long as you remain loyal."

Sabin rested a hand on the butt of his slug gun. "Do you question my loyalty?"

Giacomin started to answer, then hesitated, perhaps sensing that he was a word away from the end of all words. He had crossed into Sabin's world, where death came quickly and from the front. Kane looked to the Imperator, expecting him to intervene, but Amerdath watched the two men almost avidly, as if he were enjoying the confrontation, the prospect of blood. Pendrake had risen quietly, and Kane stood too, knowing that neither of them could act in time if Giacomin said the wrong word.

"Imperator . . ." began the compusayer.

"Belay," Amerdath hissed.

A clear cylindrical shield dropped noiselessly from the ceiling, enclosing the Imperator. Amerdath scowled and his lips moved soundlessly, but the shield stayed in place. Chuddath remained behind the cylinder, staring impassively over the Imperator's head at the two men.

Giacomin's forehead glistened. "Alvar, Alvar," he said placatingly. "Please don't misunderstand me. I had no intention of insulting your honor."

Sabin's expression did not soften, but his hand dropped away from the slug gun. The shield retracted into the ceiling. For a minute no one spoke. The Imperator's expression was composed again. "Richard DuMorgan," he mused, as though nothing had happened. "DuMorgan is my most loyal viceroy."

Giacomin turned away gratefully from the still rigid praetorian. "It is my profoundest wish," he said, "that you prove to be right, sir. But DuMorgan is also your most *powerful* viceroy. The message did come from his flagship. We *are* unable to decode it. We cannot afford to ignore the possibility . . ." Giacomin glanced at Sabin, but the commander had turned back to the holowall, and was staring with a remote expression at the image of the crowds gathered below the palace. ". . . the possibility," Giacomin finished, "that the leader of the most powerful colony has conspired to assassinate his lord and to overthrow Earth."

CHAPTER 10

Kane sat on the edge of his bed and stared down at his boots. He wanted to lie back, to forget the fiasco of the briefing, to go to sleep and stay asleep for a day, a week, however long it took. But first he knew he should take his boots off. The prospect of reaching down and tugging his feet free seemed too onerous, so he merely sat, head down, while Pendrake fussed with the library screen in the next room. The audio was set too low for Kane to make out the words. He let the annoying drone go on for a minute, then vented some of his irritation by stretching out with his boots still on. Pendrake appeared in the doorway.

"Am I disturbing you, Elias? If you wish to rest, I can use the machine later."

Kane lifted a hand from the bedspread, let it drop again.

"I fear I was not having much luck anyway," the alien said.

Kane grunted. He did not hear Pendrake move off, and after a moment the sense of being watched made him turn his head. Pendrake was leaning, arms crossed, against the door frame, his gaze wandering decorously around the ceiling. He seemed ill at ease.

"Was there something else?" Kane asked.

Pendrake looked down at him with sympathy. "It was not so bad, Elias."

Kane sighed, sat up on the edge of the bed again. "Giacomin made us—made *me*—look like a complete fool."

"It is not your fault he told you nothing about the message from the viceroy's ship."

"When you're the top banana and something goes wrong, it's your fault, regardless of the circumstances. That's what being top banana means."

"But that is neither fair nor logical."

"You've noticed." Kane started to lie back again.

"Perhaps you can help me with something," Pendrake said, a bit too quickly.

Kane said nothing, waited. Why wouldn't the alien just leave him alone?

"The library seems to say little on the subject of relations between the colonies and Earth," Pendrake continued. "Fowler Giacomin believes colonists may be behind the assassination attempt, and that they wish to overthrow Earth. I fear I do not understand."

"What don't you understand?"

"What is the source of this tension between Earth and the colonies?"

Kane hitched up until his back was against the padded headboard. The spread pointed with accusing wrinkles at his boot heels. "Get me a drink, would you?"

Pendrake disappeared at once and returned with a tumbler of whiskey over ice. The drink tasted flat but Kane downed half of it anyway. "The main source of tension between Earth and the colonies," he pronounced, "is that we don't like each other."

Pendrake gave him a half-smile. "I had hoped for a bit more detail, Elias. Is it because of the food situation?"

"No. That's over now."

Pendrake nodded. "I realize that the monopoly itself is ended. The psychopath plague proved that. If the colonists had not finally suceeeded in building a covert hydroponics industry, they would never have dared quarantine all Earth ships, including the food freighters. But would there not still be considerable resentment over the way Earth maintained the food monopoly for so many years?"

"No doubt, but it's not as sinister as you make it sound," Kane said. "None of the planets yet settled have much arable land. Earth has four times as much as all nine colony planets put together. From the start that left two options: setting up a hydroponics industry or running food supplies out from Earth. No colonists complained when they were spared building and tending the huge climate-controlled warehouses, the miles of nutrient tanks that would have been necessary to support each planet. They ate their prime rib and asparagus, fresh from Earth every week, and worried about other things, just like people in the big cities here on Earth have always done." Kane finished his whiskey, stared at the tumbler in the dim light of the bedroom. He saw what Pendrake was doing, and was even grateful in a listless way. Talking interplanetary politics was better than brooding about the way he was being stiffed by Giacomin. Still, being distracted was a poor substitute for being truly interested in what he was talking about. How long had it been since he'd felt enthusiasm for anything at all? It was an ill-inspired question, one to which he knew the precise answer in days and hours.

"If the food monopoly started out so innocently," Pendrake said, "how did it become such an issue later?"

Kane shrugged. "Once the colonies got established, someone got the idea it would be better if Earth couldn't hold food dependence over their heads. When they tried to end the arrangement Earth became suspicious that the colonies wanted to kiss us off, so they kept the monopoly going as long as they could with embargoes and surveillance. What difference does it make?''

"I am trying to understand why colonist plotters might now be moving against the Imperator.'' Pendrake's voice was not chiding, but Kane found a rebuke in the words. Pendrake pressed on before he could say anything. "It is your view, then, that growing mutual suspicion brought things to the present unhappy state?''

"It was in the cards,'' Kane said.

"How would you pose the central issue?'' the alien persisted.

Kane sighed. "Three words or less, my friend. That's what you get today: Independence versus Unity.'' Kane set his glass on the bed table and slumped down until his knees blocked the alien out of his sight.

"Very interesting,'' Pendrake said. He moved so that he was again in Kane's line of sight, and sat down on the corner of the bedroom's writing desk. "Independence versus Unity. And the answer will be decided by who has the dreadnaughts.''

"You've got it.''

"And Earth has the dreadnaughts.'' Pendrake gazed at him, the dark eyes calculating, and Kane knew the alien was determined to keep the thing going, that he was thinking how best to coax his poor moody human friend into another spoonful of medicinal talk. Part of him wanted to tell Pendrake to go to hell, but that would have been harder than pulling off his boots. There was no escaping his friend's good intentions. The only way out was to perk up a bit, convince Pendrake that he'd been a help.

"Dreadnaughts seem a poor way to settle a difference of philosophy,'' Pendrake said. "Surely the very presence of Imperial ships off every colony planet can only exacerbate the problem.''

"The ships are there for a reason,'' Kane said. "It was an Imperial battle group that staved off the alien attack on Alpha Centauri. Someday an alien species a little stronger and smarter and better organized than the Andinaz raiders will come along. Right now the ambassador from Moitan is here dealing with Amerdath over the issue of a disputed planet. We don't have any reason to think the Moitan are warlike, but what if they are? They could prey easily on a scattered collection of independent frontier planets, pick them off one at a time.''

"One could make the point," Pendrake said, "that Imperial ships defended Alpha Centauri IV only because the colony did not have its own big warships.''

"It had warships.''

"A mere police force, with no ship above the cruiser class, as is the case for all colonies.''

"Your pacifism seems to be slipping," Kane said.

Pendrake grunted. "Surely you know, Elias, that I profoundly wish there were no such thing as a dreadnaught ship. But I still must ask the justice, thinking as much as I can like an Earthman, of the great warships being entirely in the hands of Imperials.''

Kane laughed sourly. "What do you want? A good fair fight or peace?''

"You know the answer to that, Elias.''

"Sure, I know. Don't mind me.''

Pendrake was silent a moment, his face thoughtful. "What has kept the colonists from making their own dreadnaughts?" he said.

"Economics," Kane answered. "Earth had a monopoly on food, and that monopoly is gone now because hydroponics is a simple science requiring basic materials. Eventually the colonies scraped together or diverted enough of those materials despite the embargo. The making of a warship—even a single ship in the corvette class—is an incredibly complex science, requiring huge outlays of money, technology and manpower." Pendrake nodded encouragingly and Kane pushed on with it. "The parts that go into a single Imperial warship come from hundreds of different factories. The subprocesses of the guidance system alone require technologies and theories from a dozen different branches of math, physics and engineering. The construction costs of a single paradoxical drive unit equal the total monetary value of a month's output of raw materials by Alpha Centauri IV, and that's our oldest and most productive colony. The forty or so manufacturing plants where sub-components of such units are turned out would cost many times that to build from scratch, assuming Earth would sell all the various pieces of high-tech machinery necessary. The colonies can afford to buy some ships when they are allowed to, though the expense even of that is very high. They can't yet afford the purely physical costs of building their own warships, even if they could put together the army of brainy types needed. So Earth is the only dealer in the warship trade.'' Pendrake tried to say something, but Kane rode over it. ''You can argue whether Earth should ever have tried to maintain a monopoly on food. But you can't argue that Earth should dole out dreadnaught class warships.''

''So instead it will use those warships to force its will on the colonies.''

Kane shrugged. ''What we can or cannot force is open to question. Stopping a combined revolt of all or most of the colonies would be a dicey proposition, dreadnaughts or no dreadnaughts. It's a delicate balance of power. There are loyalists in the colonies, but there's a growing faction determined to break loose. The colony planets were settled in the first place by restless adventurers, free spirits, misfits who've had their share of fights, many of them started by their own belligerence. Amerdath knows this. To be human is to feel a certain perverse admiration for it. But putting planet-killer ships into the hands of such people is a different matter. The Imperator, whoever holds the office now or in the future, must walk a high wire. The challenge is to channel the independent spirit of the colonies, to keep it pointed out toward the discovery and taming of new worlds, while keeping a unified human race, at peace with

itself and everybody else. If Beta Tenoris had a few
dreadnaughts in its navy, the Moitan ambassador might not
be on Earth today, trying to diplomatically settle its differ-
ences with the colony.''

"A telling point," Pendrake agreed. "Do you believe
Gregory Amerdath acts from these high motives, or for the
aggrandizement of his own power, his personal ambition
to rule over the entire human race?''

Kane swung his feet to the floor and sat on the edge of
the bed. "I'm not sure his motives matter as long as he
walks the wire," he said. "But sure, I think he wants
what's best for his people—all of them. But he can fight,
too. He seized power in the unification wars. Earth was
destroying itself with its nationalistic feuding, and it was
carrying those feuds into space. Amerdath didn't win the
war so he could then sit by and watch while the new union
breaks apart under the feuds of planetarism. But he is also
a proud and ambitious man. He has immense energy and a
shrewd mind. He likes his power. . . .'' Kane noticed
Pendrake's suddenly averted face and realized he was
talking about the man as he had been, a man with arms
and legs, a beating heart, questing loins, a joy for life. The
phrase was glassy and frictionless, and Kane was unable to
move off it. *A joy for life.*

A minute passed and then he got up and walked past
Pendrake to the door of the suite. "I need . . .'' He stood
at the door without turning, trying to think what it was that
he did need. "I need to get out of here," he finished.

CHAPTER 11

Kane stood on top of the palace and stared down at the arid stretches of rock and desert. He had chosen a south tower, because none of Chronos, the city that spread on the plain below Amerdath's palace, had yet expanded to this inhospitable side of the man-made mesa. Pendrake, knowing he wanted solitude, had withdrawn to the other side of the deserted tower, but for some reason lingered there instead of leaving altogether. The vertical drop of over three hundred meters down the smooth outer wall of the palace pulled Kane's blood, spun it over the nerve tips of stomach and eye. Smoothed by distance, blasted by a million brutal summers, the Nevada desert beckoned like a hard cleansing sea. There was no wind. The sky, cloudless and brilliant, floated above, and Kane had the conviction that if he were to jump he would not fall, but would spiral away to a dot, a mote of dust freed by gravity to drift timelessly. The idea refused to pass out of his mind. It stuck in place, vivid and seductive. He saw himself to be individual immortal atoms, as indestructible as the rocks

below. He felt time stop, understood the lie of his beating
heart, and knew the silence would accept him.

"Elias!"

Kane stood for a moment longer, his feet on the second
rung of the railing. The top rail pressed against his knees.
Pendrake's hand held his belt as his upper body arched
over the desert far below. The stones of the tower jittered
into focus, receding to tiny curling lines where they met
the top of the mesa. Kane gagged and tried to straighten.
Pendrake hauled him back to safety. His knees wobbled
and he bent over, propping his hands on his legs until he
was sure he could stand. He stared at Pendrake. "I was
. . . I . . ."

The alien's face was full of pain. "You wish to die?
Because I desire that you live."

"I don't know what came over me," Kane said.
"I didn't plan it. One minute I was just looking out, and
then . . ."

"She would be angry to see you on that rail."

"Stop." Kane said it harshly, then rubbed at his throat.
"I know," he said more quietly. "I know she would. But
she's *gone,* Pendrake."

"She is not gone."

"What kind of talk is that?"

"She is in our minds, Elias, where she always was. It is
the only place she or anyone else can be for us. If you
destroy that, then truly you destroy her."

The tears came, hot and bitter. Kane turned away from
the alien, but did not try to escape the hand on his shoulder.
He sobbed, dried his face on his sleeve and then broke
down again. When at last he got it under control, he felt
emptied, a cell with the door flung open, something huge
and dark gone while his eyes were pinched shut. Perhaps it
had flung itself on the rocks without him. He turned back
to Pendrake. "Why do I suddenly feel so good?"

"Because you are alive and need no longer feel guilty
about it. You did try most earnestly to kill yourself. I

stopped you or you would have succeeded. Your sacrifice is accepted, Elias.''

"By God?"

"By the god that is within you."

"A harsh god."

"This is a harsh time."

Kane finished drying his face. "I haven't cried since I was a boy. Frankly, it's overrated."

Pendrake smiled. "You are a terrible liar, Elias." There was a sound behind them, the pneumatic whoosh of the roof door. Kane and Pendrake turned as the Princess Briana, attended by two praetorians, emerged from the elevator.

"Ah, there you are, Kane. I was told by your room that you might be up here." Briana strode toward him, and Kane watched her come, hoping his eyes were not too red. He was surprised at the pleasure of seeing her walk, the pure aesthetic enjoyment. A moment ago he had tried to kill himself, and now he felt life bursting in him. He sensed that it would not last, but he was grateful for it. Briana stopped a short distance from him, as though deliberately allowing him room to inspect her. She was dressed in a one-piece suit of dazzling white that matched her hair and molded itself to her easy movements. The Amerdath tree emblem was stitched in silver, the branches spreading to her shoulders and the trunk descending between her breasts to root itself in a belt of silver links. Kane bowed, imitating the courtly gesture of Pendrake.

"Princess, I'm honored that you would seek me out."

"Flattery, Kane? I hadn't thought it like you."

Kane shrugged and gave her a smile, realizing as he did it that he must look like a simpering fool to her.

"I want to talk to you," the princess said.

"If you'll excuse me," Pendrake said, picking up quickly on her meaning. "Elias, there are some matters for me to attend. I will be in our rooms." He bowed to Briana. "Princess."

She watched the alien depart. "He's quite impressive, your Cephantine friend. So powerful looking."

"I've seen him rearrange the bars in an ImpSec prison cell."

"Yes, I recall the story of how you escaped the death cell in time to face down the Chirpones in front of my father. I had always assumed that the part about the bars was myth."

"It's no myth."

Briana looked more closely at him. "Are you sure you want to talk right now?"

"Talking is exactly what I want to do."

"Fine." Briana's expression became businesslike. "You've held my father's highest esteem since the end of the plague. That is why I ask you for help now. Perhaps you can influence him."

Kane felt shaky, almost high. He tried to put what he had just come through totally out of his mind. He could think about it later, and he knew that he would think about it, that he would have no choice. Now there was Briana, demanding his attention, demanding that he listen. It was a demand that fit his needs. "In what way would you like me to influence him?" he said.

Briana gestured, and the two praetorians stepped back, out of earshot. "Dr. Reik arranged for Father to be treated by a psychiatrist."

Kane nodded. Reik had told him that Amerdath would be scheduled for psychiatric treatment.

"Father talked with the doctor briefly and then ordered him out. He refuses now to see any kind of therapist."

"Something made him angry?"

"He was quite calm about it, actually. He just thanked the man for his concern and said that he was fine and didn't need any therapy."

"And you want me to persuade him otherwise?"

"Yes."

"But if he doesn't want . . ."

"Mr. Kane, surely you see how *crazy* that is, refusing all psychotherapy. My father had his body blown away, cremated out from under him. He is the only human being in history to suffer so grievous a wound and live. Can you imagine what a victim of the guillotine would have suffered if the head had remained conscious for even a minute after? That's what my father faces every minute he's awake, every minute that they don't sedate that bottled blood that keeps circulating through the plastic tubes."

Kane hesitated, wondering what she really wanted. Didn't she realize that his relationship with her father was not friendship, not the kind of intimacy that could permit him to tell Amerdath that he was shattered—that he needed a psychotherapist to help him patch together his sanity. And even if he was such a close friend, Amerdath did not seem shattered to him. He seemed, in fact, to be coping almost unbelievably well with his calamity. Perhaps Briana wanted to undermine his confidence in Amerdath's ability to go on ruling. But why would she care to influence the opinion of a sometime private investigator, a man who had come to court only weeks ago? If it was the throne she wanted, she should be concentrating her intrigues on those of her father's lieutenants with real power. Perhaps she was setting him up. Perhaps she knew that if he tried to persuade her father to accept psychiatric treatment, Amerdath would become angry and dismiss him. She might have reasons for wanting him off the investigation.

Kane felt the palace below him again like quicksand, sucking at him with its intrigues. He had come to the rooftop seeking escape, a more permanent escape than he had known. Pendrake had pulled him back from the edge, and before he could fully realize what he had almost done, Briana had come, a dazzling vision of beauty and life, and he had felt elation at escaping death. Now the rest of what she represented imposed itself on him again. The elation was gone and reality was back. He looked at the edge of the rooftop, the rail he had climbed, and suppressed a shudder of revulsion. There was short death and long death, the only two choices open in life. Still, he was glad to be afraid again of the short death. He looked back at Briana, found her gazing at him with a directness unleavened by social courtesy. She said much in the way she looked at him. She was comfortable with her impulses. Now she wanted to study him, so she studied him, not caring how he took it. The sun had reached its zenith above him. The white stones of the roof glared up into his eyes. He began to sweat.

"Do you see that I am right, that my father needs therapy?" Briana asked.

"Perhaps he prefers to deal with his loss in his own way."

"You refuse to speak to him about this?" The jade eyes grew cold with punishing swiftness. Kane felt himself weakening. He did not have the strength to deal with her now, he realized. "I want an answer, Kane."

"I'll be seeing your father regularly in my role as investigator," Kane temporized. "I'll think about what you've said. If it seems appropriate . . ."

She moved close to him, so close that her perfume enveloped him, subtle but compelling, a hint of rose, a suggestion of silks molded against satin skin, dewy with the oils of her body. "If you persuade him," she murmured, "I'll not forget it." He fought the impulse to pull her to him, to press the length of himself against her. He felt at the same time drawn and repelled. He hated his own weakness—in failing to say no, in letting her obvious use of her sexuality arouse him. And still he could not throw off an image of the two of them on the vast satins of her bed, overhung with silver canopies, scented fountains in the background, the measured bootsteps of praetorians sensed rather than heard in the hallways outside. The scene gathered force in his mind, heavy with the weight of destiny, a stone still far above him but falling inexorably.

She let him edge back from her, showing with a half-smile that she was aware of it. "I think my father refuses psychotherapy because he is clinging to a false hope," she said.

"A false hope?" he said thickly.

"That a body can be restored to him. That he'll walk again, pick things up with his hands; bed a thousand more women, like that doctor of his. Poor Elias, do I make you uncomfortable? But surely you've heard the gossip. How he used to court Dr. Reik and how she refused him over and over. How they had it out, shouting and screaming, with the servants cringing in the next room. You're sweating, Elias."

"You said your father hopes to get a body back. Is the artificial body finished, then?"

"Reik has scheduled the surgery for tomorrow. By the way, Father wants you there."

No, Kane thought, the force of it sounding like a voice inside his head. The idea of watching Amerdath's neck being attached to the plastician's simulacrum, to the network of myelon nerves, revolted him, causing a feeling near panic. Or perhaps it was the thought of going back into the surgery room.

"He probably wants you watching Reik," Briana said. "Not that you could do anything if she decided to make a fatal slip."

"I'm sure Dr. Reik will do the best she can," Kane said.

"You're quite impressed with her then?" Briana's voice was heavy with private amusement.

"I see no reason to be at the surgery," Kane said stiffly.

"Nevertheless, you will be there." She waited for him to reply. He said nothing. She gave him a half-smile, acknowledgment or contempt, and let it pass. He savored his foolish little victory, the feeling of having located his spine in the sweating mass between his shoulder blades. Briana sighed. "Poor Father. Even if this body, this artificial body, works, there will be so much he can't do. But still he clings to his hopes. What do you think that means, Mr. Kane?''

''I haven't thought about it.''

She nodded enigmatically. ''Even if the transplant succeeds, Mr. Kane, how long do you think my father, Gregory Amerdath, Imperator of the Terran Empire, will be content with an *artificial* body?'' She turned and the two praetorians fell in on either side of her as she strode to the elevator.

CHAPTER 12

Because he did not want to be there at all, Kane got to the operating room early. He took a mean pleasure in ordering aside the praetorian who guarded the entrance to the O.R.'s small steep observation balcony. The guard was young and duty-stiff, and did not at first recognize this tall wolfish man dressed in grays so drab by palace standards that they must draw suspicion.

The balcony was deserted. Kane chose a seat in the backmost of the three curving rows. He turned himself inward in an effort to escape his surroundings, but inside waited the knowledge that yesterday he had tried to kill himself. The remembrance terrified him now, much more than it had immediately afterward. How could he have attempted such a thing? At least his terror was reassuring, proof that his instinct to live was back in place. Something had been exorcised. But he had not been healed; it meant only that he must live with his sickness. He tried to empty his mind, to be neither inside himself, where there was so little comfort, nor in this room.

A few blank moments passed, a meager success, and

then Kane began to let in the clamor from his senses—a faint smell of disinfectant, the unnatural sparkle of glassware and chrome and steel under searing overhead lights; the headless body on the table in the center of the room. The plastician had done a good job, so good that Kane had to look away and then back, building up the image by increments. He had not prepared himself for the sight of the headless body because his mind had classified it differently—a clever machine and nothing more would be grafted to Amerdath's head this morning. But the eye saw a well-muscled corpse, fingers curving in repose, tracts of white hair on the chest, the forearms, the legs. The eye saw a corpse with no head or neck, and Kane felt the meager contents of his stomach turn sour and reach, prickling, for his jaws. The plastician had given the body a penis, and Kane smiled grimly despite the mood of his stomach. No Cromwellian portrait, this body that the Imperator had commissioned. The penis was modeled on a lore that had not changed in centuries of male insecurity. It would impress anyone who looked and did not think. It would give feeling, but it would not feel. It was the ultimate symbol of the body from which it hung—a symbol of potency to all but its numb bearer. Kane thought about the Princess Briana's last words to him on the palace tower, and the foreboding of that moment returned. *Surely Amerdath would not aspire to take a human body, a live human body for his own.*

Doors swung and a figure came into view below the curve of the balcony. The man or woman, masked, capped and amorphous in a rumpled gown, began to check the equipment around the body. More O.R. technicians began to appear and the room took on sound and life, and Kane settled back into the padded seat, feeling better. When Reik entered, he recognized her at once, though there was nothing in her appearance to mark her off from the others. The red hair was bound up beneath the cap and she wore the same shapeless blues as the technicians, but she brought focus to the room. If she moved, the figures around her gave way; when she stared at the body Kane could feel the force of her thoughts, the intensity of her preparation. The others were putting the room in order; Reik was putting herself in order. She turned and looked up at Kane, and he saw her forehead pull into a frown. She spoke up into a hidden microphone.

"Elias, what are you doing here?" The voice sounded unnaturally loud in the glassed confines of the balcony.

Kane shrugged. "There was nothing on trivee."

"Not funny."

"The Imperator requested the honor of my presence."

Reik's frown deepened. "This isn't a good place for you to be."

She was only showing concern, Kane knew, so he controlled the obscure anger and said mildly, "Tell that to our boss."

The doors behind Kane opened and Alvar Sabin entered, brushed past Kane without a word, and settled hunched over in the first row of seats. Sabin sat with absolute stillness, his face almost pressing the glass. From behind, Kane could sense the focus of his gaze, the way he tracked every movement of Reik below. Then the Imperator was brought in on the life support cart. Amerdath's eyes rolled up, stared at the observation balcony until they found Kane. The Imperator grinned and blinked. "Thanks for coming, Elias. I know it's not easy. Hello, Alvar. Will you please stop scowling—no, make that an order. No more scowling until I'm under anesthetic."

Sabin sat back. Kane watched the reflection of the praetorian's face screw into a stiff parody of good humor.

"Now you look like you need to sneeze."

"Sir, I . . ."

"Forget it. It's all right. Elias, you watch Martha, here, and make sure she gets my head on frontwards."

Reik glanced up at him, her eyes impassive above the

mask. Kane smiled. "These days, sir, it might be better to keep an eye out behind you."

Amerdath stared at him, and the technicians seemed to wind down where they stood, and then the Imperator laughed. "Too true, my boy. Too true." He turned to the technician beside his cart. "All right. I'm ready. Don't be too long now or Chuddath will come barging in."

Reik looked at him. "You want fast or you want good?"

"A point, Doctor."

The anesthetist approached the cart, lifted a panel and attached a bottle of clear fluid, running a trailing tube into the mouth of a stopcock. He turned the cock and Amerdath's eyelids drooped then closed as the anesthetic filtered into the blood supply. Two technicians rolled the cart into position at the head of the table on which the artificial body lay. Martha Reik extended her arms to the side, then brought them around in front, rotated her wrists, shook her fingers. She stepped to the table.

"We'll build an anastomosis," she said, "between the nerves and blood vessels of Amerdath's neck and the myelon nerves and blood vessels of the body. From the moment we detach the head from its present life-support system to the final vascular interface must take no longer than two minutes. Then we'll go directly to the nerves. Are the rest of you ready?"

Reik's assistants around the table nodded or murmured assent, and Reik motioned for Amerdath's cart to be brought close. Her body screened the Imperator's head as she detached the stump of the neck, and Kane was glad that he did not have to see. Sabin stood and hurried to the side of the balcony, trying to get an oblique view of the procedure. Reik continued to talk in a calm, lecturing voice as she worked. She connected the arteries and venous returns to the body's artificial vessels well within the two minutes, and the heart pump located in the top of the chest cavity took over the function of its disconnected twin in the life-support cart. The artificial vessels were elastic and remained extended through the gap between neck and body as Reik set about the much more difficult task of connecting the nerves. Immediately after the assassination attempt, severed nerve trunklines had been packed in anesthetic gel to eliminate local pain and to prevent the desiccation and withering that would have drawn the nerves permanently up and out of reach. Now it was necessary to tease out the severed nerves and fuse them with the artificial ones of the body. The procedure was carried out under extreme magnification and required a delicate and practiced touch. Any mishandling, the slightest gouging by an instrument, the barest misalignment of nerve and myelon, and the fusion would not pass nerve impulses.

Even if the procedure was totally successful, only the motoric functions could be restored. By the late twentieth century, microsurgical techniques had existed for the fusion of nerve to other natural nerve tissue. But no one had yet developed myelon nerves capable of registering sensation or translating feeling into feedback which could be decoded by the brain. If the operation worked, Amerdath would gain muscular control over his body, as he would in the case of natural nerve fusion. He might learn to walk, to grasp, to sit and stand, but only by watching each movement and relying on the gross external feedback provided by his eyes. With myelon tissue there could be no receiving, no internal feedback. Amerdath would not be able to feed himself without watching the spoon, or brush his teeth without looking in a mirror. In a dark room, he would always be helpless.

Reik bent over the neck for almost two hours. From his seat in the balcony, Kane could detect almost no movement in her. It was as though she had hardened into stone. And yet, he knew, her fingers were moving in fractions of millimeters, moving and stopping and moving again as she aligned the fusion, jacketed the trunkline with a micron-thin sheath of artificial material. She lectured calmly throughout the procedure, drawing off body tension into the release of chatter. Occasionally one of the technicians would vacuum the sweat from her face with sweeps of a suspended tube.

At the two-hour-and-sixteen-minute mark Reik's monologue cut off in mid-sentence. She straightened, stepped back and almost fell. Two technicians steadied her. The mike picked up her gasping, and Sabin and Kane were both on their feet, and then Kane realized it was over. She was finished, taken by her reaction.

"I don't know, I don't know," she moaned. Kane saw that her hands were trembling out of control. One of the assisting surgeons motioned to the technicians, who helped Reik from the room. Another surgeon began the close-up work of melding the exterior junction of neck and body.

"She doesn't know?" Sabin turned to Kane and his face stretched with tension. "What does that mean? Has she done it or hasn't she?"

"She's good," Kane said. "She's very good. Let's hope it's going to be all right."

Sabin stared blindly at him for a moment and then turned away.

Within twenty-four hours of the surgery the anabolic accelerators pumped through the tissue of Amerdath's neck had done their work and the nerve-myelon junctions were ready to be tested. A surgical pin wedded the bottommost vertebrae of Amerdath's neck to the artificial spine. The plastiflesh of the body's neck formed a cuff around the real flesh, hiding the juncture between neck stump and body and blending into the skin under Amerdath's jaw and hairline. Much of it was merely an extension of common plastic parlor technique. The one part that was not—the attempted fusion of real and artificial nerves—was the only part that mattered.

Kane had slept only fitfully the night after the operation, but he felt sharp, almost jittery, now. Pendrake put a

calming hand on his shoulder and Kane glanced at the
alien, tried to smile a reassurance he did not feel. He
looked back at the table. The lower half of Amerdath's
body was decorously covered, the need for modesty in-
vested in the artificial body with the attachment of the
living head and its taboos. Across the foot of the biotable
from Kane and Pendrake stood Alvar Sabin and the Princess Briana. Briana seemed subdued, the normal brash
aura that could command a room gone from her. Her face
was pale, watchful. Chuddath had positioned himself at
the foot of the table. Conspicuous by their absence were
the Empress Eunice and Amerdath's son, Lucian.

Martha Reik reached down with a syringe to the left
nipple of the body. Kane felt a sympathetic twinge as she
plunged the needle through. Beneath the nipple, he knew,
was a loop of the mechanical circulatory system, but the
entry of the needle made his teeth clench nonetheless.
When Reik removed the needle, the artificial flesh closed
over the puncture. Amerdath's eyelids fluttered and rolled
up. Before he could react, Reik said, "Lie still, please."
Her voice sounded hoarse and flat and Kane wondered if
she had slept since the surgery.

"How long?" Amerdath asked.

Reik looked relieved. The artificial speech bellows system,
activated by transmitters in the forehead muscles, had been
transplanted intact into the mechanical body, but this was
the first test of it since the operation. "Twenty-four hours,"
she said, "just as we planned. Lie still. Don't think about
moving. You're getting no feedback, but you should be
able to move. We'll start testing in a minute."

Amerdath squinted up at her. "The operation was a
success, then?"

Reik deflected the overhead light and managed a tight
smile. "We'll know shortly. I just don't want you trying
any movements before the anesthetic flush is completed."

"Martha, if you've really brought this off, there'll be

nothing you can't have. You want my villa on Centauri IV? It's yours. My estate in Florida? Just ask . . ."

"Sh-h-h-h!" Reik's face reddened and she busied herself checking Amerdath's pupils. Pain registered in Kane's fingertips and he realized he was clutching the thin underedge of the table. He dropped his hands. The blanket began moving, trembling across Amerdath's legs. The trembling grew more pronounced, and Amerdath's knees began to jerk. Reik looked down from the head of the table.

"Stop," she said, "stop moving."

"I'm not doing anything," Amerdath protested. The arms began to tremble too, and Kane looked at Reik for reassurance, saw instead the spread of horror across her face. She turned to the medical cart behind her as Amerdath's face distorted and the whole body began to buck and slam against the table.

"Grab him," Reik yelled. "Grab him, hold him down."

Pendrake leaned across the torso, pinning it to the table as Chuddath pinioned the artificial legs. A second later, Sabin reacted too, grappling for a hold. Briana stood back, a look of revulsion on her face. Kane ran to the head of the table and tried to steady the Imperator's head, which was twisting back and forth, thudding on the biotable with each violent jerk. A gargling noise came from Amerdath's throat. Reik pushed at Pendrake's shoulder. "Move lower down. I've got to get at the chest." Pendrake shifted and she centered a syringe over the chest, plunged it home through the access nipple. Seconds crawled by and then the convulsions subsided, the strangled noises died away.

Reik straightened and turned to two technicians who had been summoned by the room's compusayer. "Get him to surgery right away," she said.

Briana grabbed her arm. "My father. The body . . . is it . . ."

Reik's face was white, the lips bloodless. "There's too much distortion. If we leave him this way he'll never be anything but a violent spastic. We have to disconnect at once.''

"Then the operation is a complete failure," Briana persisted.

Reik jerked her arm free of the other woman's grasp and hurried from the room.

CHAPTER 13

The great hall outside the Imperator's private chambers returned Kane's footsteps, skeletal tappings shorn of boot and flesh. The stark echoes preyed on him, raising his awareness to swoop fearfully among the dark corners. He stopped and the hall went silent. At the other end of the chamber, perhaps thirty meters away, Chuddath stood in front of the entrance to Amerdath's quarters. The entrance was closed, massive double doors inlaid with carved jade and gold. Kane knew Chuddath must be watching him with those opaque insect eyes, but there was no nervous movement, no shifting of the body as a human would have shown. The warrior simply watched, and perhaps wondered what this frail creature hoped to gain by pacing about while the palace slept. If he came closer, Kane knew, the warrior would choose his moment and respond to his presence. Until then Chuddath would not move, a piece of bizarre statuary with a quicksilver core.

Kane looked around him at the hall, seeing in the sensory clarity of midnight what he might have overlooked in the preoccupations of day. The chamber soared up like the nave of a cathedral, crossed at the top by flying buttresses, hung high along either side with flags of the old nations of pre-Imperial Earth. At intervals along the walls, gargoyle faces peered down from mazelike designs of cut stone. There was purpose to the hall, a message: *This is but the anteroom of Amerdath, ruler of the nine planets, Imperator of the human race.*

Today, seven days after the Imperator's heart had stopped beating forever, he had held court in the chambers beyond this hall. He had seen members of his family, had welcomed Richard DuMorgan, Imperial viceroy of Alpha Centauri and possible plotter of his death, and had assigned a royal page as liaison for a visiting representative of the Moitan fish people. His face had appeared pink and healthy atop the life-support cart. There had been no sign in his speech or expression that the day before he had been severed from a second body. Amerdath could not command his own hands, but he could still command an empire.

Kane walked on toward the magnificent carved doors, toward the figure of Chuddath. The Ornyl's stillness grew more unnerving as he approached. The hairs on Kane's neck stirred and he saw again why Chuddath must be so hated and feared, even by a strongman like Alvar Sabin. Being in the warrior's presence was like being watched through a curtain, knowing that someone or something, perhaps demonic, was there; that they could see you but you could not see them. Kane stopped a few meters in front of the alien and said, "Good evening."

The vocal arms remained as still as the rest of Chuddath's body.

"I couldn't sleep, so I thought I'd take a walk," Kane continued, determined to show no discomfort at the warrior's stony reception. "I know very little about your race. Do you sleep?"

"No." Chuddath flipped the word off and was still again. His head continued to face straight down the hallway. Obviously he did not want to talk.

"You don't sleep ever?" Kane persisted.

Chuddath did not acknowledge the repetition.

"Do you mind my being here?"

"Yes." No hesitation.

"I need to talk to you."

"Because you couldn't sleep?"

"That was just a way of breaking the ice—you know, starting the conversation."

"Do not break . . . ice with me."

"All right," Kane said. "No small talk. It's hard to get you alone. You're with the Imperator whenever he's awake, and the praetorians are always around. They're standing outside every door to this hall right now."

"I know this."

"Do you also know whether they have listening devices outside this door?"

"The praetorians, no . . . but Fowler Giacomin listens . . . always; everywhere. What does it matter?"

"I'd prefer our conversation to be private."

"I do not hear . . . as men hear. You may speak in . . . the smallest way."

Kane nodded. "I want to know about Amerdath's son, Lucian," he said in an unvoiced whisper, so low that his own words were lost to him. "I'll try to ask questions that you can answer briefly and without using the prince's name. Do you hear me?"

"I hear."

"You're with or near the Imperator all the time. Before the assassination attempt did he see much of his son?"

"By human standards, no."

"And since?"

"Not at all."

Kane frowned, incredulous. "Not even once? Lucian hasn't been to see his father a single time?" Chuddath made no answer and Kane realized that the alien would not repeat himself. "Would you say that Lucian hates his father?"

"I cannot answer."

"Because you don't know?"

"Correct."

"But you're physically closer to Amerdath than anyone. You see and hear almost everything that goes on."

Chuddath paused a long time, the vocal arms poised over the chitin as if in indecision. "I am not man. I do not judge . . . love."

"But what about hate?"

"Hate is human."

"Aren't the Ornyl partially human?"

"In form only. Your word is . . . humanoid."

Kane studied the alien, trying to find the feelings behind the words. The Ornyl's face was incapable of expression, and the eerie violinlike tones of his voice, while intriguing and varied, were too alien to plumb for hidden meaning. "How do you feel about Clemis, the assassin?" Kane asked.

"He is the . . . Imperator's enemy."

"Damn it, Chuddath, how do you *feel?*"

Chuddath stared down the long hall. "Always man sees . . . with single eyes."

Kane shook his head in exasperation.

The scream issued from a speaker grille above the double doors, beginning low and swelling in volume. It did not break and renew itself, did not build on human lungs, but continued and grew, freezing Kane with its alienness even as Chuddath turned and burst through the doors into Amerdath's chambers. Then, as doors clanged in the hall behind Kane, he thought of the forced air vocal system on Amerdath's life-support cart. He followed Chuddath on the run.

Amerdath's scream was dying out as the alien and human reached what had once been the bedchamber. The bed had been removed and Amerdath's cart positioned against one wall. The compusayer had turned up the room lights, and Amerdath's face was pinched into a squint. The sound that came from his throat now was a sustained gasp. The skin of his face had turned the color of dough. Chuddath stood, helpless, his head swiveling in a vain search for intruders, while Kane rushed to the life-support cart and pulled open the access panel. He saw the problem at once. "Call Dr. Reik," he shouted.

"I have already done so," replied a calm voice from the ceiling. "She is at this moment running down corridor C-16. Have you other instructions, Mr. Kane?"

Kane did not answer, but eased his hand through the thicket of oxygenating tubes to the main arterial feed. Thin streams of blood, bright red with their load of oxygen, were spraying from leaks in the tube just below its entry into Amerdath's neck. Kane grasped the section of tube, blocking off the leaks with the palm of his hand. His skin began at once to itch where it pressed against the tube. The itching quickly turned to a burning sensation, but he held on. "Compusayer," he snapped. "Are you familiar with the Imperator's life-support system?"

"Of course, Mr. Kane."

"Contact a technician who is as close as possible to the nearest supply room and have him bring tubing here immediately. . . ."

"Specify tubing."

Sweat sprang out at Kane's hairline. "Damn it, I don't know. The kind that takes blood to and from the Imperator's head."

"At once, Mr. Kane."

"And inform Dr. Reik that blood is leaking from Amerdath's circulatory system." Kane blinked the sweat from his eyes and peered into the maze of tubing until he located the dark red venous returns. They did not seem to be leaking. Something wet hit his face and he reached in with his other hand to pinch off another leak in the arterial tube. Drops of blood were oozing through in several more places and he began cursing softly.

"What are you doing?" Chuddath demanded.

"Just keep away from me. I do this or he dies," Kane rasped. The palm of his hand felt like a hot knife point was being drawn along it. Footfalls sounded behind him, but he dared not turn for fear of pulling the tubing loose. Feet skidded for purchase and someone grunted. There were two heavy thumps, like bodies hitting a wall.

"Stay back." Chuddath's command blasted through the room with the force of a siren.

"Praetorians, the Ornyl is correct; Mr. Kane is helping. You must not molest him," the compusayer said.

Kane gritted his teeth. *Damn it, where was Reik?*

Then she was beside him. She reached beneath his hands, turned some cutoffs. "All right, Elias, let go."

Kane released the tubing and looked for the door to the suite's bathroom. Two technicians ran in. One was carrying a bundle of tubing. "Here," Reik commanded. "Quickly."

Kane found the bathroom, ran the cold water taps over his hands until they grew numb. He stared at himself in the mirror. Stringy patterns of the Imperator's blood draped his forehead and one cheek. He saw that his lower lip was cut, though he didn't remember biting it. Without looking at his hands, he patted them dry on one of the thick hand towels that hung through gold loops around the sink. He reentered the bedroom. A physician was kneeling beside a praetorian who was holding his ribs and muttering, "Damned roach," over and over. Other praetorians stood at the door, 'ruptors held across their chests. Kane saw Fowler Giacomin and Alvar Sabin behind the techs and doctors who were working around Amerdath. The only space close to Amerdath was next to Chuddath. Kane stood next to the alien, even in the chaos of the moment feeling the forbidding aura that had kept the others away. Amerdath was blinking sleepily. Some of the color had returned to his face. Reik straightened from the life-support equipment and turned to Kane. "Let me see your hands."

"Never mind that," Kane said. "How is he?"

"He's going to be fine, thanks to you. Now don't be more of a hero than you already are. Stick out those hands."

Kane let her see them, and when she grimaced he changed his mind about looking at them himself, because the pain didn't need any more of an edge than it already had.

"What do you think?" she asked.

"Probably one of the off-planet cataplastics," he said. "I'd guess industrial cattaric acid. The tubing is plastic-based, right?"

She nodded and turned to one of the technicians. "Get a couple of liters of polymer flush here as fast as you can, and some of the alkaline salve."

"What are these people doing in here?" Amerdath's voice was low and hoarse.

Reik turned back to him. "You're all right now, sir."

"What happened?"

"Someone tried to kill you by throwing acid on the circulatory tubes of your life-support system. Don't you remember anything?"

Amerdath stared at Reik as if waiting for her words to make sense. "No," he said. "I remember feeling strange and then . . . screaming. I think I screamed. But there was no one in here."

"Compusayer," Kane said. "Before Chuddath and I came in, was there any intruder in this room?"

"Certainly not. I would have stopped and detained any intruder, Mr. Kane."

A hand closed with spidery delicacy on Kane's shoulder, and he turned to find Fowler Giacomin appraising him. "It seems you were in just the right place at just the right time," Giacomin said.

"Elias saved the Imperator's life," Reik said stiffly.

"Isn't that overstating it a bit?" Giacomin said. "I thought the brain could survive several minutes of stopped blood flow. Surely the compusayer would have summoned you in time.''

"Decreased or stopped blood flow wasn't the most critical problem," Reik said. "If Elias hadn't closed off the circulation leaks when he did, the pressure in the tubes would have dropped to the point that air could have bled back through the leaks and formed massive emboli. The Imperator would have suffered multiple CVA's—his mind would have been destroyed by strokes.''

"Nevertheless," Giacomin said, "it seems oddly fortuitous that Mr. Kane should be outside the Imperator's door at midnight, having a secret conversation with the Imperial bodyguard.''

"Is it illegal to have a private conversation in this palace?" Reik asked coldly.

"It is also interesting that you feel you must defend Mr. Kane.''

"Your suspicions will have to wait, Giacomin," Kane said. "Imperator, do you feel like talking?''

Amerdath's full color had returned. He hesitated only a second. "To the man who saved what is left of my life? Of course.''

"You saw the Empress Eunice, Richard DuMorgan, your daughter, Dr. Reik and Alvar Sabin today. Is that correct?''

"Yes.''

"Did you see anyone else?''

"I called in a page and assigned him as liaison to Manoster, the emissary from Moitan.''

"Right, I remember that. Was anyone else in the same room with you today within a distance of ten feet?''

"Only you, Pendrake and Chuddath. Why do you ask?''

"That's nine people," Kane replied. "One of them tried to kill you tonight.''

CHAPTER 14

"You're talking garbage."

Kane recognized the voice of Alvar Sabin behind him. When he did not turn to face the praetorian commander, Sabin was forced to edge around the medical people to get in front of him. "You just heard the compusayer deny that any intruder was in this room," Sabin went on, "so how can you say that one of the nine people the Imperator saw today tried to kill him tonight?"

"Not tonight," Kane said. "Today—or rather, yesterday, since it's now past midnight. One of the people who got close to the Imperator at the audiences yesterday sprayed acid from a concealed source through the ventilation grille of the life-support cart."

"But the compusayer has poison-detecting abilities," Sabin protested.

"For food and drink or the topical poisons that can kill through skin absorption," Kane said. "But cattaric acid is a relatively mild industrial solvent used to etch the new harder plastics. The plastic ornaments in this room would collectively contain more cattaric acid in residue form than

119

would be needed to dissolve the circulatory tubing—especially since the acid was probably diluted in water or buffered so that it would take several hours to eat through the tubing.'' Kane's hands began to burn again, and he wished the technician would get back with the salve.

The compusayer interjected its mild voice. "I'm afraid Mr. Kane's scenario is most plausible. My sensors could not have detected cattaric acid, which, according to my data banks, is little stronger than human saliva, except for its unique effect on plastics and certain irritant qualities when in contact with skin. I'm afraid it would indeed be very difficult, under existing technology, to add screening for such a threat to my repertoire."

Giacomin gave Kane a sour look. "I commend you, Mr. Kane, on your rapid and precise deductions. One might almost wonder how you reached your conclusions so rapidly."

Kane displayed his palms to the security chief. "I believe the compusayer mentioned certain irritant qualities."

Giacomin paled slightly and looked away from the burned flesh. The techs appeared with the salve and some gauze gloves, and Reik tended to Kane's hands. Her fingers felt cool against his knuckles as she steadied each hand in turn and gently swabbed the skin first with the polymer flush and then with the salve. He looked down on her hair as she bent over his hands. The overhead lights picked out a spectrum from deep auburn to lighter strands that were almost blond, and Kane realized that the color was her own, not the uniform product of a beautician.

"All right," Sabin said. "So one of the nine people who saw the Imperator sprayed acid through the life-support system grille. Why didn't the compusayer at least see it?"

Kane shrugged. "A small atomizer concealed inside the clothes, activated by a certain gesture when the assassin is in position in front of the cart."

"You're all missing the point," Amerdath growled.

"Sir?" Sabin inquired.

"This proves that there *is* a conspiracy to assassinate me. We were ready to accept that Clemis might actually have acted alone. No longer."

No one said anything. Reik finished pulling the protective gloves on Kane's hands. The skin of his palms felt cool and pliant now. There was no itching or pain. He flexed his fingers gratefully then turned back to Amerdath. "If you'll excuse me, sir, I'll begin questioning the people who were here yesterday."

"No, you will not do that."

Kane stared at the Imperator. "But it has to be done."

"Alvar," the Imperator said, "please clear the room of everyone but Chuddath, Kane, Fowler and yourself. Post your men outside the door."

"Sir . . ." Reik protested.

"Sorry, Martha," Amerdath said. "I'd rather confine this conversation to the people who *must* hear it. I'm feeling fine now. You can wait outside and if I need you, you can be here in seconds."

Reik left with the others, shaking off the guiding hand a praetorian tried to put on her arm. When the door closed, Amerdath frowned but did not quite look at Kane. "Damn it, Elias, I can't have you questioning my wife or my daughter like common criminals. You can rule them out."

"With all respect, sir, I'd be serving you poorly if I did. I'll be very diplomatic . . ."

"I forbid it. It would be an intolerable insult to them."

Out of the corner of his eye Kane saw Giacomin and Sabin exchange glances, and the thought came to him that the two men, antagonistic as they were, were tied together by Amerdath and his needs. "Very well, sir, I'll confine my inquiries to the others."

"Not DuMorgan."

"But Imperator," Giacomin protested. "Richard Du-Morgan is the one man who *must* be questioned. We already know of the transmission from his ship that arrived near the palace just before the attempt. He's the planetary administrator on Alpha Centauri IV, a hotbed of colonial resistance to your authority. . . ."

Amerdath said, "I'm well aware of the rebellious elements in the colonies, but DuMorgan is my chosen man, my viceroy. If I permit you to interrogate him, he will think that I suspect him. It'll undermine his position. If he's loyal, he'll be hurt and offended, and if he's not, it'll only warn him."

Sabin said, "I've always felt Giacomin was paranoid about the colonies and I still think so, but I agree now that we must suspect DuMorgan."

"Suspect him, then. Elias, make discreet inquiries, but not directly. You other two, stay away from him."

Kane hesitated. "That leaves Martha Reik, Alvar, myself, Pendrake and the page you assigned to the Moitan emissary."

"Start with the page," Amerdath said. "As far as I'm concerned, the rest of you are above suspicion."

Giacomin inclined his head. "We're grateful, sir, but you mustn't think like that. . . ."

"Yes," Amerdath cut in, "I *must*. The three of you may think what you like, or what you must. Investigate all you like within the guidelines I've given you, but I—I *must* put you all above suspicion."

The security chief and the praetorian commander bowed together and Kane inclined his head. Amerdath's message was clear. He intended to protect himself from paranoia. He would rely on them to be loyal or to guard him against the one of them who might not be loyal. He was also doing one other thing, a thing Kane dared not let himself ignore: He was making it harder for them.

The quarters of the page were in the city that sprawled most of the way around the base of the palace rock. Chronos was a new city, established after Amerdath had won the unification wars and sheared off the top of the rock to build his palace. The name Chronos derived from the granite formation that towered in its midst like the gnomon of a sundial. To reach the city, one merely walked or took a shuttle through a traffic corridor to the outermost ring of the palace and then descended in an elevator down the face of the cliff. There were no checkpoints at the city termini—only at the palace end of the elevators did praetorians stand ready to screen would-be entrants.

Kane descended to Chronos in a clear alpha-glass shaft. Pendrake stood beside him, silent and alert, though Kane had wakened him only a few minutes before. In the three years Pendrake had been with him, Kane had never found a point in the Cephantine's sleep cycle from which Pendrake would not come instantly and fully awake. This fact had, on occasion, been a point of obscure irritation with Kane, but not now, not when he needed the alien's perceptiveness and clear head to balance his own sometimes byzantine logic.

The stars aimed down at them like lancepoints. The desert beyond Chronos was a moonscape of purples. Kane had always loved the desert. The closeness of its clean arid vastness would once have added its own edge to this moment. That was before, when he had let himself love only what he could bear to lose.

"It is interesting," Pendrake said, "that neither Alvar Sabin nor Fowler Giacomin insisted on accompanying you to question this page."

"It's also interesting," Kane retorted, "how you have an uncanny instinct for when to interrupt my silences."

"You did seem to be brooding."

"You might try it yourself."

"I miss her, too, Elias."

"I'm sorry."

"No apology is necessary."

There was an awkward silence. "Giacomin did make noises about coming along," Kane said, "but I refused, and Amerdath backed me up. It all seemed very *pro forma*."

"Do you consider that a clue?"

Kane smiled in the semidarkness of the elevator cage, making sure that his face was turned away from the Cephantine. "My friend," he said darkly, "everything is a clue."

The elevator touched bottom. The compusayer had coded a walking stick for the page's apartment before they'd left. As they stepped out of the elevator, the stick—outwardly identical to the knobbed canes currently favored by the fashion-conscious—said, "Straight ahead to Duke Street."

The city, home of thousands of clerical and administrative workers in Amerdath's government, was nearly as lively at night as during the day. Holographic marquees advertised nightclubs, theaters and bars with swirls and sky-bursts of colored light. Well-dressed people with the good looks that could be bought more easily than birthed strolled along the sidewalks on either side of the broad avenues. Gaudy electric cars, open at the top, noiselessly carried people along the streets on computerized paths that made traffic lights unnecessary. Muted symputer music drifted from open cafés. As they progressed, a dozen aromas mingled to blunt the crisp air of the desert night. Kane walked quickly, intent on his thoughts, barely aware of Pendrake gazing around with his customary polite curiosity. The pleasure center of Chronos gave way to palatial, brightly lit residential streets as the walking stick continued to murmur directions in its diminutive copy of the compusayer's voice. There were fewer people now, and less traffic.

"You are approaching the Moitan embassy behind the high wall on your right," the stick announced. "Directly across the street is the temporary apartment of the page, assigned as long as he continues as the official liaison. He lives in Unit 312."

The building indicated by the stick was an elegant three-story structure of chrome and glass, which was now mostly opaqued against the night. Lush shrubs and fruit trees alien to the desert grew up from fertilized beds around the building's perimeter. Kane and Pendrake took the elevator to the third floor. When they were at the door to 312, Kane paused. "What is the page's name?" he asked.

"I am sorry. The compusayer did not impart that information."

"You are some smart stick, do you know that?"

The walking stick remained silent. Kane knocked on the door, waited, knocked again.

"It appears he is not at home," Pendrake said.

Kane nodded and withdrew from his pocket a thing shaped like a flattened egg. He'd taken the device from storage in his special suitcase before leaving the palace. He squeezed the egg and a tiny filament extended from the smaller end. Carefully he slipped the filament into the lock.

"What are you doing?" Pendrake asked.

A light winked on the egg and Kane withdrew the filament. It retreated into the egg, then reemerged in the shape of a key. Kane waved the key around a second to cool it, then slipped it into the lock.

"Is it not improper to enter another man's private dwelling?" Pendrake asked.

"Aren't you droll. You know very well that it is. Stay outside if it makes you feel better." The key turned and the door swung open, and Kane started to step through into the apartment. He brought his foot down short. Something was wrong, something registering at the outer limit of his senses. A very faint smell. He drew the air in slowly, careful not to blunt his capacity to smell with too forceful an inhalation. And then he realized that the precaution was unnecessary. As soon as he entered the apartment the smell would grow stronger, the smell of raw sewage.

"If you feel we must go in," Pendrake whispered with a resigned expression, "I will accompany you."

"You stay here," Kane said sharply, knowing that there
was no reason to whisper, but Pendrake was a step behind
him as he entered the apartment. The page was in the
corner of the living room beneath a globular cluster of
ceiling lights, and it almost seemed that he was leering
roguishly at them, his face canted, his eyes slits, his
tongue sticking out. The illusion was heightened by the
fact that he seemed to be standing on his tiptoes, swaying
mockingly. But the rope was just visible under the angle of
his jaw, and there was a definite gap between his toes and
the floor.

CHAPTER 15

Kane felt Pendrake rush by him. Only at the last second was he able to shout, "Stop!"

Pendrake hesitated beside the body, his fist around the rope above the man's neck. He stared back at Kane, his face made harsh by the cringing muscles around his eyes and mouth. "You'll disturb evidence," Kane explained.

"Elias, this man may be alive."

"No," Kane said, but he hurried over anyway and tried to lift one arm away from the body. It resisted stiffly. The skin at the wrist was cool and doughy. Pendrake stepped back and rubbed at his face; turned away from the dead man. Kane watched him with concern. "Are you all right?"

"I can function. I have seen such things before, too often, but never can I seem to . . ." Pendrake shook his head.

"Okay," Kane said. "I know." He turned back to the body feeling sick and disgusted and guilty because he had too many times been the link between Pendrake and scenes of death. Guilty because he could look at the page and feel horror, but not the same crushing shock to his sanity that the Cephantine was fighting. He could understand what had happened in this room, and Pendrake could not, and his ability to understand made him feel dirty.

He bent down and inspected the distance between the page's toes and the floor. The apartment ceiling was high, the four meters favored in a world that was no longer crowded. Behind the body was a fallen bar stool, apparently kicked over by the page's thrashing legs. Controlling his repugnance Kane knelt and gripped each wrist of the corpse in turn, twisting the stiff arms so that he could inspect the fingernails. They were long and appeared clean and unbroken. He inspected the rest of the body as thoroughly as possible without disturbing the clothing. There were no obvious wounds. He turned his attention to the man's head, probing the skull gently through the hair. Something on the man's tongue caught his attention.

"Pendrake, see if you can dial up the light," he said, deliberately holding back from doing it himself. If he could get Pendrake moving the alien's shock might recede. At first Pendrake did not respond, then his hands dropped from his face and he looked around for the light switch. Kane saw with relief that the membranes around the black eyes had receded out of sight. Pendrake found the rheostat and dialed a bright glare from the cluster of overhead lights. Kane brought his eyes to within a few centimeters of the protruding tongue and stared at the dark shred until he was satisfied. A faint odor of garlic receded as he leaned back from the dead face.

"Could you bring me another stool from the bar, please," he said to Pendrake. The alien complied silently. Kane placed the stool in front of the body, climbed up to stand on it. Pendrake steadied him with a hand at the belt as he studied the rope. It was made of nylon and another synthetic fiber woven in the usual way. He looked up to where the rope was knotted around the shaft of the light before it fanned into the smaller shafts that supported each globe. The light glared into his face now, and he had to squint, but he could see the knot, and by fingering it he was able to confirm that it was tight. He could also tell that it was not tight enough.

He got down slowly and walked to the wall of the apartment, clearing to transparency the section in front of him. He gazed out over the city at the colossus of rock that soared up from its center. Light bathed the rock face and reflected from the unipolarized elevator housings, giving the rock a warm golden appearance, striped vertically with silver. At the summit, the beta-steel ramparts of the palace ascended tier upon tier, softened here and there by hanging gardens lit in continuously changing hues. From here the palace looked remote, a place of fantasy, Babel and Babylon both.

"Elias, perhaps you should look at this."

Kane joined the alien, who was bending over a low table by the door to the apartment. On the table was a handwritten note that read: "I can't stand it. Please tell the Imperator I'm sorry." Kane frowned and reread the note.

"An inconceivable thing," Pendrake said, "for a being to destroy its own life."

"It is terrible," Kane agreed, "but this man didn't kill himself. He was murdered."

Pendrake stared at him. "I do not understand. Are there other wounds on the body?"

"No, when they take him down they'll find a single bruise around his neck where the rope bit in and a dislocation of the cervical vertebrae. Perhaps a crushed windpipe, perhaps not."

Pendrake looked ill. He swallowed with obvious difficulty. "But has this man not been strangled by hanging from the rope?"

"It appears that way. He may have died from either strangulation or a broken neck, just as he would have if he'd gotten up on that stool, tied the rope around his neck and jumped off. The only problem is that he didn't. This man weighs seventy-five kilograms, give or take five. That

weight suspended from rope like this will result in some
stretching, which is detectable as a slight separation along
the helical seams of the rope. This rope shows that
separation. But if you tie seventy-five kilos to the rope and
drop it, the stretching that occurs when the weight is
brought up short by the rope is magnified many times. The
force applied to the rope would be equal to the man's mass
multiplied by his acceleration due to gravity through the
length of his fall. I'm betting an autopsy will confirm that
the cervical dislocation in the man's neck is not consistent
with a one-meter drop or jump from that stool.''

"Then what did cause it?'' Pendrake asked.

"I'd guess a blow to the back of the neck.''

"You discovered all of these things merely by looking
at the rope?''

"Not entirely. There are some other clues, too. For
example, there appears to be a bit of meat on the man's
tongue, and I noticed a piece caught between his top center
incisors. The meat showed hardly any signs of softening or
discoloration due to digestion, indicating that the man's
salivary flow stopped very shortly after he'd eaten.''

"Just before he died he ate something.''

"Yes. An odd thing for a presumably distraught or
depressed man to do just before he kills himself. When
Giacomin's men get here, I'm betting they'll find traces of
fresh cooked steak around the rim of the man's disposal
unit.''

"But what about this note? Surely this is an authentic
suicide note. It is in handwriting, which can too easily be
verified for any but the most ignorant or careless killer to
have forged it.''

"It's no forgery,'' Kane agreed. "I'd bet my last credit
it's in the page's handwriting.''

"Then you must think that he was somehow forced to
write his own suicide note. But under what conceivable
threat could this be done? He would surely realize that if
he wrote the note he would certainly be killed, while if he

refused, the killer might be frustrated. The killer could not threaten him with painful injuries, since these would later be detected on the body and reveal the deception.''

"Your reasoning is impeccable," Kane said, "but I don't think it was obvious to the page that the killer planned to fake his suicide. Take another look at that note."

Pendrake reread the note. "It is ambiguous."

"Right. What does it really mean? 'I can't stand it. Tell the Imperator I'm sorry.' What couldn't he stand? Suppose the killer or killers came to him and told him they wanted him to disappear—that they didn't want him acting as the Imperator's go-between with the Moitan emissary. The Moitan fish people are strange, smelly, ugly, and so on to a lot of Earth people."

"They are *alien*," Pendrake said pointedly.

"Right," Kane said uncomfortably. "And they're here to contest our claim to a planet also claimed by Moitan. The page could have been flimflammed into writing the note if whoever set this up played the xenophobe angle. Let's say the killer offered him money to write the note and disappear. When the page wrote 'I can't stand it,' he didn't realize the phrase would be taken as remorse rather than repugnance, remorse for the acid attack on the Imperator."

"This is guesswork, Elias."

"Granted."

"We do not even know that this man had anything to do with the attempt on the Imperator's life."

"Unless you count the acid atomizer in his belt."

Pendrake gaped at Kane.

"I found it when I was searching the body for other wounds. The whole belt's a thin reservoir for the acid. The nozzle is concealed in the buckle, and probably is activated by tensing the diaphragm or abdominal muscles in a certain way."

"I am impressed," said a voice from behind Kane.

Kane whirled toward the door, straightening from the jujitsu stance when Fowler Giacomin and two of his agents stepped into the apartment. "What the hell are you doing here?" Kane demanded.

"Preparing to conduct an investigation of this man's death," Giacomin replied in a reasonable, slightly aggrieved tone.

"How . . ."

"Please, Mr. Kane. Your walking stick is programmed, as are all extensions of the compusayer, to report any crime immediately to the central banks. It's part of the attraction of the stick, don't you think? You can be fending off a street mugger with it, while it calls the authorities for you. Of course, you don't want to hit anyone too hard with the stick until after it's made the call."

The two operatives behind Giacomin smirked. Their chief's face remained bland. "Besides," Giacomin went on, "you were about to call me anyway."

"How long have you been standing out there listening?"

"Long enough to be very impressed with your deductive and perceptual powers, Mr. Kane. I must take our recruiters to task for missing you in their yearly sweeps of the university criminology programs. But then, you never actually graduated from one, did you?"

"Your recruiters didn't miss me," Kane replied. "I turned them down."

"A pity."

"I don't think so. I think I like being your boss better than I'd like it the other way around."

The security chief stiffened. The men behind him looked at each other. Then Giacomin made an exaggerated bow. "With your permission, Mr. Kane, I'd like to do my job."

Kane nodded, deliberately ignoring the sarcasm in Giacomin's posture and voice. "We're through here. I'll expect your full report, including lab analysis of the rope, when you've finished."

As Kane followed Pendrake out the door, Giacomin said, "One thing, Mr. Kane."

"Yes?"

"I'm sure you understand the importance of remaining good friends with the Imperator."

Kane smiled, but he felt coldness at the back of his neck. "May he live forever."

The bar was crowded, smoky, redolent of stale beer and sweat. When Kane sat down and put his elbows on the plain wood bartop, his sleeve stuck in the varnish left by decades of neglected drink spills. He pulled off the gauze gloves Reik had put on him and inspected the skin of his palms. It looked red, and he knew the skin would begin peeling in the next few days, but the salve had already done its work. The healing process was well under way and there was no pain. He looked around, glad he'd been able to find this place at the far fringe of the city, this smelly, close, ordinary place where common men and women came because it was better than home.

Pendrake sat down gingerly on the round stool beside Kane, half rising as the stool wobbled on its loosely bolted shaft, and finally settling with a resigned sigh. A burly man on the other side of Pendrake frowned at the alien, and Kane felt a stirring that was half warning, half déjà vu. There had been another bar a few years before, in a casino where he had just won Pendrake in a million-credit crapshoot called GalTac. The man at the bar who'd frowned at Pendrake then had been better dressed, and his face had been done by a top plastician instead of remodeled by a dozen barroom brawls. That man had slapped Pendrake's face. Kane felt his back muscles tense now in anticipation. But the man's expression changed slowly into a grin that gave his scarred face an ursine charm. "Say," he bellowed, "you're a Cephantine, ain't you?" He pronounced the last syllable "tyne" and Pendrake winced slightly as he turned.

"That is correct, sir."

"Well, I'll be shivved, put 'er there."

Pendrake shook the proffered hand and suffered his back to be thumped while the man ordered him iced tea—a correct choice, made without asking—and then regaled everyone near him with a story of how a Cephantine had saved his "chamber-potted arse" in an asteroid-belt mining accident. Kane half-listened, amused at the alien's discomfiture, and oddly let down. What had he hoped? That the man would start something and give him a chance to break the crooked nose once again? He drank off the first raw whiskey the bartender brought him and tapped the rim of the glass, impatiently signaling for a double, because something else had happened that day three years ago in the posh casino. He had seen a beautiful black-haired woman for the first time. A woman with pale skin and the grace and strength of a lioness in her walk. She had been followed by a plump waddling Chirpone and its Krythian bodyguards. Her name had been Elizabeth Tyson, and she had wanted to take away the pain of the world.

At five-thirty in the morning dawn began to ooze up in the east like spilled wine into the edge of a napkin, and Pendrake came out of the bar with Kane's arm pulled firmly around his neck, and began the long silent walk back through Chronos to the foot of the rock.

CHAPTER 16

Kane awoke after only four hours. The clock on the wall at the foot of his bed read 10:34 A.M. He remembered beating on the top of the bar in time with the raucous rhythm of the symputer. The symputer had been an old model, and Kane recalled the high frequency hum that became audible during quieter music. The rest of it was missing. In the bar, and now here in his bed in the palace, and no memory of in between.

Kane rolled onto his side. The bed stretched away taut and unrumpled. What was the use, what was the damned use of so much bed? He would have it removed today and replaced with a narrow military-style bed like he had used during his days as a navy lieutenant. One of those beds barely wide enough for one person.

He got up and sat with his feet on the floor, feeling nothing but the strands of carpet between his toes and a queasiness that should have been much more severe. He should not be awake at all, not with all the booze. He went into the bathroom, splashed some cold water on his face,

then stood propped on locked elbows, staring down at the
gold ornamentation on the handles of the faucet.

"How do you feel, Elias?"

Kane turned. Pendrake stood in the doorway. The alien
was wearing the immense ankle-length robe of brown
velvet, and Kane remembered how Beth had argued with
the tailor, insisting that the brown would go best with the
Cephantine's coloring.

"Ah, how do I feel, was that the question?" Kane
squeezed past the alien into the bedroom. He called for
morning lighting and squinted around in the surge of cheery
yellow brilliance, spotting a crystal pitcher and two glasses
sitting on the bartop. He walked over and inspected the
pitcher, hefting it, while Pendrake came up beside him.
"This should do," he said. He eyed the wall across from
the bar. It was made of dark-veined marble. He threw the
pitcher with all his strength. It seemed to tumble through
the air in slow motion, flinging brilliant motes from its
facets and collapsing into the wall with a sunburst of
silvery shards. He threw the glasses too. "I feel guilty,"
he said.

A vacunit extended from the base of the wall and began
with snakelike motions to sweep up the glittering debris.

"No," Kane shouted. "Leave it there, damn you."

When the vacunit kept up its busy motions he ran over
and kicked it until it withdrew into its recess with an angry
ratcheting sound.

Someone began pounding on the door. Kane looked at
Pendrake and the alien shrugged, a non-Cephantine gesture
that he always did with amusing awkwardness. The knocking stopped and the door shuddered. The palmplate began
to glow, then blew inward and landed on the carpet.
Pendrake moved in front of Kane as the door slid brokenly
aside. Two praetorians ran half crouching into the room,
blasters low and waving out front. Curls of smoke eddied
up around the fallen palmplate where it had scorched the
carpeting.

"What the hell is going on in here?" one of the praetorians, a sergeant, demanded. "We heard noises."

"You just happened to be passing by?" Kane asked.

The praetorians straightened and holstered their weapons. "No, sir."

"You were standing outside my door, then. Why?"

The praetorian saw the fragments of crystal lying at the foot of the marble wall. "Excuse us, Mr. Kane. We'll have the lock replaced right away."

"I asked you a question, Sergeant."

"We've been assigned to guard you, sir."

"By whom?"

"Our orders come from only one man besides our Imperator," the praetorian said stiffly.

"Alvar Sabin? But why?"

The praetorians turned to leave.

"Stop. I don't need any guards. Get the lock fixed and then clear out."

"We can't do that," the sergeant said.

"I'm ordering you, under the special authority given me by the Imperator . . ."

"I'm sorry, Mr. Kane. You'll have to take it up with Commander Sabin or the Imperator."

"Take up what with my father, Sergeant?"

The praetorians came to attention. Amerdath's son, Prince Lucian, entered and faced the two men. "At ease, for God's sake." The soldiers complied, glancing at the prince then staring ahead with sullen expressions. "What is going on here?" Lucian asked.

"Alvar Sabin has, for some reason, decided that I need protection," Kane said. "I dropped a pitcher and they burned my door down. Perhaps, sir, you can make them understand that I don't need or want guards."

Lucian shook his head disgustedly. "You men are relieved of your duties as guards for Mr. Kane."

The praetorians looked uncomfortably at each other. "Sir . . ."

Lucian's face reddened. "I said you are relieved. Report to Sabin at once and tell him my orders. If he questions them, let *him* come to me. I won't stand here and argue with trenchers."

The men bowed and backed, stone-faced, out of the suite. The infusion of blood drained back from Lucian's face, leaving it a sickly white. He laughed shakily. "Was I convincing?"

"Very, sir."

"You can drop the 'sir' business with me. May I come in?"

"Of course." Kane gestured at a chair near Lucian. "Sit down and make yourself comfortable."

"Does my discomfort show that much?"

Kane did not answer and Lucian sniffed. He sank down. "That's all right, Mr. Kane. My father said you were honest. It's a relief, actually, in this den of sycophants. They're such cretins, the praetorians. So proud of their black and silver. They put on that uniform like a scrotum. It turns them into perambulating balls." Lucian frowned contemplatively. "Not a bad image. Perhaps I'll do a sculpture off it. The praetorians would never catch on."

Pendrake looked bewildered and Kane smiled, because the alien rarely missed archaic or colloquial expressions. The prince gazed around the suite. Amerdath's only son looked even thinner than he had at Beth's funeral. His elegant white satin jumpsuit, tailored slim, nevertheless hung loose at the knees, elbows and shoulders. His hand tapped restlessly at the armrest. The skin above his knuckles was grooved around the tendons and heavily veined.

"I'd have dropped by sooner," Lucian said, "but I've been working on an especially demanding piece."

"We're honored by your visit," Kane said. "Perhaps we could see the work when you've finished."

Lucian gave a short laugh. "*If* I finish, perhaps, Mr. Kane. This one has me beaten so far. May I call you Elias?"

"Of course." Kane felt vaguely embarrassed. As prince of the Terran Empire, this man could call him anything he liked. Where was the assurance that should have been trained into Lucian since babyhood? How could any nature, however unsuited, escape the imprint of power in Amerdath's household? And then Kane had another thought—that the escaping of such an imprint was itself a form of power.

Lucian noticed the mounds of broken crystal. "That must be the pitcher you . . . dropped."

Kane nodded.

"And your vacunit is broken?"

"I think it managed to escape in time."

Lucian studied Kane. "I see," he said, and Kane had the unsettling conviction that Amerdath's son did see and understand—if not the precise details, the emotional topography of what had happened. The prince continued to look at Kane, who gazed back, defusing the steady eye contact by studying the peculiar split of color in Lucian's left eye.

"Do you know, I was four years old before my father noticed it."

"I didn't mean to stare."

"Quite all right."

"Your eye *is* striking," Pendrake said. "On my planet all eyes are colored as mine, except for rare Cephantines afflicted with a condition similar to albinism."

"I've read much about Cephan," Lucian said. "I'd like very much to visit your planet. I find your people the most admirable we have yet encountered."

"You are kind."

"The pacifism, the gentleness and refinement of the Cephantines should be models for us all, though, alas, they are not. Last night . . ." Lucian's voice hitched. "I had begun to believe that Clemis had acted alone," he finished finally.

"Apparently there is a conspiracy," Kane agreed.

"Apparently?"

Kane smiled. "You'll have to forgive me, but I always

hedge my bets. Even proven facts are often more apparent
than real.''

Lucian nodded vigorously. "You're so right, Elias. I've
had this problem in my work, as you have. There is a
sense in which our occupations are the same, you know. I
take a block of stone and start chipping. The stone is
amorphous and therefore its meaning is unclear. Somewhere inside the stone is a certain shape, a form of truth, if
only I can find it. You look for the murderer of my father
in almost the same way. You chip away at the stone of a
past event seen clearly only by one person. You are looking for that person, because he is the truth of what happened.
The rest of your stone consists of matter that hides and
confuses. You must strike your stone over and over in just
the right places, with just the right implement and just the
right force in order to find your truth—my father's murderer,
to be precise.''

"But your father has not been murdered," Pendrake
pointed out.

It seemed a trivial omission, the words "would-be"
accidentally left out, and then Kane realized that Pendrake
had perceived the reason for Lucian's mistake. The prince's
face underwent a subtle change, skin tightening, lips flattening over teeth in a wince held just below the surface.
"Hasn't he?"

"Is that why you haven't been to see him?" Kane
asked. "Because you think of him as dead?"

"Who told you that I haven't been to see him?"

"Chuddath."

"Yes, the Ornyl would know." Lucian's tone was
abruptly subdued.

"You look like you'd like to say something else," Kane
prompted.

Lucian laughed sourly. "Very good, Elias. I come here
to pump you for information about your investigation—I'm
sure you've recognized that by now—and you end up
pumping me. I was a fool to think myself more subtle than

you, but then, reputations can be misleading, and I hadn't really met you yet, had I? Yes, I would like to say more about Chuddath, but I don't know precisely what. Don't trust him, Elias. Suspect him always.''

"He seems fanatically loyal to your father."

"Their bond is very deep. Almost unthinkably deep in ways I can't bear to talk about. What my father did . . .'' Lucian stopped, and Kane sensed he had drawn back at the edge of an important revelation. He wanted to prod Lucian, but the man's expression stopped him. There was pain, loathing, the pallor of nausea in the aristocratic face. "I can say only, what is loyalty?'' Lucian continued. "The truth of many things is clearer than the truth beneath what we perceive as loyalty. But that's enough, or I fear I'll be sick.''

Kane suppressed his frustration. "You said you came to pump me about my investigation. You don't have to pump me. I'll tell you all I can right now, under one condition.''

Lucian leaned forward. "Which is?''

"Come with us afterward to see your father.''

The prince gave a laugh edged with hysteria. "What is this? Are you playing the priest, the healer of some imagined schism between me and my father? Or is it some other game? You want to see how I react, perhaps. Will the sparks of patricidal hatred perhaps blaze in my eyes? I could order you, you know.''

"Yes, you could order me.''

Lucian stared at him. "All right. Tell me and I'll go with you.''

The Princess Briana was with her father when Kane, Pendrake and Lucian entered the audience chamber. Amerdath's eyes betrayed nothing at seeing his son for the first time since Clemis' assassination attempt. Briana smiled coldly at her brother. "Well, well. What have we here? The mighty prince favors us at last.'' She stressed ''mighty'' just enough to give it the opposite meaning. Lucian ig-

nored her, or perhaps he did not hear. He stared at his
father's head atop the life-support cart, his eyes jerking
from cart to head to the Ornyl warrior behind, as though
he was afraid to let them come to rest and see.

"Hello, Son," Amerdath said. "I'm glad you came."

"How are . . . no, I'm sorry."

Amerdath smiled. "I'm quite all right, and it's fine for
you to ask. How are you? How is your . . . work coming?"

Lucian acknowledged the pause with a bitter smile.
"My *work* is not going well."

"I'm sorry to hear that."

Briana snorted and looked at the ceiling as if it could
commiserate. "Listen to you two."

"Perhaps you can stay after Elias briefs me, and we'll
talk," Amerdath said. Lucian did not reply, but stared
glassily at his father. Kane edged nearer Briana's twin,
afraid that he was going to faint. He remembered his own
first reaction to being in the presence of Amerdath's
disembodied head.

"Well then, Elias. What did you discover last night?
Who is it that wants my head, too?"

Lucian made a strangled sound. Tears spilled and he
turned away from his father. "I'm sorry," he choked.
Kane watched Amerdath's face as his son ran from the
audience chamber. No emotion registered; none at all.

"You see?" Briana said as soon as the great double
doors closed behind her brother. "He's weak. He has
always been weak. You cannot afford the chance that he
will take over should you . . . become too ill."

Kane realized that they had interrupted Amerdath and
Briana, that he should offer to leave, but he said nothing,
ignoring Pendrake's restless movements beside him.

"But I am in perfect health," Amerdath said. "What is
left of me has few vulnerabilities, medically speaking."

"The assassins, then. They could strike again at any
time. If you transfer power now, you may stop being their
target."

"And you'd be willing to become their target in my place," Amerdath said dryly.

"Yes, I would . . . Father." Briana's voice was abruptly soft.

"I thank you for your altruistic offer, but I'm quite fit to rule, and rule I will."

"Then pretend to pass power to me. No one outside your closest advisors would know that you had not stepped down. You could give me your commands and I would implement them as my own."

"Your concern is appreciated, but my answer is no. There are ramifications . . ."

"You're afraid the colonies would revolt as soon as you appear no longer to rule, but you're wrong."

Amerdath gazed at his daughter. "I'm wrong, am I? You see the obvious and yet you say that I'm wrong?"

"You *are* wrong. The colonies have stayed in line—barely—because they fear you. They know what kind of a strong man you are. Now they will wonder if you are weakened by your terrible injury. They will want to move, and they will move, to test you. If they expect succession to go to that piece of whimpering meat that just ran out of here, they'll more than test you. I'm the only hope you've got. Their spies know me and see what you do not see."

"We will discuss this at another time," Amerdath said with a glance at Kane and Pendrake, "but my answer will be the same."

Briana stared at her father. The Ornyl bodyguard shifted behind Amerdath, a potent gesture from one whose every move meant something. The princess stalked to the door of the chamber. She looked back at her father. "You are a strong old man," she said, "but I am strong, too."

Then she was gone, and the sound of the bronze door ringing from her fist died slowly in the great chamber.

CHAPTER 17

"You must excuse my daughter," Amerdath said. "She is headstrong."

"She appears to have the iron will of her father," Kane said.

Amerdath gave an enigmatic smile. "You mean you think she is like me. I've been told that before, many times. What do you think, Pendrake?"

"I do not know the princess, sir."

"An excellent answer, my friend." Amerdath fixed Kane with a cautionary look. "Do not mistake Pendrake's answer for mere diplomacy, Elias."

Kane nodded even though he did not see the point. Of course Briana was like her father. One did not have to know her well to see that. Perhaps Amerdath wanted to think otherwise—so much so that he read too much into Pendrake's careful answer. It was always hardest to see the self, no matter where one looked, inside or out. And yet there could be something to Amerdath's warning. Kane did not know Briana, and he discovered in himself now the truth that he was afraid to know her. The realization disturbed him. It was his business to know Briana, to know them all, these people who might want to kill Gregory Amerdath. Knowing people was what made him good at what he did. Wanting to know was what had brought him out of his inner deserts each time to this bizarre form of intimacy between hunter and hunted.

" . . . often get the idea that you are not listening to me," Amerdath was saying.

"I'll be happy to wait until Dr. Reik has come," Kane said almost absently.

"But then," Amerdath continued as though Kane had not spoken, "you always dredge up what I've been saying from that idiot videotape recorder you call an eidetic memory."

"Yes, sir," Kane said.

"Just once I'd like to catch you. As I was saying, Dr. Reik is going to supervise something I think will surprise you. Ah, here she comes now."

The bronze doors through which Briana had stormed out swung open and Martha Reik entered. Kane watched her stride across the polished parquet of the audience chamber, hardly noticing the man in the yellow uniform of the dietician's staff who pushed the cart behind her. Each long step caused Reik's hair to flare from her head and the muscles of leg and arm to suggest themselves beneath the glossy jumpsuit the way a cat's body will slide beneath its coat. Kane made himself look at the cart. It was loaded with food—pastries iced with sugary white swirls, a pot of steaming coffee, hot sausages fragrant with spices, slices of bread lavishly buttered, a bowl of red and yellow apples glistening and flawless.

Kane looked up from the cart to catch Reik's gaze sliding off him with a shyness he had not noticed in her before. She nodded at him and greeted Amerdath. "Good morning, sir. Would you care for some breakfast?" She gave the words the weight of high ritual.

The Imperator smiled broadly. "Indeed I would. You

remembered everything, I see." He glanced at Pendrake and laughed. "You look absolutely pop-eyed."

"I beg your pardon, sir, but I do not understand how you can hope to eat these things."

Reik turned to the alien. "The past week I've been preparing a link between the Imperator's natural esophagus and an artificial one. The link leads to a food sack within the life-support cart that can be . . ."

"Please, my love. You'll spoil my appetite."

Kane felt an irrational pang at the term of endearment. He watched the Imperator eat a pastry fed to him by the dietician.

"Ah, that's good, that is good," Amerdath moaned. "Mind your fingers, man, I haven't eaten for weeks. I think next the sausages and then some coffee." Amerdath ate steadily for the next twenty minutes, a look of mingled greed and pleasure concealing any awareness he might have had of the three humans and the two aliens. Occasionally he would murmur some instruction to the dietician, but would otherwise show his readiness for the next bite with looks that made Kane think of a feeding infant's rapport with its mother. Amerdath finished everything on the tray and let the dietician dab carefully around his mouth with a linen napkin.

"Good," he said. "Martha, you're a genius. I feel like a real man again. Funny thing, though. I don't feel a bit full. Maybe you'd better throw a few antacid tablets into that stomach." Amerdath laughed with huge enjoyment.

"I do not understand," Pendrake said, "why you wanted these things, sir. Is hunger not a function of gastric motility, blood sugar levels and other signals that no longer affect you?"

"Hunger, yes. Appetite, no. Ask any fat person—any *honest* fat person. Appetite is strictly up here." Amerdath signaled by raising his eyebrows and Kane thought how a normal person would have pointed to his head. He felt a resurgence of pity for the man so horribly maimed.

Amerdath's blood sugar and nutrient balance were now controlled by machines. There was no stomach to send squirming signals to his brain. Until today there had been nothing in its place but a small absorbent receptacle to catch the steady drain of saliva through Amerdath's throat. Even with the artificial stomach, he would never again experience hunger—or fullness. But today a sense had been restored to him, a simple thing that Kane in his lean man's objectivity toward food had always taken for granted. Amerdath would never again walk through his garden or feel a woman along the length of him, but today lust had been restored to him.

"Martha, if you'll excuse us now, I believe Elias has some business to discuss with me."

Reik nodded and motioned the dietician out, then turned to Kane. "Let's have a look at those hands before I go."

Kane held them out. He had forgotten the acid burns of the previous evening and it seemed petty and self-indulgent to display them now in front of Amerdath, as though they were real injuries. She held his hand longer than necessary— or perhaps it was his imagination—and nodded finally. "You'll lose a bit more skin before you're through. Why don't you come by after you're finished here and I'll get you something to retard the peeling and irritation."

"They're fine . . ."

"Don't argue with your physician."

"She's right, Elias," Amerdath said. "I'm damn glad I was on good terms with her that day in the garden."

Kane saw that she was waiting for him to agree. "Okay," he said. "I'll drop by."

After she'd gone Kane found Amerdath looking at him shrewdly. "She's a fine woman, Elias."

"Yes, sir."

"Don't keep closing yourself off to her."

Kane said nothing and Amerdath's expression firmed. "All right. What have you got for me?"

Kane briefed the Imperator on everything he had discovered in the murdered page's quarters the previous evening. He did not mention the side trip he'd made afterward to the run-down bar on the outskirts of Chronos.

"So you think my page was set up?" Amerdath said.

"We'll know for sure when Giacomin reports the lab results to me, but yes, sir, I do. It's too unlikely that the page cooked himself a steak, ate it, then wrote the rather distraught note and hanged himself, wearing the belt with the acid atomizer to clear up the ambiguities in the note."

"It's damned unlikely when you put it that way," Amerdath agreed. "So one of the other people who saw me that day used the belt and then planted it on the page after persuading him to write the note and killing him. What do we do next?"

"Next I question the other people who were in the same room with you yesterday—*all* of the other people."

Amerdath frowned. "I told you . . ."

"Yes, sir. Excuse me, but you also told me to find out who's trying to kill you. Now you'll have to decide which order you want me to obey, because I can't obey both of them."

"Bilge. There are a dozen different ways to go about this thing. You don't have to harass my family. They wouldn't be involved in something like this."

Kane glanced at Pendrake, who raised his eyebrows and drew in his breath sympathetically. "Sir," Kane said. "Your daughter . . ."

"Nonsense."

"Your daughter just challenged . . ."

"That's enough!"

Kane gave Amerdath a hurt look but said nothing more. Time became a presence in the room. The Imperator stared at Kane, his face expressionless, his attention focused on some inner vision. Kane stared back, aware of something that had eluded him until this moment. It was there in Amerdath's vacant expression, a factor so huge it must loom over the whole investigation. The factor was emotion.

All people were creatures of it, even in their most rational moments—the professor who greets a tardy student with an irritated pause, the chess champion who fumes at his opponent's tapping fingers, the mathematician who snaps the chalk correcting an error on the blackboard. But what about Amerdath? He had just seen his son for the first time in weeks, but there had been no tears, no fumbling for the right words, no agony when Lucian had run from the room. His daughter had just issued a veiled threat, but Amerdath had shown no anger. Last night, only moments after someone had tried once again to kill him, Amerdath had spoken calmly and rationally. Kane thought back over the time since the first assassination attempt. At some points there had seemed to be emotion in the man's behavior, but how could he be sure? What was emotion—a release of biochemicals from the endocrine system? A certain pattern of neural impulse in the brain? Kane knew only that he did not know, that no one knew, except perhaps for Amerdath himself. The answer would affect every dealing with the Imperator, even as it must be affecting the present disagreement. Why didn't Amerdath want his wife and daughter investigated? Because of his love for them or because he could no longer comprehend their possible hatred of him?

Amerdath's eyes focused again, jogging Kane back from his own musings. "All right, Elias. But there are several conditions. First, you will wait until Giacomin brings you the full analysis of the murder scene. Maybe there will be some clue to who's behind the assassination attempts, a fingerprint or something."

Kane nodded, though he knew from the pattern of the page's death that no such clue would be found.

"Second, you begin with Richard DuMorgan. Only if you are satisfied that he did not spray the acid into my life-support system will you proceed to my wife and daughter."

"Fine, sir."

"And for God's sake be careful. Use the light touch. It's crucial that none of these people think *I* mistrust them. If they complain to me, I'll not back you up. I'll tell them you acted against my wishes and I'll order you to stop. I don't know what you can hope to gain from talking to them, anyway. Or do you plan to take one of those fancy snoopers of yours and scan them for residues of cattaric acid while you chat about the weather?''

Kane suppressed a smile. "No, sir. Whoever used the belt is squeaky clean by now.''

"No doubt." Amerdath peered over at the food cart, left behind by the dietician. "All right, Elias. You can begin on the viceroy tonight. I'm having a state banquet for Manoster, the Moitan emissary. Richard DuMorgan will be there, and by that time you should have Giacomin's lab report. I'll introduce you to DuMorgan, seat you next to him at the table. Pendrake, we'll put you next to my daughter.''

Pendrake inclined his head. "I shall be honored.''

"Perhaps you can get to know her better," Amerdath said dryly.

"Will you be eating with us, sir?" Pendrake asked.

"Damned right I will." Amerdath's face showed such pleasure that Kane felt reassured about the Imperator's emotions. Surely no man could fake delight as vivid as that on Amerdath's face. And if he could, why should he? Still, a question remained. The human race had always identified its emotions with its flesh, separating geographically the source of feeling from the source of thought. Perhaps it was not merely a poetic device—a metaphor for something not understood. For centuries man's language had reflected the division—between mind and body, spirit and flesh, head and heart. Now a man had survived a real severing of the two. *What was that man really like?*

"One other thing," Amerdath said, "before you go. I've given the order for Mark Clemis to be executed." Amerdath did not look at Kane but stared, instead, at the food cart. "The execution will be one week from today. It will take them that long to get him back into good physical condition."

Kane stared at the Imperator, rejecting the implication, not wanting to understand. Pendrake looked pale. "Sir, if you plan to kill the man, why do you wish him to be physically rehabilitated?"

"Death will be by surgical excision of Clemis' head under anesthesia," Amerdath said. "As soon as it is done, Reik will perform surgery. An eye for an eye, Elias. A tooth for a tooth. A body for a body."

CHAPTER 18

As soon as they were out of Amerdath's presence, Pendrake turned to Kane. "Elias, you must persuade him not to do this thing."

"How? You saw him. He wouldn't even look at me. He sure as hell isn't going to listen."

"He will not survive as the man we know now. To possess the body, the hand that destroyed his own flesh. It will drive him mad."

"He clearly doesn't view it that way." Kane felt a terrible weariness mixed with anger—anger that events could have brought Amerdath to such a precipice. He turned to the praetorian that guarded the door. "You have a way of monitoring the audience room?"

The guard stared straight ahead and made no reply.

"I asked you a question. Do you know who I am?"

"Elias Kane."

"The Elias Kane who can break you down to private."

The guard looked at him with contempt. "You wish me to help you spy on our Imperator?"

"I wish to examine Amerdath's security measures. Shall

I tell him that one of his guards is trying to impede me? One of the same guards who stood by while another praetorian blasted his Imperator with a shattergun?''

The guard's contemptuous expression vanished, replaced by resentment and fear. He clearly had not expected Kane to recognize him as one of the eight who had been so deeply shamed.

"Commander Sabin . . .''

"Is under my jurisdiction in this matter. Now show me the monitoring room.''

The guard pointed sullenly to a door leading off the anteroom.

"See that we're not disturbed.''

The closet sized room was semidark, lit only by the greenish glow of the monitor screens. There were five screens, one for each wall of the audience chamber and one showing the central dais, where Amerdath looked down from the life-support cart. Only Chuddath and the Imperator were left in the room. The insect-man moved around in front of the life-support cart. As Kane watched, he leaned down, touching the narrow triangular strip between his compound eyes against Amerdath's forehead.

"What's he up to?'' Kane muttered.

"The S'edhite merging,'' Pendrake said.

"What?''

"It is a form of mind touch. Only the Ornyl and the race from which they originally descended can initiate the link. Few outside the Ornyl even know of the phenomenon.''

"How do you happen to know about it?'' Kane asked.

"My former master once hired two Ornyl as bodyguards,'' Pendrake said with some distaste. "Is this important, Elias? Should I have told you earlier?''

"I could have asked. It makes sense out of some rumors I had trouble believing—rumors that Amerdath and Chuddath are very close personally.'' Kane watched the merging. The warrior was totally still. Amerdath's face was partially obscured, but the corner of his mouth hung slack and open. The tableau reached through Kane's rational mind and set loose hidden dreads. It was as if the insect was sucking at Amerdath's brain. Kane shivered and turned from the screen. "Tell me all you know about this."

Pendrake continued to watch the monitor, apparently unshaken by what he saw. "It is an interesting process, Elias. An Ornyl from the warrior caste may establish the S'edhite with only one other being in his lifetime. Actually, the merging of minds is accomplished from a biological basis that is not considered mysterious by the Ornyl themselves. A small gland atop the Ornyl's brain is surgically removed and implanted within the chosen recipient's skull."

Kane's stomach turned uneasily. "You mean Amerdath has had a piece of Chuddath grafted onto his own brain?"

"Not on the brain, merely adjacent to it. When the gland is removed, it encapsulates itself in tissue that is inert. The result is a very small spherical mass that could fit comfortably between the cranium and the brain without causing tissue rejection. Of course, the process is usually carried out between Ornyl, but there is nothing to prevent a human recipient."

"How does it work?"

"I am not a xenobiologist, Elias, but in simple terms, the Ornyl maintains empathy with the displaced tissue. The tissue acts as a receptor for the recipient's cortical activity, conscious and unconscious thoughts and emotions. Thus it acts as sort of a telepathic bridge between donor and recipient."

"Are both parties aware of their own separate identities during this . . . this S'edhite merging?" Kane asked.

"Oh, yes, Elias. Really, it is merely a shorthand but very intimate way of conversing."

Kane looked back at the screen. "What could have made Amerdath do such a thing? Why would he open his mind to . . . to . . ." Kane let it hang, afraid that Pendrake might misunderstand.

Pendrake looked shrewdly at him. "Chuddath is, indeed, an alien creature, Elias; alien to us both. You need not be ashamed of your repugnance, since you cannot help yourself. Fear of the insect is instinctively embedded in your race and, to some extent, in mine. The insect is, after all, our foremost evolutionary rival. And to see one of such size is unnerving, though we must remember that Chuddath also shares humanoid features with us."

"So why would Amerdath do it?"

"I do not wish to appear cynical. What the Imperator has done, I very much admire. I would like to believe that I could take such a step myself, in order to better understand another creature, however distasteful he might be to my eyes."

"But you think Amerdath might have done it for another reason," Kane prompted.

"Perhaps. The Ornyl donor in a S'edhite arrangement becomes psychologically bound to the recipient. Once surgery has been carried out, the donor becomes incapable of the slightest disloyalty to his chosen partner. In the ancient history of the Ornyl race, the warrior caste would often become donors to their tribal kings for just this reason."

Kane gazed at the monitor. Cynical or not, Pendrake was no doubt right. Gregory Amerdath must have established a S'edhite link with the Ornyl warrior for this self-serving reason above all others—to have one creature at his side that he could trust absolutely. Every aspect of the alien's appearance and behavior proclaimed that Chuddath was dangerous and unpredictable. But if he was biologically bound to Amerdath by a loyalty that could not be broken, then he could not be implicated in plots against the Imperator's life.

Kane turned from the screen. Chuddath had been one of the nine suspects, and he realized now that he had wanted it to be Chuddath. *Let it be the ugly one, the one we can all loathe so easily.* Abruptly Kane felt ashamed, voyeuristic at having watched from hiding the scene of bizarre intimacy. He knew the scene would cling to his retinas, that it would taunt him with its indefinable grotesqueness. Kane switched off the monitors. The greenish glow died and he sought the strip of honest yellow light under the door. "Let's get out of here."

CHAPTER 19

As befitted their minor official standing, Kane and Pendrake were among the first to enter the banquet hall. Like so much of Amerdath's palace, the hall was immense, soaring five open stories above the long table. Spark points of thin laser beams drifted across the dark ceiling in arcane patterns. Helices of silver, each supporting a hundred candles, blazed at intervals along the white damask of the table. The thousand flames dived and swam in gold cutlery and bone china. Standing motionless as soldiers on review, uniformed servants lined the walls of the banquet hall. Within the walls, behind the tapestries of forest scenes, a symputer produced infinite variations on a theme, soothing without being bland.

Kane and Pendrake stood with a growing number of elegantly dressed men and women as each new guest was announced. Kane stared over the carved back of his chair into the yellow warmth of the candles as the list of names ascended in political importance. An admiral of the Imperial navy, an ImpSec undersecretary, Dr. Martha Reik, Commander Alvar Sabin, his Excellency, Richard Du-Morgan, Imperial Viceroy to Alpha Centauri IV.

Kane watched as DuMorgan made the long walk from the door of the banquet hall with a stride of casual and unselfconscious elegance. It was time to pay attention. This man was the real reason he had come to the banquet. The viceroy wore a uniform of light blue, with the dark blue sash of the Imperial rajinate and two rows of medals. The plain rustcolored sphere of the Legion of Mars was pinned above the medals, making a stark contrast to the glittering diplomatic honors and proclaiming that DuMorgan had suffered grievous wounds in military defense of the Empire. Kane wondered at the irony of a colonial wearing an Imperial medal. But DuMorgan was, at least officially, an Imperial. The medal had been won in defense of Alpha Centauri IV against an armada of Andinaz raiders. Despite Fowler Giacomin's distrust of the colonies, no blood had yet been shed between colonials and the legions of the mother planet. An Imperial medal worn in the court of Amerdath was not yet an act that would damage DuMorgan's popularity on Alpha Centauri.

DuMorgan gave Kane a congenial nod as he took his place behind the chair on Kane's right. Kane nodded in return and then glanced across the table at Pendrake. The alien was studying the Centauran viceroy in the unobtrusive way that was such an ingrained part of Cephantine manners. DuMorgan was a striking man. His lean muscled body was hardly the usual physique of an administrator; his face bore equally arresting contrasts. Scars curved symmetrically down from above the temples over each cheekbone, scars such as sabres might make. But the dark eyes between the scars were urbane, full of barely suppressed mischievousness. DuMorgan's jaw was firm and clean shaven, but an almost dandyish mustache spoiled the hawkish masculinity just enough to defy attempts at pigeonholing the viceroy. As administrator for the oldest and most powerful of Earth's colonies, Richard DuMorgan seemed to reflect with his appearance the complexity and ambiguity of his position. It would not be easy to draw from this man an explanation of a certain subspace message beamed from his cruiser to the vicinity of the Imperial palace on the day of Amerdath's near murder. And yet, Amerdath had been firm on the point: DuMorgan was to be handled with the greatest delicacy—the explanation could only be teased out, not demanded.

Only one guest remained to be introduced before the entrance of the Imperator himself. This was the guest of honor, Manoster, emissary from the Moitan fish people to the Imperial court. After an auspicious pause, the alien was announced, and even the most phlegmatic guests turned to gawk as Manoster entered the hall. The Moitan's home planet was a world of lavender-tinted potassium seas, and it was in a tank of native water that the alien entered. The tank was about two meters in height and rode on a cushion of antigrav suspensors steered by biofeedback sensors planted in Manoster's pectoral fins. Filtration equipment sent fine clouds of bubbles up from the bottom of the tank. The alien resembled a dolphin except for its reddish skin, the greater cephalic bulge and the ventrally located vestigial limbs. The Moitan floated upright in its tank in an imitation of the posture a man might take, its head bent forward with more suppleness than a dolphin could have shown to face out of the tank. There was an opening above water level at the top of the tank and a speaker grille in front that would carry conduction vocalizations from the tank into the gaseous outside world. It was said that the Moitan had learned in an astonishingly short time to speak English, a fact of ominous significance to the more militaristic of Amerdath's xenobiological advisors. No human had yet succeeded in speaking Moitan.

Kane reviewed what he had read that afternoon in the palace library about the Moitan. Little was known except that their home planet was approximately 0.7 parsecs beyond Beta Tenoris, which was the most remote of Earth's colony planets. The Moitan "fish people," as the popular press insisted on calling them, were an industrialized and

highly technological race that had, several millennia in the
past, developed anaerobic and low aerobic techniques for
working with their periodic table of elements. This enabled
them to progress into their own version of the iron age and
thence to the high science and technology they now enjoyed.
They were experts in mining the mineral deposits from
beneath the rock floor of their seas, and mineral rights
were thought to be the primary reason why Moitan was
contesting Earth's claim to the planet just discovered by
both races.

Manoster glided up to the table, surveyed the assembled
guests with eyes that looked faintly incredulous because
they were so round and then executed an unmistakable if
abbreviated bow. There was a delighted murmur among
the guests and several of the closer ones bowed in return.
Then trumpets sounded, high and slashing, a primitive
sound in an age of electronically perfected music. Several
people started at the first brassy scream; the last echo fell
five stories into complete and rigid silence. Every face was
turned toward the door when Amerdath came through. The
Imperator of the Terran Empire was sitting in a thronelike
chair of carved oak and gold inlays. A collective intake of
breath whispered through the assembly as people realized
that Amerdath *was* sitting, that he seemed to possess a
powerful-looking masculine body. He was dressed in boots,
pants and tunic of Imperial white. The tunic was open at
the chest where the silver tree emblem of the Amerdath
family hung on a chain. Amerdath's chair was settled for
this occasion on a mobile antigrav bed that conceded
nothing to the technology supporting Manoster's tank. Two
praetorian majors stood behind the chair, guiding it at a
stately pace to the head of the table, and as the chair drew
closer the guests could see the mat of white hair on
Amerdath's chest, the pattern of veins on the backs of the
hands that rested on the armrests. Kane recognized the
body as that made by the plastician for the failed operation,
and yet the effect was still startling. Amerdath looked like

a man again, instead of a pathetic monstrosity. Even the cuff of plastiflesh that surrounded and supported Amerdath's true neck looked real, bullish and powerful.

Kane glanced at Manoster, found the alien as mesmerized by the sight of Amerdath as the others. It was a master psychological stroke aimed at them all: *I am Amerdath, Imperator of the human race and its nine worlds. I am he who has ruled, who rules and who will rule all, nine planets or ninety. If your eyes seek weakness, they will find only strength.*

Farther down the table Briana, at Pendrake's left hand, was regarding her father thoughtfully. From the far end of the table, the gray-haired Empress Eunice gazed at him with the same impenetrable look that she seemed always to wear. Of all the people at the table, only Lucian was not looking at the Imperator, but staring instead at his plate. Kane checked DuMorgan last and the viceroy glanced back at him with a brief crinkling around the eyes, a message: *I know who you are, and I know you will be watching, and do not forget how the act of measuring always distorts what is measured.*

"Ladies and gentlemen, do sit down, please." The Imperator's voice seemed louder and firmer than usual, but Kane reminded himself that he was second from Amerdath's right, while the voice must carry to the end of the table. As everyone took their places, Kane realized that Chuddath was not present. Perhaps Amerdath had ordered him to remain outside the banquet room out of deference to the sensibilities of his guests. Kane knew only that he was relieved at seeing the Imperator again in an entirely human context, a man with a body and without the looming alien presence; relieved that nothing present need remind him of the huge insectoid head pressed against the Imperator's face with the closeness of a lover.

The first course was served by the ranks of servants, a cold potato soup, thick and flavored with scallions and pepper, and the guests received their second shock of the evening as Amerdath picked up his spoon and began with great care to eat. Like the others, Kane forced himself not to stare but to eat his own soup as he thought how it must be done. The plastician's body had been wired with myelon nerves when it was thought the body could be joined to Amerdath's head. Remote signal transducers could have been added to the body and an electronic jacket-type arm devised for a remote operator. Then the operator, a man of the same size as the artificial body, could sit in another room wearing the arm jacket, could hold a spoon in his hand and could "eat" out of the image of the soup bowl conveyed to him, along with the image of Amerdath's artificial arm, by laser holography. The operator's own arm would be concealed beneath a nose level shelf to eliminate confusing visual feedback from his own jacketed arm. The holographic video broadcaster could be concealed inside the chest of the artificial body with the other life-support equipment. The artificial arm would mimic whatever movements were made by the remote operator, who would know when to act and what to do through subvocalized instructions transmitted from Amerdath by sensors in the plastiflesh neck.

Kane watched as much as he dared while the Imperator finished off the bowl of soup. It was obvious that Amerdath had practiced. The effect was quite natural. A wet pressure built up around Kane's eyes. It was like watching a blind man recover his sight, or a deaf man leap up and keep time with a symputer.

"Quite a man, isn't he," DuMorgan said.

"Yes." Kane knew he should be more gracious, but the intrusion of the viceroy into his thoughts and the casual clairvoyance of the remark annoyed him. He reminded himself that it was time to stop playing the open book; time to start reading DuMorgan.

"We haven't been formally introduced," DuMorgan went on, "but I've heard much about the famous Elias Kane."

"You're too kind."

"Not at all. You saved us all from a nasty interplanetary crisis when you solved the psychopath plague."

"I'm sure the colonies were delighted to lift their quarantine of Earth," Kane agreed dryly.

DuMorgan laughed. "Touché."

The second course was served, a filet of red snapper, broiled in oil, and Kane wondered at the symbolism of serving fish, and a red fish at that, in the presence of the Moitan emissary. But Manoster gave no appearance of noticing. The alien was eating special food imported at great expense from Moitan by a speedy Imperial corvette. The food resembled frog, and Kane thought of the alien's own possible symbolism as a servant dropped a fresh and apparently live morsel, arms and legs kicking, through the opening at the top of the tank.

Kane realized he was neglecting DuMorgan. "You don't hear touché as an expression much anymore," he said. "One would almost think you obtained those classic scars in a nineteenth-century sabre duel."

"Is that the derivation of the word?" DuMorgan asked. His eyes seemed far away, as though he was recalling an unsavory memory.

"The scars were popular among the ruling class youth of several European countries as badges of honor," Kane explained.

DuMorgan's smile seemed forced. "I see. Actually, I got these in an even more foolish way, several years before I became viceroy. The Andinaz warriors have these great crablike pincers on their top set of arms. I never expected to get that close to one, but they actually boarded my cruiser. Clumsy of me to get caught that way."

Kane felt suddenly drab in his own navy lieutenant's uniform, with the barren place on his chest where DuMorgan sported the Legion of Mars.

"But tell me," DuMorgan said. "What put you onto the solution of the psychopath business? You really are quite highly thought of on Centauri IV, you know. We were all quite frightened that the bug was going to spread to our planet, too.''

Reluctantly at first and then with more ease, Kane began to tell DuMorgan about the events of three years before. The third course was served, a savory loin of lamb with haricot beans, garnished with carrots and onions. A dry red was poured with the entrée, replacing the sparkling white that had accompanied the second course. The symputer music picked up in tempo as the conversation around the vast table became louder and more animated. Twice as Kane glanced along the rows of blurred faces, one stood out, the Princess Briana, looking across at him with a speculative half-smile that was somehow inviting. Each time this happened, he glanced at Martha Reik; each time, she appeared to be paying close attention to the man next to her, a handsome marine colonel.

Kane paused in his account of the plague for more of the red wine, conscious from the heat in his ears and the way the candle flames kept smearing that he was drinking too much and too fast. DuMorgan paid rapt attention to everything he said, and when the viceroy suddenly looked toward the Moitan emissary, his distraction was therefore all the more apparent.

''Your concern is abbreciated,'' the emissary was saying in his high-pitched voice, ''but we could, I am sure, find ways to mine the hard rock of the new blanet with berfect safety.''

''Yes,'' Amerdath replied. ''I've heard about your expertise at subsurface mining. Tell me, how do you cope with the problem of noise and concussion effects of tunnel blasting being magnified in the dense medium of the water in which you live?''

Kane saw that the viceroy was staring intently at the alien, his eyes fierce with concentration. It was an expression startling in its sudden intensity. The alien appeared unaware of DuMorgan. ''Let us just say that noise and concussion are not a broblem for us," Manoster said. The Imperator made some reply. The conversation continued, and Kane realized that DuMorgan's attention was again entirely on him. He was forced to resume his conversation with the viceroy before he could properly analyze the momentary current of tension. He tagged the moment in his memory, determined to pull it out and examine it later.

The courses continued to follow each other, red-sleeved arms of the waiters appearing deftly over the shoulder with joints of meat, roast pheasant, cheeses, each with its own wine. There were toasts: To the distinguished visitor from Moitan—may his people find many planets and much wealth and as part of that wealth come to count the friend-ship and goodwill of the Terran Empire. To the Imperator of the great Terran Empire—may he find great joy in his reputation throughout the solar systems as a gracious and fair potentate, and so on, back and forth, jockeying for diplomatic points, planting the barbs carefully, a game that brought a glitter to the Imperator's eyes and caused the laughter and good cheer around the table to grow sharp and glassy with the excitement of the internecine chess game.

After dessert the symputer faded and an archaic key-board instrument called a pedal harpsichord was wheeled in. The harpsichord was made of walnut, with cherrywood keys. It was played by a man with a badly deformed and hunched back. Reading Kane's expression, DuMorgan leaned over and spoke in a low confidential tone. "It was the princess' idea. A . . . *special* entertainment for her father's first official fête since the attempts on his life." Kane saw Amerdath frowning over at the harpsichord player and whispering to one of his praetorian majors. Shortly after that the deformed man stopped playing and slipped out of the hall. The instrument was removed and the symputer played again, and no one seemed to notice except Briana. She smiled up the table at her father, and the smile was a terrible thing to see.

CHAPTER 20

"Does it not strike you as odd," Pendrake murmured, "this invitation for a private audience with Manoster?"

Kane glanced around the anteroom of the Moitan embassy, delivering a warning look to the Cephantine. "Did I ever tell you the story about the girl scouts and the embassy of Beta Tenoris?"

Pendrake frowned. "I do not think so, Elias, but what . . . ?"

"A troop of Nevada girl scouts had planned a field trip to the Tenoris embassy in New York to learn more about our outermost colony. A high official of the Terran State Department, which is headquartered here in Chronos, got wind of the trip and sent along a large plaster wall hanging—a decorative replica of the Imperial seal—with the compliments of the mother planet. When they got to the Tenoris embassy, the girl scout troop presented the seal to the Tenoran ambassador. He patted their heads, thanked them and hung the gift in one of his embassy's anterooms. Five years and a number of episodes involving apparent state department clairvoyance later, the ambassador took

166

down the seal and had it smashed with a hammer. There was a bug inside.''

"I take it you do not mean a six-legged creature with three body segments," Pendrake said contritely. "That is a humorous story.''

"I thought you'd find it amusing." Kane squirmed in the sculpted plastic chair, trying vainly to get comfortable. The chair had not been manufactured with his leanness and height in mind. He occupied himself with Pendrake's observation. What *did* Manoster want with him? Since the invitation, Kane had rubbed the question to a rhetorical polish. Before he could waste more time with it, the door to the Moitan ambassador's office slid open and a voice issued from inside.

"Mr. Kane and Bendrake, blease come in.''

Kane squinted as he entered Manoster's working quarters and Pendrake, apparently bothered even more by the lighting, bumped against him. The room glowed in a red aura, its few furnishings seeming to jitter within their hazy outlines. Kane stared with slitted eyes until the alien's tank firmed up from a blur across the room. "I hobe you are not uncomfortable," Manoster said. "The bortion of the sbectrum favoring Moitan vision is, of course, somewhat different from that for humans.'' The alien was facing them in his tank, and Kane realized as he had not at the banquet that Manoster was capable of rotating his eyes from the typical monocular side vision of the fish to coordinated binocular vision.

"The lighting is fine, Excellency," Kane said.

"Good. Blease sit down.''

Kane found the blurred shape of a bench beside Manoster's tank and lowered himself onto it, sliding aside as Pendrake almost sat on top of him. Kane tried to focus on the bubbles rising with hypnotic slowness through the alien's tank. When that did not work, he looked up at the ceiling, which was a glowing lavender color that made the backs of his eyeballs itch.

"You are looking at what we see on our world," Manoster said, "whenever we raise our eyes toward the *tisren*—the meeting of heaven and hell. I understand that in your culture hell is below."

"To those who believe in it," Kane said.

"And you do not believe in it?"

Kane laughed without humor. "I can't afford to." He wondered what perverse instinct had caused the alien to touch on the topic of afterlife. They were not here to discuss what happened to someone after they died. He closed his eyes and saw a silver cannister of ash.

"But you do believe in evil, I bresume?" Manoster continued. "A man who seeks killers . . ."

"I believe in evil."

Manoster shifted almost languidly in his tank. "The death of the bage who was assigned to me. Most distressing. I talked with him only that morning. I understand that he might not have destroyed himself as it abbeared?"

"May I ask what makes you think that the page did not commit suicide?"

"Rumors. A diblomat must have a keen ear for gossib."

"Your concern about a human you had just met is admirable."

"Not just any human, Mr. Kane. One who was to work in close connection with me in delicate negotiations. If the bage was murdered, I must ask myself, why? Was it, berhaps, so that one dedicated to the murderer's ultimate goals could reblace him? If so, what are those ultimate goals? I and the few who came with me are quite vulnerable in your environment."

"I think I can assure you that the murder was not related to your Excellency."

Manoster moved again in his tank, this time more abruptly. Kane's attention was drawn to the alien's vestigial hands, which appeared through the red-smeared vision to be squirming restlessly. "Your assurance is a comfort. I'm sure you understand my concern."

"Yes, Excellency." Kane looked up from the hands to find the Moitan ambassador's head angled away, a single eye staring at him with fishy coldness.

"You are investigating not only the bage's death, but also the attembts on your Imberator's life."

Kane nodded, in part to see if the alien understood the gesture.

"I am informed that you think it quite likely the braetorian assassin was not acting alone."

"You are well informed, Excellency."

"I also understand that the assassin has refused to reveal his accomblices even under severe torture. It is a bity you cannot embloy the Moitan technique."

"And what is that?"

"Why, holding the brisoner's head above water, of course."

Kane laughed and Pendrake frowned. "You must excuse my friend," the Cephantine said stiffly. "Elias, I fear, has a rather grisly sense of humor."

"You do not find my joke amusing?" Manoster inquired.

Pendrake looked nonplussed. "I beg your pardon, Excellency. I fear your humor is rather more human than Cephantine."

"Quite all right, Bendrake."

Kane's smile hung on his face, incongruous, as somber possibilities occurred to him. After only a brief period of known contact between the human race and Moitan, Manoster understood human language and culture well enough to make ironic jokes. It pointed to tremendous intelligence—or extensive prior contact with humans that no one on Earth suspected. The latter explanation could only mean that the Moitan had had extensive unreported contacts with colonists. It was surely possible, and just as surely against the interests of the Empire. Kane realized the ambassador was staring at him. The vestigial hands had turned placid.

"It is unfortunate that the braetorian has revealed nothing. Have you any susbects?"

"Several," Kane said.

"That is encouraging."

"I'll like it better when I'm down to one." Kane stared back into the single eye. Manoster turned slowly in his tank until both eyes were again bearing on Kane. It seemed almost a deliberate gesture, as though the alien were flaunting its superiority. *You see in only one way. I see in two.* Kane remembered the remark Chuddath had made on the night of the second attempt. *Always man sees with single eyes.*

"Thank you for coming," Manoster said.

Kane stood and found his way through the blood-colored light to the door.

When they reached the tree-lined avenue outside the embassy, a praetorian lieutenant was waiting for them. He informed Kane that the Princess Briana desired his presence. A military aircar was waiting. There was little time to think what the summons meant; before Kane's eyes had adjusted to the brilliant sunlight outside the embassy, he was back in shadow in the cool dusky corridors of the inner palace. They stopped outside the hallway leading to Briana's private quarters. The lieutenant cleared his throat. "Uh, Mr. Kane, the princess wishes to see you *alone*." The praetorian glanced at Pendrake.

The alien smiled slightly at the lieutenant's obvious discomfort, perhaps enjoying the joke of this trained killer being afraid of him. "I shall find my way back to the guest levels, Lieutenant." Pendrake turned to Kane. "Remember your manners, Elias."

The lieutenant led Kane down the hall. Crystal sconces gave just enough glow to light the way to the end. Then he was on the other side of Briana's door. The room was dim and unnaturally still. A trace of honeyed perfume drifted past him and was gone. As his eyes adjusted Kane saw her, sitting motionless in a peacock chair across the room.

She wore a fawn-colored suit, tight at the body, loose and sheer around the arms and dancer's legs. The jade eyes surveyed him for an uncomfortable interval.

"Come in, Elias."

"I thought I was in."

"I want you . . . all the way in." Her pause after "you" was just long enough to make it two phrases, her meaning unmistakable. Kane felt his toes digging into the carpet, his breath tingling in his lungs as it waited to be expelled. There were ways not to hear such invitations, and a lifetime of well-hidden shyness had made the ways automatic with him—a smile, a bland answer, a skillful change of subject. But now he said nothing. His mind went scarily blank, and the blood pounded down from his heart to a place that had been numb since Beth died. He had walked in the door and Briana had offered herself to him, and she was beautiful and a trigger had pulled behind his eyes and he wanted her.

He walked to her, feeling light-headed. The rest of the room blurred as she stood to meet him. She did not smile, and that was good. There was hunger on her face, but it did not destroy her poise. She stopped his dreamlike advance with fingertips on the chest and gazed at him, concentrating on the look of his own hunger. She drew her hand back, leaving it upraised, and Kane found her fingers. Their hands fit together, nerves seeking each other through the insulating pads of skin. They fingered each other's clothes, finding routes beneath, places where fabric yielded warm smooth skin. The floor accepted them. Clothes disappeared, the motions of removing them peaks of awareness. He pressed himself to her, feeling the exquisite shape of her, the firmness and vitality in her muscles. He smelled her, the flesh and its oils, the odor of desire, musky and rich. He wanted it to last, knowing when it was through they would feel diminished. He drew it out, the ache, the sublime, almost painful dams of blood and nerve breaking, breaking, two rivers crashing together. Unvoiced screams, driven inward to the core.

They didn't bother to move for many minutes, except to roll apart onto their backs. Briana murmured, "Thank you for not saying anything. I hate it when they talk." Her hand still lay on his stomach and his on her thigh. The floor existed again, the room, words, and all the other things with which the time in between is passed. *Of course he had not said anything. What was there to say?* He looked over at Briana, at the perfect profile, the beauty that now receded like a spent wave. He had needed to end the celibacy of grief, and she had needed him for her own reasons. Now he felt spent and, though he could not fathom why, only slightly guilty.

"Now that we've broken the ice," he said, "why did you want to see me?"

She rolled into a sitting position, then stood and began to pull on her clothes. He dressed too, thinking how it was harder to lie to someone when you were both naked.

"What are you smirking about?" she demanded.

"I don't think there could exist a good answer to that. Let's just say I'm a happy-go-lucky person and leave it at that."

She shook her head, then smiled slightly. "In time, I think I could grow to like you."

"Did you ask me here to get the latest on the investigation?"

"Silly Elias. I know all about the investigation. I asked you here for a *de*briefing, if you'll pardon the pun. You debriefed me very nicely. We must do it again sometime."

"What's in it for me?" Kane asked.

Briana laughed delightedly. "Oh, you *are* a treasure, Kane. Not only do you spurn small talk, you insult me. I suppose we could call what just happened 'hard' evidence that men do fake orgasms. You don't know how refreshing it is not to hear a man fawning over my beauty. But I don't think you faked it, and I guess that cancels all debts."

"I guess it does." Kane took a step toward the door.

"You don't have to rush off. Aren't you going to ask me if I sprayed that acid on my father's new plumbing?"

"Not while you have your clothes on," Kane said.

"Fair enough. Remember this. My father is gallantly trying to protect his family from your investigation, but don't try to handle me with discretion. I don't like it. If you want to question me, come right out with it."

"I'll remember." Kane opened the door to the hall.

"One more thing," Briana said. "You've been neglecting my brother. I'm not sure you should do that."

Kane closed the door softly behind him. He made his way past two praetorians to the elevator. He rode up to the guest levels, and walked past his own doorway because he wasn't thinking. He wasn't thinking about anything at all.

CHAPTER 21

The note was on the bar, as though Pendrake had known he'd go straight for the drink as soon as he got back to their rooms. Kane grunted at this little watermark of cynicism. What was it the alien had said before leaving him to walk alone in Briana's lair? *Mind your manners, Elias.* If the big alien had a flaw it was seeing too much. Kane shrugged, poured himself a whiskey, then gave in and picked up the note. It read: "Elias, I'm going down to the bar in Chronos where we drank the other night. I'd appreciate it if you'd join me as soon as you get back. There's something very interesting we need to discuss."

Kane thumped his drink on the bar, spilling half of it. He hurried to his bedroom, opened the special suitcase and tossed aside the shirts that he'd never unpacked. He touched two inner corners in a patterned sequence and the false bottom of the case popped up. He withdrew the parts of the slim navy-issue needler and snapped the handle and snout into place, checking the charge. An image came unbidden of what had happened to the last needler he'd drawn from this case. There had been the other guest room, the one in the casino hotel; the hand of Pendrake holding the needler by the tip of its snout as though it were a dead fish as he deposited it in the room's flashunit disposal. The world had been going mad then, but Beth had been alive. The pain of a billion other human beings could never be as real for him as what he'd endured since she had been killed. Knowing it made him feel small and selfish but changed nothing.

He slipped on the V-coat, the one he'd hoped would hang in the closet unworn, snugged the needler into a slim holster tailored in where the left inside pocket should be. He checked himself in the mirror of the bathroom, making sure that the padding around the holster hid the bulge the weapon would have made. The other side of the coat was padded, too, balancing the hidden holster. If he tried to bring the needler back into the palace after his trip to the city, the praetorians at the elevator checkpoints would stop him, but that did not concern him now. Searches of people leaving the palace were not routine.

As he hurried through the curving corridors and waited impatiently in the elevator that crawled down the side of the mesa, Kane tried to think who might have dictated the note to Pendrake. He let it occupy him until he reached the run-down bar at the outskirts of Chronos. A page had been made to write his own suicide note, and Pendrake had been made to write a message luring him here, and guessing who wasn't half so likely to help him as the needler.

The bar was closed. Kane looked up and down the street. It seemed unnaturally quiet, too empty for three in the afternoon. A dry hot breeze blew in from the desert beyond the dead end of the street. Kane tried to see through the glass of the bar window, but the sun was wrong, and all he saw was a worried face and a hand edging into a V-coat. He wondered if behind that face, wearing it like a mask, was another face, another hand drawing a weapon. A man behind the glass could be aiming at the rivulet of sweat that ran down his forehead and stopped in the crease between his eyes. Had they planned it right to the time of day, the positioning of the sun? He was only unnerving himself, so he cut it off and tried the handle of the door. It was unlocked. He considered getting to a phone, calling Sabin and demanding a squad of praetorians to back him up. But they had Pendrake and if they saw praetorians, they could kill the alien on their way out without losing a step. He had to keep the rendezvous and keep it alone, keep it now.

He went in low, the needler out in front, diving and rolling out of the mat of sunlight, feeling exposed, and then, when nothing happened, foolish. The bar seemed deserted, mummified except for the motes of dust that his entrance had set tumbling slowly through the sunlight. He got up and looked for the next door, remembering too little about the place for a man who had spent four hours in it. The door to the back was an iris-type, and they were waiting behind it.

He counted three of them as he came through and took out the first with a spread of anesthetic darts from the needler. A fist bounced off the top of his head, making his nose prickle and giving him hope, because a trained fighter wouldn't have wasted energy on such a blow. There were more than three, coming out of the shadows. Before he could get the needler around for another shot, someone got his wrist, no leverage or pressure at the vulnerable elbow, just a viselike grip. He tried to go with the motion, use the man's own strength against him, but the man was standing still, just holding on, and Kane glimpsed a swarthy, bearded face, calm eyes, before the fist descended again on his head. That was tiresome, so he lashed out with a foot, and someone yelped, began to blubber. But there were more. They started piling on and he went down.

Kane let go of the needler, and went still, and hoped they would get off him before the brain got tired of waiting for its next dose of oxygen and went into withdrawal.

"Okay, he's decided to be smart," someone growled, and the mass of bodies shifted. Kane pulled a breath at last and the red mist cleared away from his eyes. "Hold him, now. Hoist him on his feet." Hands jerked him up. He tried to gasp silently, not wanting to give them a show.

When he got his breath again he said, "Lucky you came to your senses. I was about to get mad."

"Don't be a comedian." It was the swarthy face. Kane saw in the eyes an intelligence that did not go with stereotypes of huge men with hamlike shoulders and hands as hard as mailed fists.

"You can let go of my arm now," he said. "I won't hurt you."

"I said don't be a comedian."

The man Kane had kicked was writhing on the floor and moaning. The bearded giant let go of Kane's wrist and gave the man a reproving look. The moaning stopped and two of the others bent over the man, began carefully straightening the leg Kane knew he had broken.

"Was it necessary," the giant asked, "to come charging in here and attacking us?"

"You tell me."

The man frowned and then nodded grudgingly. "I suppose it was. What tipped thee off about the note?"

"Contractions," Kane said, noting the colonist accent, the archaic use of "thee" typical of the large northern continent of Alpha Centauri IV. "Pendrake never uses contractions. It's part of his obsessive nature."

The giant glanced at one of the men beside him, who looked defensive. "How was I to know, Dalt? That's not typical of Cephantines who've learned English."

"They be individuals too," the big man called Dalt said. "Thou could have done thy homework better." He turned back to Kane. "Thou knew and yet thou came. Admirable."

"Not really. I knew the only way you could get Pendrake to write the note would be to tell him you'd hurt or kill me

if he didn't. I'm a big baby about pain and being killed.
Can we get on with it?''

"If thou art the baby about pain thou claims, it will be
over soon enough," Dalt said. There was no malice in his
voice, no satisfaction, and Kane began to think that under
different circumstances he might get along with this man.
But the circumstances were not different.

"Let me at him," said the man on the floor.

"No," Dalt said.

"It's the code."

An eye for an eye, a tooth for a tooth, Kane thought.
Only a few days ago he'd heard the Imperator say it about
Clemis' body, the body Amerdath planned to take for
himself. It was the part of the old Christian Bible that the
people on the great colony outbacks understood best. It
was a prominent part of their code, but Dalt had said no,
and . . .

"Not until we get him below," Dalt continued. "It
would be stupid to break it now and then have to carry
him. Bad enough we've got to carry both our comrade
who is sleeping from the gun, and thee, oaf."

There was another door at the rear of the back room,
weathered wood on one side, steel on the other. The tunnel
at the bottom of the stairs was short and steeply graded.
The temperature dropped several degrees as they descended.
The injured man grunted with each step of the men carrying him, but there was no more whining. Each time Kane
glanced at the man he found the pained eyes centered on
him with snakelike concentration. No one spoke during the
short descent. One of the men kept the needler propped
between Kane's shoulder blades. Glow-globes lit the way
around a single bend in the tunnel to another steel door.
The door opened as the party approached, admitting them
to a large room with concrete walls and a low ceiling that
sweated with condensation. Pendrake sat with stiff dignity
in a forcechair, a guard with a 'ruptor standing behind
him.

"Good afternoon, Elias."

Kane saw with relief that the Cephantine showed no obvious injuries. "Pendrake. Maybe we should have tried someplace new."

"The service does seem to have deteriorated since our last visit," the alien agreed. "How was your meeting with the princess?"

Kane smiled at Pendrake's slight emphasis on the word *meeting.* "My friend, you're becoming a master of sly euphemisms."

"I had hoped to be a master of sly notes."

"Oh, I got the message, all right. These guys aren't really that much. Couldn't you have just tapped them lightly . . ."

"Please, Elias. You know that I could not do violence. If you understood the note, you should not have come."

"Enough talk," Dalt said. "Mr. Kane, sit." The big man indicated a second forcechair with the point of his beard. Kane sat and felt the field close around him. The effect was claustrophobic, suffocating, as though he'd been trapped in a cave-in. He felt dizzy and realized that he'd begun hyperventilating in response to the pressure on his chest. He forced himself to relax.

"I want to break his leg," said the injured man, who had been deposited on a cot along one wall. "Now. You promised."

Dalt flicked a hand in irritation. "Thou will have thy chance. The leader will say when. Now be quiet or I'll have to move thee again."

The man sagged back on the cot as a tired-looking bald man entered from a side room and bent over the leg with a syringe. Someone else brought an ice pack. Dalt loosened the force field slightly on Kane's chair and waved most of the squad he'd used to capture Kane out of the room. When they were gone, he studied his captive. "Thou hast said that thou fears pain. 'Twould be better if thou did. In my experience, men who make jokes about their cowardice are the bravest.''

"Not me."

The big man stared at him with an unreadable expression. ''Thou knowest from my manner of speech that I be colonist. Perhaps thou knowest already what I want from thee.''

"English lessons?"

The man's expression did not change. He reached through the unidirectional field with both hands and curled his index fingers around the back edges of Kane's jaws, just beneath the ears. The fingers felt hard and sandpapery against his skin, and then the big man began to press. A low fast beat drummed inside Kane's ears as the pain grew and grew and the sweat ran into his collar, and he knew he would have to scream. The pressure ended. ''Mr. Kane, thou *will* stop joking. We know of thy investigation, and we know that thou hast accused the colonies of plotting against the interests of Earth. What hast thou learned, and what hast thou told Amerdath?''

''I'd rather discuss that with your leader.''

Dalt placed a hand on Kane's chest, probing, measuring the ribs. The padding of the jacket flattened out under the powerful fingers. Then the hand cocked back about three inches and rammed in, and Kane felt the rib crack as the air was punched out of him. The left side of his chest felt like it had been skewered with thin hot wires. The pain burned down very slowly until it smoldered, the way it was going to smolder until he healed or got a shot of something or they killed him. He needed oxygen, but breathing hurt, so he had to sip the air. He tried to scan the room, moving his head to each side as much as possible within the force field. The big man sighed. ''There be four men besides myself,'' he said. ''One behind thee holds a 'ruptor, then there is the doctor, the man whose leg thou broke and one other who helps the doctor set the leg. But thou art in a forcechair, and there will be no escape. What have thy investigations revealed?"

"I'll talk to your leader now." Kane's voice came out hoarse and pinched, from the throat, because the diaphragm didn't want to move any more than it had to. "You'll not be letting us go in any case, and I don't like the habit you have of talking with your hands. Your leader and I have already established a better rapport anyway, at dinner last night."

Dalt reached again into the field, and Kane saw in the big man's eyes that the guess had been right. As the fingers began to press on the broken rib, the door through which the doctor had entered opened again.

"That's enough."

The big man stopped and stepped back and Richard DuMorgan, Imperial viceroy to Alpha Centauri, took his place.

CHAPTER 22

"Somehow I'd marked you down for more finesse," Kane said.

"I apologize," DuMorgan replied. "But these are desperate times. A few bruises . . ."

"My broken rib will be relieved to hear that it's only bruised."

"What? Are you certain?"

"I don't think this particular one has been broken before, but yes, I'm sure."

The viceroy's expression darkened. He turned on Dalt. "I told you, nothing serious."

"He broke Sol's leg. Did thou want me to tickle him?"

The exchange discouraged Kane. DuMorgan was a civilized man, and he would no doubt be the top kick in any colonist conspiracy, but his control over his men would seem tenuous if Dalt could talk back to him at will. Military discipline might not be the strong suit of the colonist mentality, but DuMorgan was a soldier before he was viceroy. If he could not control his forces, hotter heads than his would likely prevail.

DuMorgan turned back to Kane. "Perhaps Dalt has done you a favor at that—unless you'd rather have a broken leg than a cracked rib. The code is satisfied."

"I'm sure Sol will be glad to hear that when he wakes up," Kane said.

"He'll accept it," DuMorgan replied. "Make no mistake, Elias. These men are good soldiers, not undisciplined rabble."

Kane nodded in salute. DuMorgan had managed to rebuke and praise Dalt in the same breath. On the big man's face Kane could see the real truth—DuMorgan's men might speak their minds, but they'd follow the viceroy into a star core.

"This doesn't make sense," Kane said. "Why have you snatched us? There are sure to be repercussions."

"I think you know why we had to take you," DuMorgan said. "You were getting very close to us. I only hope we're not too late."

"What makes you think I was getting close to you?"

DuMorgan smiled wearily at him. "Perhaps you and I should change places."

"You do look like you need to sit down," Kane said, "and these chairs are irresistible." Kane noted the puffiness under the other man's eyes, the feverish redness of the twin crescent scars. DuMorgan was on thin ice—a drug-hardened surface of alertness over a black lake of fatigue. The surface had cracks, and soon DuMorgan would either rest, spend dreamless, deathlike hours at the bottom of the lake, or he would go psychotic. "How long since you've slept?" Kane asked.

"Sleep's overrated, Elias. Waste of time, really. Can we talk? Will you answer my questions?"

Kane thought about it. There was very little he could tell DuMorgan and much he might learn from the viceroy. "If you'll answer mine," he said.

"Thou art in no position . . ." Dalt fell silent at the viceroy's sharp hand motion.

"Yes, he is," said DuMorgan. "You see what playing rough got you. We need his cooperation. I have a feeling that if Mr. Kane got the drift of what is really going on with us, he might even consider joining us. In any case, as he has pointed out, he'll not be leaving us, so nothing I could tell him will make much difference."

"We have the drugs," Dalt said.

DuMorgan closed his eyes. "Let's hope they won't be necessary. All right, Elias. I'll tell you what I can as long as you keep giving me straight answers."

Kane glanced over at Pendrake, wincing at the pluck of pain the movement caused in his side. The Cephantine was staring straight ahead, his eyes glazed. It was the beginning stage of the *Tropos* meditation. The alien had heard DuMorgan say that they would not be leaving, and he was doing the only thing he could, but Kane felt dismay. If it worked it might destroy his best chance at information, and there was still the man behind them with the 'ruptor. But he could say nothing to the alien, could not give him even an oblique warning, because in the trance Pendrake would not hear him. Kane turned back to DuMorgan, filled with urgency because death might soon hold a lottery in the room, and he and Pendrake held the short straws. "Fire away."

"Let's start," DuMorgan said, "with what Marin told you."

"Who's Marin?"

DuMorgan and Dalt glanced at each other. "Elias . . ."

"I do not know who Marin is," Kane said firmly.

"Perhaps he was using a false name, though I'd assume you'd have checked."

"I don't know what you're talking about."

"There's no use in your protecting him," DuMorgan said. "He's blown. We've already taken him out. We just want to know what he told you last night and whether you've passed it on yet."

Kane frowned. "Are you saying one of your own men is supposed to have contacted me to betray you?"

"It's no use trying gentle ways with this man," Dalt cut in. "We should use the drugs."

"I'm telling you, *I don't know.*"

DuMorgan took a deep breath, exhaled slowly, rolling his head around as he rubbed his neck. "Elias," he said at last. "We *do* know. We have a man in Giacomin's office. He overheard one of Giacomin's field agents making a report on Marin. The agent saw Marin, who was your waiter at the banquet last night, pass you a note. This morning, our man in the Special Branch uncovered the 10,000-credit payoff deposited in Marin's account on Tenoris. Those funds were transferred by you, Elias, from your own account. You paid Marin off to turn traitor on us. No doubt the Imperator will reimburse you. What did Marin tell you about our organization, and what have you passed on to Amerdath?"

"You've been suckered," Kane said.

"What do you mean?"

"Giacomin. He maneuvered you into picking me up. The waiter never told me anything, never passed me any note. I never saw him before the banquet and I didn't notice anything but his arm last night. Giacomin must have known or suspected that Marin was a colonist who had infiltrated the palace household staff. He probably suspected, too, that you had an agent hidden in his own Special Branch. In fact, he must have specifically suspected your man. So he deliberately had his field agent make his report on Marin so that your man could overhear. Then he kept his eye on this Marin. When you pulled him out, you confirmed that both he and your man in Giacomin's office were colonist spies. Now that Giacomin's game has worked, he'll also expect you to pick me up to find out how much Marin told me. You'd better hope Giacomin didn't have agents following me here."

DuMorgan rubbed at the puffiness under his eyes, and

Kane realized that the viceroy must have been on stimulants since before the banquet for the reaction to be this intense now. Things were coming to a head, and no one in the palace knew it. Only Giacomin even suspected. "As it happens, you *were* followed," DuMorgan said. "Two of Giacomin's people. We bagged them as soon as you entered Chronos. If there were more, we'd be hearing from them about now."

"Thou believest this man?" Dalt said incredulously.

"What about the money?" DuMorgan asked.

"For someone with Giacomin's resources, it could be arranged. He'd have my account tampered with and then assign the man in his office he suspects of being a spy to investigate it. Again, the fact that you snatched me blows both Marin and your man in Special Branch."

DuMorgan shook his head slowly. "If what you say is true, we can't save him. Giacomin already knows we hamstrung his two bird dogs, so he's no doubt put my man in custody already. We can't let you go, and when he confirms you've been snatched, he'll put the screws on the man we had in his office. He was one of our best."

"Did that man know you are leading the show?" Kane asked.

"No. Very few people know that. We work on the cell system, only a few people in each cell. There will be time to pull out his other cell members, but our Special Branch feed is finished. And he made us blow our own men. Damn! Damn him to hell." DuMorgan's eyes closed again, and he swayed slightly as, for a second, he dipped toward the sleep he needed so desperately. Dalt's hand came just short of the viceroy's elbow, but held back. One pretended not to see weakness in such a man unless there was no choice. Kane glanced at Pendrake. The alien's eyes stared across the room, glassy as onyx. It would come any second now. Kane tried to will the pain in his side away, to reduce it to discomfort, to a mere nuisance that he could ignore when the moment came.

DuMorgan straightened and stared at Kane. "If what you say is true, we are hurt but not so badly as we might have been. Marin is not a traitor, and no one knows the rest of his cell. I didn't think he could have slipped you a note without my seeing, and I didn't think Marin would ever turn on us." Kane looked beyond DuMorgan. The doctor had left the room. One man still squatted by the injured man's cot. There were Dalt, DuMorgan and the man with the 'ruptor. The 'ruptor would have to go first.

"We can't be sure," Dalt said, "unless we use the drugs. Now."

DuMorgan gazed down at the floor. "I'm sorry, Elias, but he's right."

"We have a bargain. I've told you the truth," Kane said. "Now I want you to tell me just one thing. I'm familiar with colonist grievances against Earth—the tax rates, the high-tech monopoly and so on. But Amerdath trusts you, and Alvar Sabin seems to have a moderate attitude toward the colonies too. I've heard Alvar ridicule Giacomin for his obsession with colonist conspiracies. If Amerdath dies of old age, there's a chance that Lucian could take over, especially if things have been reasonably peaceful. The prince hardly seems the type to make things harsher for the colonies if he does get the throne. But if Amerdath is killed, Briana is almost sure to take the reins. Under her flag, Alvar Sabin would lead the full military might of Earth in a vendetta against the colonies, starting with Centauri. Giacomin's secret police, who've been leashed to a tight heel by Amerdath, would go on a rampage . . ."

"I don't need a lesson in interplanetary politics, Elias," the Centauran viceroy said.

"Then *why?* Why in God's name are you trying to assassinate Gregory Amerdath?"

DuMorgan stared at him. "What makes you think *we're* trying to kill him?"

"For openers, the fact that you beamed a secret message to the vicinity of the palace on the day of the attempt."

DuMorgan looked surprised but recovered quickly. "Giacomin," he muttered. "He's a *devil*. Sure, we beamed a secret message. It had to do with . . . with some of what's been happening. The existence of this room and these men around me has already told you that something is happening. But not that, Elias. I can assure you, that message from the *Sentinel* had *nothing* to do . . ."

There was a sound like a sheet ripping and Kane turned as Pendrake tore through the grip of the forcechair. Tenths of seconds framed each part of it—the force field collapsing onto the chair with a pop, Pendrake reaching for the switch behind Kane's chair, Dalt beginning to move while DuMorgan stared, slowed by stimulant fatigue. Kane pushed up as the field released him and pains shot through his ribs. Pendrake caught the barrel of the 'ruptor before it could bear on him and tugged the gun free as though the guard's fingers were boneless. Kane hit Dalt, two knuckles in the side of the head as the big man lunged for Pendrake. Dalt grunted and dropped to hands and knees, settled forward on his face. The punch recoiled through Kane's arm to the cracked rib. Dizzy with pain, he leaned on the arm of the dead forcechair. The man who'd been beside the cot froze halfway to DuMorgan's side.

"We've got the 'ruptor," Kane said between clenched teeth. "Nobody move. If anyone's monitoring in the next room, stay put. If the door opens, the viceroy dies first."

DuMorgan stood very still, shoulders sagging. "I congratulate you, Elias. No one's ever knocked Dalt off his feet. And you, Pendrake. I knew about the *Tropos*, but not that it could make you capable of this. You can't escape, by the way. My men will follow as soon as you're out the door."

Kane motioned Pendrake toward the tunnel entrance, holding out his hand for the 'ruptor without looking away from the viceroy. He saw DuMorgan's eyes widen. Metal groaned and snapped, and Kane turned as Pendrake finished bending the 'ruptor into a U-shape and dropped it on the floor. Kane swore, and the adrenaline shot into his legs, and he raced for the door as DuMorgan began to react. The door was a sliding one that disappeared into a wall when open. It was steel, three centimeters thick. Pendrake got it open and Kane made it through about two meters ahead of DuMorgan. The Cephantine slammed the door shut again, pivoted gracefully on one leg and kicked the door in its center, bowing it in and freezing it shut on its runners.

Kane leaned against the wall of the tunnel, holding his ribs. "Damn it, you big . . . you big . . ."

"Pacifist?" Pendrake suggested.

"Somehow that lacks the right flavor. All you had to do was give me the 'ruptor."

"Guns are dangerous, Elias. Someone might have been hurt or killed."

"So what do we do if there's a guard waiting for us in the bar?"

"We run, unless he is armed. If he is armed, we surrender."

"Surrender. That's perfect. Why didn't I think of it? We'll just surrender." The door thumped and vibrated as the men behind it tried to batter it flat enough to slide it open. Kane tried to draw a deep breath, coughed as the pain of it burned his chest. Pendrake moved to help but Kane waved him off. "I can make it. Let's go." When they got to the top of the stairs and opened the door to the back room of the bar, the needler was pointed at Kane's face. He could see the trigger finger tightening, knew the spread of darts would go straight into his eyes.

CHAPTER 23

"You're beautiful," Kane said.

"The paracaine's made you giddy," Martha Reik replied.

Kane thought about the snout of the needler, perfectly round, a perspective that even in memory prickled against the fragile drum-tight membranes of his eyes. The paracaine was beginning to erase the pain of his cracked rib, and the relief was a mild high. But she *was* beautiful, and he might have lost the chance to see her or anything else, ever again. "It's not the paracaine," he said.

Reik stopped probing his ribs for new injection sites and looked at his mouth. He found it arousing, a breaking of taboo, and the thought came to him that people watch each other's eyes as a social truce, a mutual restraint of curiosity and desire. The truth of a person displayed itself in other places: in the hands, in the distance kept or shortened, in the way the body arranged itself. Her hands had not left his ribs. Through the paracaine he could feel their light pressure, the fingers spread, drawing heat. They were alone in the small infirmary. The room began to play on his senses, the shining glass of the drug cabinets behind her, the light pooling beneath a table lamp, the whirring of an air conditioner, the scent of alcohol and disinfectant, These things were a part of her, of Martha Reik, healer. Kane let his fingers close around her forearms. The white sleeves of her coat wrinkled under his hands, transmitting the lean smooth cords of her arms, and a sense of knowing something more of her because of the contact.

Kane leaned forward on the examination table, watching her lips until they blurred. It was a chaste kiss, a slight opening of the mouth, almost sad in its sweetness. He pulled back and gazed at her. What was wrong with him? Twice in one day, two very different women, two acts, two meanings, which in each case he should have been able to hold away from himself. His body was acting without waiting. It was not like him, and that was frightening. It was not simply lust that had moved him to Briana, nor was it lust at all that strained in him for contact with Reik. Never in his adult life had he hungered to be held, *cradled*. His physical contacts with women had been for pleasure or, with Beth, for love, but always as a man. Now, when he needed all his strength, the thing inside wailed like an abandoned infant.

"You *are* giddy, Elias."

Kane took the out as quickly as she offered it. "You're the one giving the shots."

She held up the syringe and thumped the bubbles up to the tip and her hands were steady. "That man who brought you in. I've seen him around the palace."

"One of Giacomin's people," Kane said. "He almost shot me in the face. I'm surprised he didn't."

She stared at him. "What are you talking about?"

"Giacomin's agents were closing in on the place where Pendrake and I were being held. We were escaping and we ran into their point man. He could have fired away and claimed he had to react first and check I.D.'s later."

"You think Fowler resents you enough to want that?"

Kane thought about how Giacomin had used him and

Pendrake as bait. There would be an accounting, as soon as the security chief gave up combing Chronos for the rebels and returned to the palace. But he was alive, and if Giacomin had wanted him dead, he would be dead. "No," he said.

"How did the colonists get away? You said they had you and Pendrake underground, and that you were making a break for it when Giacomin's people were moving in. They should have been able to sweep down the tunnel and gather everyone up."

"They got down the tunnel all right. Then they found three centimeters of steel door that Pendrake had smashed shut. By the time the security forces had brought down the cutting torches, the colonists had slipped out through another tunnel—the first rule of the ground hog. Giacomin didn't net one prisoner, and I don't think he's going to . . ." Kane stopped, realizing that his voice sounded almost gloating. Was he that angry at Giacomin—so angry that he wanted the man to fail even if it meant that the enemies of Amerdath would escape? Or was it something else, a wedge of doubt Richard DuMorgan had slid into place during the last seconds before Pendrake had broken free?

Reik withdrew the needle a last time, and Kane realized he hadn't even felt it going in. He patted his ribs, suppressing an instinctive anxiety at the lack of feeling, at the sensation that he was touching dead meat instead of part of himself. "That's great," he said. "Not even a twinge. I feel good enough to go dancing tonight."

"See that you don't. The rib *is* cracked, and it doesn't need any unusual stresses put on it, or any usual ones either. As you know, paracaine is a very long-acting anesthetic, the effective period depending on stored fat and metabolic rate. Unfortunately, you're short on the first and fast on the second, but you should still be all right for several days. After that I can give you oral painkillers. Try to breathe normally and forget about the rib."

"Okay, thanks." Kane eased himself off the table. He stood looking at her and the moment for just walking out passed.

"Are we going to act like it didn't happen?" she asked.

"What would you like to do?"

"Don't give me that."

Kane felt a flash of anger, hot and irrational. "Why the hell not? Is everything up to me? Do I take all the risks?"

She took his anger calmly. "I didn't lay the snares waiting out there for the two of us. Beth Tyson's death did that. I wish the risks were mine, but they're mostly yours, Elias, and I can't change that, no matter how much I might want to. I want you to think about yourself and your own wants and needs, and then be as honest as you can with both of us."

Kane walked to the door and back, hardly aware of his movement. He felt her watching him, her face reposed and attentive, and finally he gave up trying to keep the words back. "Briana summoned me to her private quarters today . . ."

"And you had sex with her."

"Damn it, am I wearing a sign around my neck or did you and Pendrake watch through a peephole?"

She smiled. "You're not wearing a sign, Elias. I'm the Imperial physician, remember? The princess is a lot like her father was, where her sex life is concerned."

"If you say so," Kane said, regretting it instantly because he realized she'd deliberately laid herself open to even things up. "I didn't feel guilty afterward," he said, feeling against all reason that Reik was the one who could hear it and help him make some sense out of it. "I expected to feel guilty and I didn't. Just a few minutes ago, when I touched you, when we kissed, I *did* feel guilty."

"Why should you feel guilty about Briana?" she asked, as though she had not heard the last part of what he'd said.

"Because of Beth, I suppose."

"Because you were disloyal to her memory?"

"Isn't it supposed to go something like that? Except that I didn't feel guilty." He searched her face in appeal. "What's wrong with me?"

She shook her head once, the movement so small he almost missed it, and busied herself with locking away the vials of anesthetic. He flushed. It had been thoughtless and cruel to talk to her about Beth, Briana, everyone but herself, after what had just happened between them. He should have said other things, but what? She'd said she wanted him to be honest, and that took away the easy words.

"Nothing is wrong with you," Reik said. She turned back to him. "Damn it, Elias, if Beth is where she can hear you she must be pretty mad at you. How could you even think of comparing what the two of you had with what happened in Briana's quarters today? *Of course you didn't feel guilty.*"

Kane knew she was right, but it gave him no relief. He'd had sex with Briana and felt nothing, and that was all right. But he'd kissed Martha Reik and his guilt was a wall protecting a dead woman from a live one. "Neither of us can forget all that's happened," he said.

"Do you really think I would want you to forget—that I would want you to cut out part of your life and throw it away for me?"

"I don't know," he said simply.

"Then find out." Reik's voice was sharp. "She's part of you, Elias. You've still got the only part of her you ever really possessed. If you do what's best for yourself you can't betray her, because she *is* you." Reik stopped, letting out the air of other, unspoken words. She looked down at the floor, hugging her elbows to her body, and Kane felt her pain, a hurt her vials could not numb for either of them. "I've broken my own rule," she said, "and it was a stupid thing to do. I've told you how I think things are, and what you should do, and you wouldn't be

human if it didn't compel a part of you to resist. There's
nothing more I can say, Elias. I'm sorry."

He reached for her hand, ignored the resistance; pulled
the stiff arm away from her body and willed a response
into her fingers. "No," he said. "I reject that. People can
help each other if they work at it." He could see the
unasked question in her face. *Can you let down the walls,
Elias?* He wanted to say that he could, but there was an
image of Beth in his mind, painfully vague, and he had to
keep it from eroding more. "There has to be time," he
said, "and I know there might not be. I'm not capable of
forgetting that."

"I know," she said softly. "But, still . . ."

He nodded. "But still."

She released his hand. "I promised Gregory Amerdath
that he could see you as soon as I'd patched you up.
There's a praetorian outside waiting to take you to him."
She turned back to the cabinets and Kane walked out
quickly.

Amerdath was in the garden, the same roof garden with
the ramparts and the watching praetorians, and Kane had
to force each step. Amerdath was supported by the same
cart that had sustained him before the elaborate charade of
the banquet. It was sitting on the spot where he'd been
struck down. Kane stood waiting in front of Amerdath,
unable to look at the ground. *Were there still stains of her
blood in the soil, broken ground where she'd fallen?*

"Thank you for coming so quickly," Amerdath said.
Chuddath stood behind the cart. The grotesque insect head
scanned the walls and the bushes around Amerdath with
slow but continuous sweeps. The Ornyl warrior did not
want to be here either, Kane saw, but some perverse need
of Amerdath demanded it of both of them.

"How is the rib?" Amerdath asked.

"Painless, sir."

"Good. Giacomin is not back yet. I'd like your briefing now."

Kane began with Pendrake's note and ended with the way Giacomin had used them as decoys.

"Richard DuMorgan," Amerdath said. "I just can't accept it."

Kane didn't answer. He wanted to ask, *What are you going to do about Giacomin?* But he knew that Amerdath's informal style with him had its limits.

"Did Richard actually admit to planning my murder?"

"No, sir. In fact, he acted surprised when I asked him about it."

"What is your evaluation of that?"

"I haven't had much time to think about it."

"Shoot from the hip."

"It's possible DuMorgan is not behind the assassination attempts. He had us, and there was no way he could have anticipated what Pendrake did. There was no reason for him to act surprised when I asked him why he was trying to kill you, and yet he did seem surprised—genuinely taken aback."

"But it doesn't make sense, does it? If he's not behind the attempts, what *is* he up to? Why did he go underground, snatch you? What was he afraid this waiter, this man Marin, could tell you?"

"I don't know, sir. There is one thing we should remember. DuMorgan went to the colonist hideaway so that he could be there to question me. If I hadn't escaped, if Giacomin hadn't found Pendrake's note and followed up on his two tags that DuMorgan's men took off my tail, DuMorgan could have left the hideout and returned to court. Whatever his game is, this forces his hand. He's a hunted man now. He's got to make his play or fold."

"I suppose we can thank Fowler for that much," Amerdath mused, "even though his methods were devious."

"He used us as live bait," Kane said, unable to hold his anger back any longer. "Even if the fish is hooked, it gets to keep the worm, and Pendrake and I were the worms. He never gave us a hint of the danger we were in.''

Amerdath looked uncomfortable. "I understand your feelings, Elias. If I'd known what Fowler was up to, I'd have stopped him. As soon as he gets back, I'm going to light a fire under him, and he's going to sweat plenty. If he endangers you again, he's finished, but the reality is that I'm going to keep him for now. I think you deserve to know why."

"You don't need to explain yourself to me, sir," Kane said stiffly.

"Yes, I do." Amerdath's voice was almost fierce. "I *need* you, Elias. I need you fully willing and for that I need you fully aware and understanding. Fowler should not have endangered you, but I can tell you what he'll say. He'll say that it was the only way to force the head of the conspiracy out in the open. He'll say that only you could have baited the trap, because you are the one to whom this man Marin would go. He'll say that he tried to protect you by being there at the snatch, and there will be nothing to contradict him. DuMorgan himself confirmed that Giacomin's men were following you."

"If he'd let me in on it, I would have taken the risk."

"I know you would, Elias, and I thank you for it, but Fowler trusts no one, confides in no one—not even me, unless I force him, and then he holds back all he can. As much as it vexes me, his discretion is the source of Giacomin's unique value to me. And he *was* right about DuMorgan, as he has been right so many times in the past. He's a cobra, Elias, and I am his keeper. He's never bitten me and he never will. When I die, the others around me will seek him out and crush him. Perhaps that's why he's so loyal, or maybe that's too harsh a judgment. Who can see into a mind like that? I'm asking you to accept this."

"Then I accept it," Kane said.

Amerdath stared at him, clearly surprised by the quickness of his answer. Kane saw that the Imperator's eyes

were rimming with tears. Embarrassed, he gazed around
the garden while Amerdath composed himself. After a
minute the Imperator made a gruff sound, and Kane knew
it was all right to look at him. "I plan to walk in this
garden again," Amerdath said. "I'm going to feel the
ground under my feet, to get thorns stuck in my thumbs,
and to curse the damned things and then laugh."

"Clemis' body," Kane said.

"Tomorrow, Elias. If it can be done, Martha can do
it."

Kane could only nod, knowing that Amerdath must be
able to read the revulsion in his face.

"He took my body, Elias. And for the murder of Beth he
deserves to die. God willing, his death will not go for
nothing. Damn it, he *owes* me." Amerdath's voice rose to
a shout on the last words.

"Yes, sir. He owes us both." *A life for me, a body for
you, and he can't make either of us like we were.*

"I want you to walk in this garden too, Elias," Amerdath
said, his voice gentle now. "I want you to walk in it with
me, and with a woman that you love. We may have to take
what the universe dishes out, but the real test of us is
whether we've got the guts to thumb our nose at it."

The Ornyl warrior's head stopped its ceaseless rotation
and the garden seemed to still itself around Kane, as
though waiting for an answer.

CHAPTER 24

Kane stared up into the dark. He arched his neck, pushing his head with punishing force back against the pillow. The tears swam up, turning the darkness liquid, making him afraid to blink. If he let the tears spill, felt them sliding down his cheeks, he knew that he would be unable to stop. His throat would burn, and the sobs would shake him, and he would wail like a broken-hearted child. He must not be so self-indulgent. But the pain. Would it never leave him? Did Beth have to fade before he could be healed? No, he must not let her fade, even to end the pain.

Today, as Reik patched up his ribs, she had said it: *"Do you really think I would want you to forget—that I would want you to cut out part of your life and throw it away for me?"* He'd said he didn't know and she had said find out. *Find out.* She had meant that he should test her, but it was he, himself, whom he must test.

He pushed himself almost violently from the bed. A thin, arctic glow from Pendrake's room caught his eye. Good. The alien was not asleep yet. There could be conversation, distraction. He stalked to the doorway. The spill of light came from Pendrake's holowall. The alien was sitting cross-legged, giant head and shoulders silhouetted against the dark luster of the wall's image. The alien had dialed a scene of deep space—a sea of stars, frozen like luminescent pearls in black ice. In the center of the wall, a large blue-green planet revolved with stately magnificence. Kane studied the pattern of stars and realized that the planet was Cephan. Though he had made enough noise getting out of bed to alert Pendrake, the alien did not move nor give any sign that he knew he was not alone. He sat with absolute stillness, gazing at the image of his home planet. There was a terrible sadness in the rapt lines of the massive shoulders, the intensity of the Cephantine's gaze.

Kane backed away quietly, feeling ashamed. He had turned so often to the alien for support, for strength, and in these last days, for comfort. What had he cared for Pendrake's pain? The giant creature was always the alien here, alone in a world of pale, murderous pygmies. Pendrake had loved Beth too, and who had comforted him? He could look only at a ghost image on a crystal wall, and grope for his own kind, shrunken and lost behind the glass.

Kane knew he should say something instead of slinking away, but he could find nothing inside himself to give. At another moment, he could find the words, but not now. He turned his back on the door to Pendrake's room. He went to his closet and dressed silently. For a while he wandered the empty, curving corridors of the palace. When the occasional guard or night worker did approach, he passed them with his eyes averted, his head down. The idea came to him slowly as he walked, emerging from the dark recess of the past, triggered, perhaps, by the sight of Pendrake staring at the holowall. He felt excitement and then horror. No, it was ghastly. He must forget he had ever . . . *You can see Beth. You can see her. You can talk to her, and she will answer you.* The words chanted over and over in his mind, smothering the horror, driving out all other thought. Yes, he could see Beth, see her move, fill his eyes with her once again, talk to her and have her answer him. Yes, he could do it, and damn the cost.

Kane ran through the corridors until he found an elevator. He pushed the button marked "Hopter Deck."

The beacon light for New York City flashed onto the screen and Kane programmed a descent for Manhattan. He sat back into the webfoam seat of the hopter and waited for the specific grid map of the city to appear on the screen. The craft jittered under him slightly as it washboarded down through layers of air turbulence. He barely felt the tremors. His mind floated with an eerie blankness, the memory of the flight across the dark expanse of the continent already fading, as though it could find no place in his mind to settle in. The city grid appeared, green on black, and he punched in his landing beam request. Instead of on-screen confirmation, there was a pause and then a voice came through on override.

"Hopter Alpha 235, identify please."

"Elias Kane," Kane said.

The disembodied voice of the controller came back, sounding bored. "We can't give you a beam to the museum this time of night, Mr. Kane. It's closed. You'll have to come in at Kennedy or some private pad, subject to owner confirmation."

"I said this is Elias Kane. I have full discretionary powers. Check compusayer central for my carte blanche, Imperial authorization, code 4377 Sigma."

There was another short pause. The screen flashed a message: PREPARE FOR RETINAL SCAN. Kane looked at the cross-hairs on the screen and waited for the ground-activated flash of blue light. The voice came again, this time respectfully. "I'm sorry, sir. I didn't recognize your name. It's been a slow night, and we get kind of dull down here. . . ."

"Let's get to it, shall we?"

"Yes sir. Beam locked in. Controller out."

Kane felt a pulse in his stomach that swelled as the hopter settled over the 4 A.M. half-lights of Manhattan. He peered down through the undercurve of the craft's dome. Towers thrust up at him like the square spines of a giant armored beast lying in the river. He could not make out the individual pad of the museum until he was nearly on it. The dark square of the rooftop swung under him, rose, and met him with a gentle thump. Footlights came on around the perimeter of the roof. A museum guard was waiting for him as he climbed down. The man was young, and looked in good shape. In the glare of the footlights, his muscles stood out under the tight fabric of the green uniform. Kane felt surprise and then understanding. Of course. They wouldn't have the usual pot-bellied retired cop here—not at this museum.

"Mr. Kane?"

"That's right."

"Controller central called and said I was to give you every cooperation, sir."

"Good. Give me the keycard to the dropshaft over there, and to the musal exhibit, and then forget you saw me."

The guard's eyes widened. "The musal exhibit? Sir, no one's been in there except the keeper since the exhibit was set up after the plague. The keeper has to wear special shielding, a helmet with faceguard . . ."

"Just *do* it, or I'll see you busted down to toilet duty." Kane heard the harshness of his voice, a remote piece of data, with no feeling attached.

The guard dug in the case at his side and handed over two plastic cards. "I guess you know your way around a musal, Mr. Kane, if anyone does," he said in a chastened voice. "That one's to the elevator, and that one is to the . . . the exhibit. It's in the bottom subbasement—level 03."

"I know," Kane said. He walked to the elevator, his stride jerking with the restrained urge to run. As soon as the door closed between him and the guard, he backed up against the rear wall of the shaft. The cage plummeted, and his hand went to his stomach, pressing against the squirming organ, holding it steady against the backbone. *To see Beth. To talk to her. To hear her answer.*

The cage slowed abruptly and then stopped at level 03. The doors slid open on a short hallway and he stepped out. He stood for a moment, looking at the polished chromium door at the end of the hall. Above the door was a sign: WARNING, RESTRICTED ZONE. ALL VISITORS MUST HAVE GUIDE AND EQUIPMENT TO PROCEED BEYOND THIS POINT. Kane felt a stirring beneath the surface of his excitement, a sluggish bottom tide of fear. He was mad to come here. If he went on now, it could destroy him. But he had to see her once again, now. The thing in there had known her, more intimately than it had known any other human being. Perhaps it still held some of her living essence, preserved in a way that no man could understand. Perhaps, if it would help him, what he would see would not merely be an image. Yes, he would go in now.

He slid the card into the door's slot, and it swung inward on a dark room. The smell of cinnamon and a trace of ether spiked like twin needles through his nostrils to the brain, triggering the old memories. Drafts eddied past his wrists and the back of his neck, hinting at a vast curved space looming in the dark around him.

"Elias Kane."

The words sounded inside his head, grinding at the bottom threshold of perception and then rising, and he realized that the musal had been asleep.

"Yes."

"What a pleasure." A small penguinlike creature popped into existence in front of Kane. It gave off its own faint light in the dark room, like a single rounded image on a black movie screen. "How long has it been?" the creature asked. "Thwee years? Fifty years? Time passes so stwangely here."

"Hysrac," Kane said. "No. I don't want to see you. You don't exist. You never did."

"Mr. Kane. I am an authentic wepwesentation. If I do not exist, who did you defeat when you vanquished the psychopath plague?"

"Please . . ."

The penguin creature popped out of existence. "Why have you come here, Kane?" said the deeper voice.

"Where are you? I can't see."

"I'm in the center of the room. They don't often provide light for me in here. Would you like me to stimulate your internal receptors?"

"Yes, but I want to see you as you really are."

"Oh, dear. I suppose by that you mean you want to see something that would not contradict your fingers were you to touch me." The voice sounded amused.

"You know very well what I mean."

The tree appeared, the squat shape he remembered. Its smooth trunk thickened just below the first branches, forming a ball out of which slender stalks grew. The stalks were covered with maroon blossoms. Among the blossoms he could see the globes of yellow fruit, so sweet and spicy, so poisonous. The tree also touched his retinas with a faint image of the room, a towering rounded cavern. The bridge of his nose itched faintly. When he reached to scratch it, the tree said, "Sorry," and the itch disappeared. "Is that better?"

"Yes, thank you."

"Now I ask again, Elias Kane: Why have you come here?"

"Do you hate me?" Kane said. "Do you want revenge on me?"

"That is not an answer to my question."

"I need to know."

"Would my answer affect your decision to be here?"

Kane thought. His stomach throbbed with a steady drumbeat of nerve. He felt the floor, vaporous beneath the soles of his boots, as if he were falling, plunging far past the point of return. "No," he said.

"I cannot read minds," the musal said. "What is it you want?"

"Beth Tyson is . . . she was killed."

The tree said nothing for a moment. "I'm sorry to hear that. Though she did not understand us and our true needs, she was a friend to the musal. And after, when she did understand, it was still she who asked that I be spared when all of my kind on your planet were cut down and burned. She acted out of the old friendship. She meant it as mercy."

The musal's words chilled Kane, more than open hatred could have done. Yes, Beth had meant it as a mercy, but what had it truly been? To be locked in this dark room, unable to know day from night, visited only by a keeper who watered the soil and carefully removed and destroyed each fallen musal seedling? No matter. He had come for one thing. He must do it now.

"I want to see her," he said. The musal's image flickered in his brain, as though some unseen force were shaking its roots, perturbing the flow of energy from it. Shock? Or laughter? He knew he had to get out of here, now, run with all the speed in his legs.

And then she appeared.

She was wearing the black dress. It was ripped at the shoulders, exposing one small pale breast, and Kane remembered how it had happened. He had attacked her that night in the garden of her estate—the garden with the musal tree in it. He had hurt her, frightened her. It had been the plague, raging in him, but that did not matter now. "No!" he shouted. "You bastard . . ."

"Elias? Elias, is that you?"

It was her voice. "Yes," he whispered. "Over here."

She groped blindly, hands raised in front of her face. "I can't see you."

"Damn you," Kane shouted at the musal. "Show her, *show* her."

"Keep talking," Beth said. "I'll walk toward your voice."

"Over here," Kane said. "Wait, I'll come to you." He stepped forward, and his shin connected with something hard. He fell heavily onto his face, scraping the palms of his hands as he tried to break his fall. He sat up and looked behind him. A low railing? There was no railing visible, but it must be there, in the dark. There was no real light in the room, only the images the musal gave him, and he must remember that.

"I don't hear you, Elias," Beth said.

"I'm here. I can't come to you, you'll have to come to me."

"All right."

A lump rose in his throat as he watched her weaving across the dim gray expanse of floor toward him, arms still outstretched, the fingers, so slim and beautiful, so full of skill, splayed as if to strain away the darkness. "I love you," he said. "I've missed you so much."

"The echoes," she said. "So confusing. Am I doing right?"

"No, over this way more, to your left, that's it—no, too much." He kept talking, watching her move back and forth across his field of vision, never seeming to get closer. He tried again to move toward her, encountered another railing. It was hopeless, he saw. He reached down and gripped the cold surface of the invisible but real railing, trying to twist it, bend it in his hands. "Do you love me," he cried in desperation.

She stopped moving and this time she looked straight at him. Her hands fell to her sides. "I always loved you, dear Elias."

"Would you have married me?"

She stared across at him, her head cocked, birdlike, her body still now.

"I was going to ask you. That night, in the restaurant, before the praetorians came."

"Were you?" she said softly. "Were you really?" Her image thinned, went dark, shone again, almost transparent.

"Let it be," the image said.

He stared at the thing the musal had summoned for him, across the room, standing there under the maroon leaves, the lethal yellow fruit, and knew that Beth was gone, unreachable.

Kane turned and walked toward the door behind him. The tears poured from his eyes, dripped off his chin, but he did not sob. His throat muscles relaxed, and he let the tears flow, making no effort to wipe them away. The rail he had fallen over was visible now, and he saw the way through, a gap to the right. Without looking back, he closed the chromium door behind him.

CHAPTER 25

The big wafer-thin blade of the surgical saw dominated the room. It was just another tool in the array of equipment, a gleaming disc suspended above the operating table on belted arms, but its purpose gave it focus. It had been designed to heal, to cleanly slice away the crushed or gangrenous arm or leg that would poison the rest of the body. Today, in less than an hour, it would kill, and Kane found himself against his will looking at it again and again. He did not have to be here, and instinct rebelled against it. But he was here. The fate of Clemis was bound up with his own life and Amerdath's. The Imperator was seeking payment from the man, and despite all Kane's certainty that payment could not be had, he was compelled to see. But there was more, too. He sat here now, knowing that he had also come to say good-bye to Amerdath. To see for the last time the man he had believed in.

The air conditioning turned the sweat clammy on Kane's face. His feet shifted on the carpet of the balcony, longing to take his weight, to carry him from the room. Martha Reik stood by the table, gowned and scrubbed, her eyes wide in the white strip of flesh between cap and mask. The others of the team were in the recovery room, where they would stay until Clemis was decapitated. Amerdath waited at the head of the operating table, ready to be separated from the life-support cart and transferred at the proper moment. An extra tube ran into the cart from a suspended bottle of anesthetic. At the turn of a stopcock, the Imperator would be asleep. When he awoke, he would ride a body once more, and the head of the man he had killed would be trash in a black polyethylene bag.

The door opened behind Kane and Alvar Sabin walked past, descending as he had the previous time to the front row. The presence of Sabin meant that Mark Clemis had also arrived, and was waiting below with a guard of praetorians that Sabin had led. Amerdath's eyes confirmed that the door to the O.R. had opened. Clemis appeared below, pinned in a mobile forcechair wheeled by two of the guard. Reik looked only at the Imperator, her eyes mirroring the minute contractions, the tightening of Amerdath's face. There was a moment of rigid silence. Then Amerdath spoke.

"Do you know why you are here?"

Clemis said nothing. Amerdath repeated the question, and the assassin wailed with a suddenness that stood the hairs of Kane's neck on end. Sabin started uneasily at the sound, then steeled himself again. Reik looked at the doomed man for the first time. In the glare of the operating lights, her tears made gleaming paths before spreading darkly into her mask.

"Mercy, mercy, oh, God, help me, puh-puh-ple-e-e-ase." Clemis convulsed in sobs, all control gone. His body jerked the chair slightly on its wheels until one of the guard eased it back so that it again faced Amerdath. The smell of urine filtered into the balcony's close confines.

The Imperator's mouth opened and closed. His head turned in jerks to Reik. "Get on with it." The breath continued to rasp through his teeth, as memorized biofeed-

back sequences in his forehead muscles frayed under stress.
"Go on, Martha, give him the injection."

Reik stood very still, captured by the horrible spectacle
of Clemis. Her hands balled into fists at her sides and her
shoulders curved in as though she'd taken a blow to the
stomach. The assassin continued to sob.

"Christ," Kane groaned. He wanted desperately to look
away, but he could not. He had come to this room concerned only for Amerdath, but here were the sights and
sounds of a man's final disintegration. Mercy, the assassin
screamed, and Kane did not want to feel mercy, he fought
it with all of his strength, and yet he felt compassion.

"Do it!" Amerdath shouted.

Reik turned on him. "No."

Sabin stood and headed toward the balcony exit, freezing when Kane's hand closed on his arm. "Let go of me!"
The commander's voice was stricken, barely a whisper.

"Sit down," Kane said.

Sabin stared at him, then looked back over his shoulder
at the scene below.

"Martha, I command you to give the injection and to
carry out the operation," Amerdath said.

"And I refuse. I'm a physician, not a murderer."

"You would do this to me now?"

"You can't go through with it."

"I can and I will. It's justice."

"The justice of animals."

Amerdath's eyes squinted, his face squirmed as if she
had slapped him. "You . . . you can't speak to me this
way. You won't be a murderer. This man is under a
sentence of death. He will feel nothing. If you won't do it,
I'll have one of the other doctors, and you'll be ruined,
finished."

Reik moved closer to Amerdath. Her voice strained at
the edge of a sob. "I know that if you will only *feel*, now,
if you will stop fighting a part of you that I know is there,
you will know that you cannot kill this man for his body."

"I'm not killing him for his body. I'm killing him for his crimes."

"Can you ever be sure of that?"

The assassin had stopped crying, was watching the argument with pathetic hope. Kane could see his hands shaking on the arms of the forcechair, a bone-deep trembling that even the tight field could not suppress. The two praetorians were looking up to the balcony now, waiting for a sign from Sabin. Kane realized that he still held the commander's arm in a token grip, but he was afraid to move, afraid that by dislodging his fingers he might release Sabin from his own inner paralysis.

"There might be another way," Reik said. "I thought of it this morning. A way you can walk, feel, do it *all* again. It will be your own body . . ."

"What are you talking about? My own body is ash because of this . . . this . . ." Amerdath paused, got control of his voice again. "If I am to have a body, it must be the body of this . . ." Once more he could not go on.

"This animal," Reik finished for him. "And then what will *you* be?"

"The body is ruled by the mind . . ."

"And if you take this vengeance, your mind will be a fit ruler for this body. And all of us whom you rule will have a new Imperator, who can never be a shadow of the one who deserves our loyalty now."

Kane watched Amerdath's face, knowing the danger of this moment to them all. At a word, the Imperator could summon Chuddath to the room and Reik would be struck down where she stood. The Ornyl would kill anyone who interfered. In time an empire might fall as well.

"You said there is another way," Amerdath said.

Reik drew a breath. "It might fail. It is dangerous. You might reject it."

Kane saw what she was doing, approved even though she was now taking force away from her own argument.

She wanted Amerdath to do it for the right reason, so that he would not question himself later.

The Imperator closed his eyes. Seconds crawled by in the frozen silence. "Get him out of here," he said.

Chuddath, Kane and Reik accompanied the Imperator back to his private quarters. At Amerdath's request, Kane dialed a vista of the eastern portion of Chronos onto the holowall. The windowless den drank the sun, an infusion of saffron limning bookcases and firing the brass supports of sling chairs. The hay-sweet odor of pipe tobacco clung to the oak walls. Kane wondered at the freshness of the smell, then remembered Reik telling him that Amerdath had taken up pipe-smoking. She had objected only mildly because there were no lungs to be damaged, and Amerdath was incessantly hungry for new forms of stimulation.

Chuddath positioned his lord beside the holowall where he could look down on the city or toward Kane and Reik with equal ease. Taking his cue from the physician, Kane remained standing. Amerdath gazed out at the illusion of Chronos. He turned back to them.

"There are two things I must say to you, Martha. The first is that if you ever defy me again in front of others for any reason, no matter how just, I'll banish you."

Reik bowed her head. "I understand."

"The second thing I have to say is, thank you. Sit down, both of you."

Reik dropped gratefully into one of the sling chairs. Kane, still full of the tension of unspent adrenaline, pulled up a leather ottoman and sat on the edge of it.

"Now, what is this other possibility?" Amerdath asked. "What is this way I can walk around in my own body again?"

Reik rubbed absently at the red line across her forehead where the surgical cap had been tied. Her hair was damp and tangled from being bound up in the cap, and her posture in the chair was a weary slump. She had never looked more beautiful to Kane. He watched her from the side, secure in gazing openly at her, because her mind was now far away, the gray eyes staring at a point above Amerdath's head. "There's a technique called electro-cortical stimulation," she said. "It was discovered more than a century ago, and has been slowly refined ever since."

Amerdath frowned. "I've heard of it. Microvoltages are applied directly to the brain during surgery, and the patient remembers things from his past."

"The patient *relives* things from his past," Reik corrected, "in absolute detail, the scene depending on where the voltage is applied. Early on there was some debate about whether the experience was more like simple memory or a full reliving, but the debate was resolved when the techniques for stimulation were refined and brought under much more precise control. The technique as it exists today produces a reliving experience that is totally vivid and convincing. Bear in mind, however, that electro-cortical stimulation of the brain has never been used clinically for this purpose."

"Why not?" Amerdath asked.

"Let me get to that in a minute. What it *is* used for is the control of seizure disorders. Here the stimulation is applied to other areas of the brain rather than those where memories are stored. First the brain is 'mapped' for the points that seemed to be involved in seizure activity. Then microscopic charged slivers are implanted at strategic 'stop-points,' usually close to the seizure locus. With a little practice, the epileptic can activate these embedded slivers to shut down an impending seizure whenever he feels one coming on."

"Wait," Amerdath said. "Are you talking about open-ing my skull, laying my brain bare?"

"Good Lord, no. I'm sorry, I should have made that clear. I'm talking about shooting the slivers directly through your skull."

"That's not funny, Martha."

"I'm serious. That's how it's done. Remember, these slivers are very small, too small to be seen. They're injected right through the pores of the scalp and the ostioles of the skull. It doesn't even mess up the part in your hair. It's done with absolute precision."

"You mentioned that the brain is mapped first," Amerdath said. "How is that done?"

"Queson particles are beamed continuously from three guns . . ."

"What's a queson particle?"

"A particle that has the penetration characteristics of a neutrino and a very slight charge. Separately, the charges carried on the beams are so weak that they pass through brain tissue without stimulating it. But at the point of intersection a microvoltage is generated similar to that which will ultimately exist on the implanted slivers. While this apparatus has been used mainly for mapping seizure sites, it can also be used on memory areas to recreate experience. Since even a single memory is often stored in several scattered locations, all sites producing a part of a given memory mosaic are mapped. The permanent slivers would then be implanted at the sites of those memories and memory mosaics that you want to experience again on demand."

Amerdath nodded. "How does a person learn to activate a given sliver?"

"Frankly, we don't know for sure. My guess is it's the same process that we use to direct our thoughts. No one has yet explained how we do that—how we can decide to think about or remember one thing instead of another. But we do it all the time. It's an empirical fact. Epileptics are able to learn very quickly how to control the slivers."

There was a long interval of silence. Kane glanced at Chuddath, found the compound eyes of the Ornyl warrior directed at Reik, or perhaps at them both. What did

Chuddath think of the proposal, he wondered? Did he grasp all of its implications?

"Elias, you've been very quiet," Amerdath said. "What's your reaction to all this?"

"I've read some of the literature on electro-cortical stimulation," Kane answered, "though I wasn't up on the latest implantation techniques." He hesitated, feeling Reik watching him. She had given the description, the neutral scientific facts, but she was leaving it to him to put a value on those facts, to say what might persuade Amerdath one way or the other. She had already pushed Amerdath into one decision he might come to regret bitterly.

"There's an expression," Kane said. " 'If I had it to do over again . . .' "

"I'd do the same thing," Amerdath finished.

"Sometimes the saying ends that way. There are moments, days I'd like to relive again . . ." Kane stopped, whatever words were next caught and held in his constricting throat. The night before that final day in the garden, he and Beth had made love, merging so well that he had almost understood what it was to *be* her, mind and body. He had marvelled at the essence of her. Everything had seemed preternaturally vivid—the body smells, the feel of satin sheets, even the pulse of blood, the tides of air in his lungs. He looked away from Amerdath. *To go beyond remembering that moment to actually reliving it . . .* "I may end up fighting you for the machine," he said.

Amerdath laughed, but Reik regarded Kane somberly.

"I could go back," Amerdath said wistfully. "I'd have the ability to do anything I had ever done. I'd have arms and legs again—my *own* body. You know, Elias, what I miss more than anything? Exercise. I used to do calisthenics—pushups, situps, weights, the whole works. I hated it, but it kept me in shape. This way I could have an exercise period every day, any time I get to feeling closed in, like my body's really there but trapped in a block of cement." Amerdath stopped and his expression became dreamy. He blinked and looked at Martha Reik. There was terrible pain, then, and longing in his face, and Kane realized that Amerdath must be thinking of her, of the moments of intimacy that he could have again—or perhaps the future moments that could never come. "Actually, I don't miss calisthenics the most," Amerdath said, and there was nothing flippant in his tone.

"I'm glad," Reik said.

Kane felt an obscure pang. Not jealousy—he had suspected already that Reik and Amerdath might have been lovers, that there had been a time or times when she had not said no. That was in the past. But it could be again, over and over, as many times as Amerdath wanted it. Not just memories of her, but the flesh itself, existing again in the same place it had existed for him the first time—in his mind. And then Kane considered the rest of it, the awful danger of what Reik was suggesting. The Imperator's expression showed that he had thought of it too.

"Martha," he said, "in the operating room you told me your idea could be dangerous—that I might reject it. Why?"

She sat forward in the sling chair seeming to gather herself. "As I said, the use of this technique for memory stimulation has been strictly experimental. Only a handful of human subjects has been tested, and I said earlier I'd get to the reason. The reason is this: In every case of electro-cortical stimulation of memory areas that were labeled pleasurable by human subjects, those subjects reported post-test let-down; depressed feelings. Most of them asked to be regressed again immediately. The animal studies have been much more extensive, but they are flawed by the animal's obvious inability to report the type and nature of sensations caused by stimulation. The principal animal subject has been the chimpanzee. Experimenters have aimed for areas of the brain analogous to memory storage zones in humans, but they can't be sure where they're hitting. So instrumental conditioning has been used to help determine which areas of implanted slivers were pleasurable for the animals. Putting it simply, the chimps were trained during the mapping phase to press a lever whenever they wanted repeat stimulation. Slivers were then implanted at the preferred sites . . ."

"All right, Martha," Amerdath said. "Forget the details. What happened?"

"In every case where self-stimulation control was given in the form of permanent embedded slivers, the animal went completely catatonic and stayed that way." She looked searchingly at Amerdath's face, and Kane knew she wanted to be sure the Imperator understood. "They went into their own brains," she said, "and never came back."

Amerdath turned away from them and stared out the window, his eyes focused beyond Chronos on the range of mountains on the far horizon. "All right," he said. "I understand the danger. Set it up. I want to begin as soon as possible."

CHAPTER 26

The praetorian guard nodded Kane and Pendrake through into the neurology lab, and Kane thought as he had before, how thoroughly the alien was becoming a part of his identity for other people. Had he been alone, the guard would have checked him much more closely. There were a few other tall lean men in the palace, but only one who walked around with a Cephantine.

The room was small, its details available at a glance. Gregory Amerdath's life-support cart was sitting against the wall, ready to be moved into position beneath the three converging guns of the memory scanning equipment. A cart loaded with fruits and pastries sat untouched next to Amerdath. The Imperator was gazing at the guns, which hung from the ceiling on a telescoping central shaft. Each gun depended from a single superstructure and could move only as a part of the fixed unit. Approximately a half meter separated each muzzle from the other two, so that the entire assemblage could be moved around the head without any gun ever touching it. Clamps for immobilizing the head extended from the wall. The queson particle generator was behind the wall, out of sight.

Martha Reik was reading some data off a display screen. She glanced up, smiled at a point between Kane and Pendrake and turned back to the display. Kane had not seen her since the day before, when she'd suggested Amerdath might find refuge in his memories. He felt a pang of disappointment at her perfunctory greeting. Beyond Reik, Chuddath stood beside the Imperator.

"Elias, Pendrake," Amerdath said.

Kane nodded. He watched Reik making her careful preparations. She frowned in concentration and nibbled at the curl of her lower lip, apparently unconscious of his interest. He had seen such intensity in only one other person. A memory came to him of Beth Tyson walking a stage, head down, hands jammed into the pockets she'd insisted on having on her everyday skirts. The memory served up a snatch of music, and Kane pinned it down more precisely. She'd taken him to an audition and then forgotten him as she paced around, listening. She'd walked into a stage curtain, got tangled up and extricated herself, without ever noticing. He had laughed then, and she hadn't heard it, and he smiled now.

"Got you!" Amerdath exclaimed. "This time I *know* you weren't listening."

Kane hesitated, replaying the words the Imperator had been saying, and extracting their meaning. "I'm sorry," he said. "You're right. I wasn't listening."

Amerdath grinned. "Ah, at last. The man is human. Don't worry about it, Elias. I'd rather watch Martha Reik, too, than listen to a lot of nervous jabber."

Kane let Amerdath repeat what he'd said about memory mapping not being such a good idea. "Do you want to put this off?" he asked the Imperator. "Think about it some more?"

Reik stopped her work on the generator and waited for Amerdath to answer.

"No, no. We're here. We'll at least give it a try."
Amerdath's head turned until he was looking at the three
guns. Kane saw that the Imperator's face was damp with
sweat, something which he had not seen since Amerdath's
head had been separated from his body. The room was
cool, and there was only one reason for the sweat. Amerdath
was afraid.

"Is there some reason you are feeling nervous, sir?"
Pendrake asked.

"I don't know. I've been over the thing many times
since Martha suggested it. I know it's safe—physically
safe." Amerdath hesitated. "I suppose I'm on edge about
how it will feel—the rays going into my head. Silly, isn't
it?"

"No, sir, it's not," Reik said. "I should have briefed
you more thoroughly. You'll feel no direct physical stimulation at all from the particle beams—they're too weak for
that. At the intersection point a memory will be activated
in exact detail. You'll think you're there. Then we'll turn
off the beam and you can tell us if it's one you like. If so,
we'll chart it for possible sliver implantation . . ."

"Yes, yes, I understand that part of it. Maybe it's not
the mechanics at all. Maybe I'm just having second thoughts
about the idea itself. The idea of going back to what was.
It . . . it attracts and repels me, both. To feel that I have a
body again would be—will be wonderful. To go back, to
substitute going back for going forward . . . I don't know."

"I understand," Reik said. "Are you sure you want to
go ahead?"

"Definitely."

"The machine is ready now."

"Then let's get on with it." Amerdath's throat corded
up as he tried to swallow. Kane looked at the generator
guns, trying to see them as Amerdath was seeing them.
Something stirred in his stomach, began to crawl, sluglike,
up the walls, a vague but persistent sense of wrongness.

Kane glanced at Pendrake. The Cephantine was frowning slightly.

Reik motioned to the Ornyl bodyguard. Chuddath moved the Imperator into position and Reik secured the clamps around Amerdath's forehead. She reached into the life-support equipment. "I'm disconnecting the biofeedback connections that enable you to turn your head, sir," she said. "That way, there will be no way you can inadvertently try to move against the clamps, and we can leave them a bit looser."

"Fine."

Reik carefully lowered the assemblage of guns over Amerdath's head until one was pointing in from behind and two from above the temples. She flipped a toggle and Kane saw the mechanism lock into place. Further movements could be made only by use of fine controls, which had been geared down so drastically that a quarter turn would shift the focal point of the three guns a distance equal to the width of a single brain cell. Reik gave the assembly a final critical inspection. "Okay, everything's set. Are you ready, sir?"

Amerdath closed his eyes. Kane felt his heart accelerating. His palms had gone damp. There was an itch between his shoulder blades, as though the spinal cord, eager to move him, was squirming within its canal of bone.

"All right," Amerdath whispered.

Reik reached for the switch that would activate the beams, sending the weak stream of queson particles through the Imperator's head.

"Wait," Kane said.

She pulled her hand back and frowned at him. "Is something wrong, Elias?"

"I don't know. The equipment . . . you've checked it over carefully, of course."

"Very carefully. Last night."

"But someone could have gotten in since then."

"Elias, this whole section has been cordoned off by

praetorians and Chuddath. No one unauthorized has gotten within a hundred meters of it." Reik's voice was resentful. Kane felt sorry for her, angry at himself, but he could not shake the feeling that something was wrong. He glanced at Amerdath. The Imperator was staring at him, his eyes intense and almost feverish.

"I'm sure everything's fine, Elias. I shouldn't have spooked everyone. Let's get on with it."

"Sir, I'd like to make just one check," Kane said. When Amerdath did not reply, Kane turned to Reik. "Unfasten the clamps."

"Really, Elias . . ."

"Please, Martha. Humor me."

Brusquely she released the equipment from fine controls, raised it away from Amerdath's head and released the clamps.

"Chuddath, would you wheel the Imperator to the side again for a moment, please," Kane said. The Ornyl complied. Kane walked over to the cart of food, selected an uncut cantaloupe and brought it back, inserting it into the headclamps. When they were tightened enough to support the melon, he lowered the generator guns until they bore on the center of it. "We don't need to worry about the fine controls," he said. "Let's just see what this thing remembers from its seedy past."

No one smiled. Reik looked exasperated. "Elias, you aren't going to be able to tell a damned thing from that. The beams are much too weak. Really, there's nothing that can go wrong. Queson particles at the level this machine can generate are harmless."

Kane nodded. He flipped the switch activating the guns. For a second nothing seemed to happen. Then the canta- loupe swelled and exploded, spattering them all with its hot blackened core.

CHAPTER 27

The warrior struck instantly. As the melon exploded, he was standing beside Amerdath, several meters from Martha Reik. In the next second he was on her, two steps, a blur of green, fighting arms extended, fingers closing around her neck. She had no time to make a sound. Kane threw himself against Chuddath as the alien lifted Reik by the neck. He bounced off the alien's back and scrambled at him again, spurred by an image of the warrior in the garden, stretching Clemis with the care of a torturer who wants his victim to last. Reik's legs thrashed against the alien's abdomen, and there was still a chance, because the alien wanted her to suffer.

Kane grappled at the carapace, unable to find a hold, lacking the weight and the strength even to distract the insect man. The room telescoped around Chuddath. Kane heard someone shouting, but it was far away, not connected with his own lungs and voice. The Ornyl staggered two steps, and Kane was thrown from his back. He sat on the floor, stunned. As Pendrake forced the Ornyl's arm down, Reik's feet hit the floor again, no longer kicking.

Kane stared, sickened, at her ankles turning easily against the tile, at her dangling arms. Pendrake held the Ornyl's free fighting arm away with his left hand, while with his right he squeezed down on Chuddath's wrist, trying to force open the choking fingers. The two aliens braced against each other, their legs angling out behind, seeking purchase. The muscles stood out on Pendrake's neck and drew his tunic tight across his back. The Ornyl's head began to jerk from side to side, and Kane got up, caught Martha as the fingers opened and she dropped. He pulled her from between the two giants, heard her gasping, felt tears of relief flooding his eyes. Chuddath threw his weight to the side and tore free of Pendrake's grip. Kane crouched over Reik, but the Ornyl had a new target. Pendrake dropped his arms and waited, undefended, for the other alien.

"Stop!" Amerdath screamed.

The Ornyl stopped his charge centimeters from the Cephantine's chest. The fighting arms rose, the hands snapped open and shut on either side of Pendrake's head, and then the warrior dropped his arms and turned away to face the Imperator. Amerdath's face was contorted. "I . . . couldn't get control," he gasped, ". . . of my voice. Is she all right?"

Kane felt Reik moving. He helped her sit up. She stopped gasping and sat, fingering her throat, staring at the Ornyl warrior. Her eyes were blank, then they focused and she blinked. Her first attempt to talk brought nothing, and then she managed a husky whisper. "I'm all right."

"I'm sorry, Martha, so sorry. It was terrible. I wanted to scream and I had no lungs. I was so shocked that I couldn't make the damned wires . . . the damned wires . . ."

Reik motioned weakly with a hand. "I understand. The stress."

Anger drove Kane an absurd belligerent step toward the

Ornyl warrior. "What are you going to do about this murder machine?" he shouted at Amerdath.

"I'm . . . sorry, Elias . . ."

"Sorry? He could have killed Beth. . . ." Kane stopped. Martha Reik looked at him, her eyes filling with tears. "He could have killed Martha," he went on in a subdued voice, "and he would have if it weren't for his cruelty."

"Elias, you must not blame Chuddath," Pendrake said. "He acted instinctively from the S'edhite link. He must have perceived that Dr. Reik was at fault for the dangerous effects of the machine—that she intended to kill the Imperator."

The Ornyl turned back to Pendrake. The vocal arms jerked angrily. "I do not need you to defend me, Cephantine."

It was the first time Kane had heard such a long sentence without pause, and he wondered abstractedly if the alien's rage had powered the small arms over their usual rest stops. Pendrake gazed pityingly at the warrior but said nothing.

Reik got up. A blackened piece of the cantaloupe stuck to her cheek. She pulled it free and stared at it. "I don't understand this."

"You checked the equipment . . . only you," Chuddath said.

"We don't know that," Kane said. "You were here too. You could have done something to the generator just as easily as she."

"No, Elias," Amerdath said. "I don't believe Martha had anything to do with this, but you must understand that Chuddath is incapable of disloyalty to me."

"Well, damn it, it could be any one of the praetorians, then. The ones who guarded the area. It was a praetorian in the first place."

"That, I'm afraid, is much more likely," Amerdath said. "Martha, get me Alvar Sabin on the phone. Elias, perhaps you should go next door and see what you can find out by looking at the equipment." Amerdath seemed in full control of himself again.

"Pendrake, stay with Martha," Kane said.

Reik turned from the phone. "That's not necessary, Elias. I'm all right." Her voice was labored and hoarse, but she backed up the words with a smile. Kane glanced at the Ornyl warrior. She waved the implication off. "He's had his fun. He won't go against the Imperator's order."

Chuddath looked in her direction. "Not fun," he said softly, the arms barely brushing.

"That makes two of us," Reik said. "If I didn't know you thought you were defending the Imperator, I'd want that hand of yours mounted on my wall."

"Only the command . . . restrains me," Chuddath said.

Reik looked from Chuddath to the Imperator, her face paling in a mixture of fear and anger. "Damn it! I will not accept this. Question me. Put me under drugs. I won't live under a cloud . . ."

"Don't be foolish, Martha," Amerdath said. "I know you wouldn't hurt me." The conciliatory words were diluted by the Imperator's unwavering gaze.

"Sabin here." The voice came over the phone's wall speaker as the image of the praetorian commander appeared on the wall screen.

"Alvar, bring your three most trusted majors," Amerdath said. "Also bring a squad of troopers. Neurology section, on the double. I think one of your men just tried to kill me."

Sabin's face blanched. "Sir, I can't see you; all I can see is Dr. Reik. Is that really you?"

Reik turned the video pick-up toward Amerdath and he glared at the lens. "Get over here, Alvar. I'll want every man presently on duty arrested and the guard doubled. I want you personally to supervise it."

"Yes, sir."

Amerdath turned his face from the lens. Reik flipped the

disconnect switch, and Sabin's face faded as a look of outrage distorted his features.

Kane turned to Pendrake. "Would you go to our rooms and bring back my case?" The alien hurried out. Kane stepped through into the semidarkness of the generator room. He squatted beside the power source and waited, calming himself with even breaths, until Pendrake returned. He took the case, removed a spray bottle and misted the corners of the cover plate around the retaining bolts. After the spray dried, he took a magnifying glass from the case. There were no prints on or around the bolts. He removed the cover. There was a metal unit the size and shape of a sausage spliced into the line from the queson generator. There were no prints on it either, so Kane removed it, taping the insulation that had been torn to splice in the unit. He held the foreign element up for Pendrake to see. "This is it. Somebody tied it into the line at a point before the beam gets fractioned for the three guns."

"What is it?" Pendrake asked.

"A piggyback power source. It could be boosted microwave or the new gigasound. I'll guarantee you this: It's not queson. It must have been put here after Martha checked last night."

"Yes, Elias." Pendrake hesitated, and Kane looked sharply at him. "I am sure you are correct," the alien added hastily. "However, we must ask ourselves why the boosted power was not detected by Dr. Reik in her tests of the guns this morning."

Kane stared at the thing in his hand. *Not Martha, please, not her.* And then he realized that it truly did not make sense—Reik would not wire in the power source and then expect anyone to believe that she did not detect the surge when checking output of the guns before the mapping process. And, in fact, she had detected no such surge. Kane popped open the access lid of the rogue source. The thing he was looking for did not seem to be there. He began to sweat. With a thin probe from his case, he teased apart the spaghettilike mass of wires and components, and it was there, a disc about the size of a fish scale. Smiling in relief, he showed it to Pendrake. "It's a remote-controlled switch," he explained. "The power source would not be tied in until a signal was beamed to this switch. Martha could test the gun emissions all she wanted and find, nothing out of the ordinary."

Pendrake looked somber. "But that means such a signal must have been sent by someone in the room—someone who saw that the Imperator was in position for the mapping. Only you, I, Chuddath, the Imperator and Martha Reik were in the room."

Kane stood. "No. It doesn't have to be that way. I'm betting that no one sent the signal."

"But, Elias . . ."

"Come on."

Sabin had arrived, was facing the Imperator. ". . . they've been arrested," he was saying. "All of them. The new guard is posted. There was no incident. Sir, I submit my resignation and offer myself for immediate arrest."

"Don't talk rubbish, Alvar."

"I've failed you. Three times."

"All of us have failed him," Kane said quietly.

Amerdath's head turned toward him. "Elias, what did you find?"

Kane showed him the power source and the remote receiver. "I think I know how the signal was sent," he said. "Bear with me a moment." He walked over to the headclamps extending from the wall, the clamps that immobilized the head during memory mapping. The clamps were unpadded, because padding for comfort would have permitted too much movement. Instead, a sandwich of two thin strips made up the bands. Embedded between the strips were proprioceptive sensors no thicker than hairs, which transmitted to the guns any minute movements of the head. The guns were compensated by this feedback system so that even if the head should move fractionally, the beam intersection remained on target within the brain. Kane slipped off a retaining piece at one end of the clamp and pried until the strips came apart. He looked at the inside surfaces then held them out for Amerdath to see.

"This is a pressure switch," Kane said, pointing. "Here, in the middle—that silver thing the size and thickness of a postage stamp. It's not supposed to be there. The thing has a microscopic point in the middle, separated from the contact wafer by a very thin membrane. When the band is tightened around the head, the point penetrates the membrane and touches the wafer. Contact is closed and a signal is sent. When the clamp is loose, the point retracts and there is no signal. Whoever rigged this last night after Martha had checked out the main generator obviously wouldn't want her to discover the power booster this morning when she tested the gun, so they rigged this. The surge couldn't come until you were strapped in, sir. You, or the cantaloupe."

"I see."

Chuddath took a step toward Alvar Sabin.

"Belay," Amerdath commanded, and the Ornyl warrior stopped just before the praetorian commander's sidearm appeared in his hand.

"Praetorian," Chuddath said. "Always praetorian."

"You . . ."

"I'm sorry, Alvar," Amerdath cut in, "but it does look like one of your men."

"Or her," Sabin said, indicating Reik with the snout of his slug gun.

"Don't you start . . ." Reik fell silent at a look from Amerdath.

"It just doesn't seem possible," Sabin said. "I know my men. I've handpicked them for your personal duty assignments since Clemis. Even if there was corruption of one or two men, it would not be the men I have picked. I'd stake my life on it."

"I mark your words," Chuddath said.

"I don't see you volunteering for the ax," Sabin shot back. "You're his personal bodyguard. You're with him almost all the time."

"Enough," Amerdath snapped. "The vital point is, *who?* Who could have enticed away two of your men?" Amerdath paused, looking speculatively at the praetorian commander. "Fowler is searching for Richard DuMorgan. When he finds him, perhaps we'll have our answer."

"It's unnerving," Reik said. "DuMorgan's on the run, and yet he may almost have gotten you."

Kane remained silent, the knowledge of failure oppressing him. Weeks had passed, and his suspects were the same, and the third attempt had now been made. How long before a fourth? How long before success?

"I will have every man questioned under drugs and torture if necessary," Sabin said in a heavy voice. His face was stricken, full of misery. Kane found it hard to believe that the commander could be behind the attempt. But if it *was* one of Sabin's men, he would become the foremost suspect. It would not be the first time in history that a "faithful" praetorian had conspired to murder his emperor.

"See to it yourself," Amerdath said. "Now."

Sabin bowed. "Sir, I think you should have someone else present at the questionings—someone not of the praetorians. Perhaps one of Fowler's men." Sabin's tone made it clear how much the statement cost him. But it was precisely what a man with nothing to hide should suggest. If one of the Special Branch witnessed the questionings, no one could say later that a thorough job was not done, or that Sabin covered up information implicating himself.

"Very well," Amerdath said. "You may go."

When Sabin was gone, Amerdath turned to Reik. "Well, let's get on with it."

She stared disbelievingly at him.

"Elias," Amerdath said. "Is the generator in proper working order now?"

"Yes, sir, but . . ."

"But nothing. You've heard the old saying about getting right back on the horse that throws you. If I leave this room now, I might never come back."

"All right," Martha Reik said when everything was once more ready. She closed the switch and Amerdath's eyes lost focus. They began to track something across the room. His lips moved and he frowned. Reik cut power. Amerdath blinked and gazed at her.

"How was that?" Reik asked.

"Uh . . . could be better." The Imperator's voice was thick, bemused. "I was on the bridge of the *Scaramouche*. The East-bloc dreadnaughts were on an attack course. The bridge had taken a hit. We were on fire. I thought we were all about to die. I didn't know that it would all turn out all right. That's one I'd like to forget. Martha . . . ?"

She nodded encouragement.

"Martha, I was . . . *there*. I was there again. It wasn't memory. I . . . Let's try again."

She changed the guns' focal point and closed the switch. Again Amerdath's eyes lost focus and then found it again on some vista forever beyond the reach of the others in the room. Kane watched emotion fill the Imperator's face. A look of wonder, a smile. His mouth opened and he made a soft, mewing sound. The back of Kane's neck prickled as he realized that someplace far away, far in the past, Gregory Amerdath was laughing.

"Looks like we hit it that time," Reik said. She flipped the power off. Amerdath looked startled. His eyes jerked back and forth, finding each face that had materialized out of his dream. He swallowed several times and, as comprehension came, he looked sad.

"Right. Hello, again. God, that's abrupt."

"Coming back?" Reik asked.

"Yes. It's like you're getting involved in a good drama, you've crawled into the set and are part of the show, then someone changes the channel. No, that doesn't describe it. I can't . . .''

"What was it this time?'' Reik asked.

Amerdath looked over their heads as though determined to reject this reality that had been forced back on him. This *alternate* reality, Kane realized, understanding a part of what Amerdath must be going through.

"When I was in military school,'' Amerdath said, "only eighteen years old, we climbed Pikes Peak, a bunch of us, and when we got to the top, we drank the beer we'd brought along, and punched each other . . . punched each other on the shoulder. The sky was eggshell blue, so bright it hurt your eyes, and there was a stiff wind. My legs were so sore. I stood on top of the peak and remembered how I had always wanted to climb it, to stand on top of the world.'' He laughed. "A memory within a memory. I want that one, Martha.''

She turned to the charting console. "Done.''

"Good. Let's go. Let's go again.''

It went on for nearly two hours. Some of the memories were bad, most were ones Amerdath wanted. The console stored each chosen locus. Each time Amerdath came back with more difficulty, reorienting himself more slowly, saying less about what he'd experienced. Reik's face became pale and stayed that way, but each time Amerdath commanded her, she sent him back to live used moments as though they were new. Reik brought him back to the present for the ninety-third time. When he at last focused on the reality that had, in the last hours, become the nightmare, he began to weep and rage. His voice was so anguished that Kane could not look at him. Reik began to cry; Pendrake covered his face with his hands. Only the Ornyl warrior stood unmoving, locked into the impassivity of his brittle face and blank eyes.

Amerdath got control again. He let Reik blot the tears from his face. Then he said, "Get me out of here.''

They took him back to his rooms. On the way an ersatz

sun shone down through the corridor ceilings and birds
warbled and sang from the hidden wall speakers. When he
was in his quarters, Amerdath dismissed everyone but
Chuddath. Kane looked back as he reached the door. The
Ornyl bent down toward Amerdath, bringing his forehead
to the Imperator's. Kane eased the door shut.

CHAPTER 28

Kane had gotten several looks at the locks and the compli-
cated security system, so selecting tools was a simple
matter: sleedeep gas, a jammer that would freeze the raster
pattern of the TV monitors while he was still out of sight
of the pick-up, leg antigrav suspensors that would keep his
weight off the pressure wires in the floor, shims to keep
the warning wires from springing from the jambs when
doors were opened, a variety of common picks, field
degaussers, and finally, the egg-shaped master key unit
he'd used earlier to open the murdered page's door. If
there were more traps, more warning systems, he would be
caught, it was as simple as that. The thought gave him a
perverse exhilaration. After weeks of groping through the
fog of words, innuendos, facial expressions, of negotiating
the currents and cross-currents of motive, of being taken
off guard by the actions of others, he was at last taking the
initiative. It was a physical act, a risk, a taking charge by
the nerves and muscles.

He felt Pendrake's gaze on his back as he slipped the
various pieces of hardware into the special vest he had put

on. He turned and snugged the vest down in front. "How do I look?"

Pendrake regarded him with disapproval. "Like someone who is about to commit a series of crimes. Elias, it is always the same. You lapse into silence and begin acting mysteriously so that I will ask you what you are doing. Very well. What are you doing?"

"Would you get me half a shot of Levian green, please," Kane said, unable to resist prolonging the game a few minutes longer. "Just a finger, now, to sharpen my nerves."

Pendrake dialed the drink on the suite's bar console. He handed it to Kane and said patiently, "Sharpen your nerves for what purpose?"

"Paying a visit to Giacomin's office, of course."

"Of course. And may I assume from the fact that it is night, and from that small laboratory you have strapped around your chest, that you do not have an appointment?"

"You may."

"Why Giacomin?"

"It's obvious. Do you remember the second attempt on Amerdath's life? Giacomin was there within minutes. Also the first time—he had agents in the garden only minutes after we left. But today? Attempt number three and he never did show up, even though we stayed in the room for hours after the attempt."

"Perhaps he did not find out until later," Pendrake said. "After all, Amerdath did not summon him."

"That can't be the reason. Amerdath didn't summon him the other times either, but he was there. Also, we know he has people among the praetorians. He probably monitors all calls to Alvar Sabin. No, he knew, and yet he didn't come. I've been asking myself why. What could he have been doing that was more important than getting personally to the scene of a third attempt on Amerdath's life?"

Pendrake stared at him. "Interrogating Richard Du-Morgan?"

"Go to the head of the class."

"But if Mr. Giacomin has captured the viceroy, why should he keep it secret?"

"So he and his sweaty sadist friend, the doctor with all the exotic drugs, can have DuMorgan all to themselves. The Imperator might lay restrictions on Fowler if he knew DuMorgan was captured. An Imperial viceroy is not an ordinary prisoner, especially when he is a hero who wears the Empire's highest medal."

"You may be correct, Elias. But why take the risk of breaking into Fowler Giacomin's stronghold? Why do you not merely alert Alvar Sabin? I am sure he would be happy to provide a squad of praetorians to go in directly."

Kane shook his head. "The security section is saturated with alarm devices. Even assuming I could get a squad of Alvar's men lined up without Giacomin getting wind, they'd trip a dozen alarms going in and Fowler would be sitting at his desk with a Cheshire cat smile before anyone could get close."

"But a thorough search of the section . . ."

"Would reveal nothing. Giacomin's got DuMorgan hidden somewhere that doesn't show up on the floor plan. Sneaking up on him is the only way. Giacomin's playing with a marked deck. He claims to be loyal to Amerdath, and yet he probably has the chief suspect in the assassination conspiracy hidden away from everyone else. Could it be because DuMorgan isn't heading up the conspiracy at all? If he isn't, but Giacomin wants to go on making it look like he is, then he'll have to keep DuMorgan under wraps. And if DuMorgan is Giacomin's fall guy, what does that make Giacomin?" Kane tipped back a swallow of whiskey.

"An interesting question." The Cephantine inspected the equipment case that lay open on the bed. "When do we start?"

Kane choked, sprayed out the whiskey.

"Do not argue, Elias. If you are going, I am going. Someone must take care of you."

"Take . . .? That's good. Listen, my acromegalic friend, this is a job for a trained professional working alone. There are pressure wires every few meters along the floor. I'll be skating over them with suspensors and I have only one pair. Your big feet . . ."

"Exert fewer pounds per square inch than your smaller ones," Pendrake cut in. "The point is moot in any case. You will go first and deactivate the alarms. I will follow."

Kane shook his head. "I appreciate it, but I don't need anyone to take care of me."

"I will remember that," the alien said dryly, "the next time we are both locked in an ImpSec prison, or trapped under a hundred meters of water in a crashed aircar, or sitting up very straight in two forcechairs."

Kane felt a flush creeping up from his collar. He reached into the case and threw a sphere about the size of a marble at the Cephantine. Pendrake fielded it deftly. "Keep your eye on that," Kane snapped. "When I've cut the alarms, I'll set it flashing."

The lighting in the entry hall was dim. Kane gave the guard a last check to make sure that he'd gotten the full dose from the sleedeep cannister. Pulse slow and even, little bubbles of saliva at the man's lips with each exhalation. He'd sleep for hours. Kane took the nose filters out and sniffed cautiously, and motioned to Pendrake that it was safe. He checked the video image on his watch face. It showed the guard as he had been a moment before, sitting in his chair, arms across the chest, staring down the corridor. If anyone was monitoring the screens inside the security section, the guard would begin to seem too still, and after a few minutes it would become obvious that he was not blinking. It was a good freeze, though, considering that Kane had done it out of sight—the man could have been scratching his head or yawning.

Kane made sure the shim was holding the warning trigger flat within the exposed doorjamb, then steadied himself against the wall and activated the suspensors. He kept his legs still above the sudden lift, careful not to let either foot slip out from under him. He baby-stepped into the corridor. It stretched ahead of him, a problem in geometry, four unbroken lines converging in the distance. The hall was cool with spillage from the giant air conditioners in the computer section. Globes lit the slightly arched ceiling at regular intervals, banding the hall in stripes of light and shadow. Glancing back, Kane saw Pendrake fussing over the unconscious guard, making sure he was positioned comfortably. Kane smiled grimly, then gave his full attention to staying upright on the icy centimeter of canceled gravity. The forces were balanced against the muscles of the leg, but too strong a step could send the wearer skidding out of control to fall on the lattice of pressure wires in the floor.

Kane inched along, steadying himself with a hand on either wall. About halfway down the hall, he saw an electric eye at waist level, worked into the wall design. He eased a disc over the receiver on the opposite wall. There would be a tiny flicker on far away monitoring equipment, but no more. Despite the coolness of the corridor, he began to sweat. The silence worked on the nerves, accumulating like ice on high wires, and Kane fought the compulsion to make some sound, to shout or perhaps whistle. He fought the urge, knowing that the corridor was silent for a reason. If a certain sound level was breached, alarms would flash in some hidden room.

Kane negotiated the corner and headed down the final hall to Giacomin's office. He edged out from the wall to avoid the cabinet of a computer-controlled fire station, and his feet slipped out to the side. He grabbed the top of the cabinet as he was going down and hiked up his knees, and

clung there while the sharp edges cut into his fingers and
sweat soaked his collar and back. His knees had come
within centimeters of the floor. He let his feet down
gingerly, breathing open-mouthed, his eyes pinched to slits
by exertion. He waited until the adrenaline aftershock
passed and then shuffled on to the door. More shims, a
pass with the egg-shaped key maker and he was inside.

The office was dark. Kane put on a pair of infrared
glasses from the vest and scanned the room until he located the minute leakage of light from the alarm box. He
studied the circuits for nearly twenty minutes before he felt
sure enough to tie in the loops that would mimic each part
of the system spread through the hallways. He canceled
the suspensors and his feet settled firmly against the floor.
He activated the signal that would cause the marble to
glow in Pendrake's hand, then bent to massage his aching
calves and ankles.

Pendrake entered noiselessly. Kane pulled off the infrared goggles and motioned to the light switch. "It's all
right. I've cut the alarm systems out."

Pendrake flipped the switch and Kane blinked against
the glare. He pulled a thin glove from a pocket of the vest
and tugged it on. The glove was woven in a mesh of soft
wire. There was a disc on the back just above the knuckles.
The glove worked by boosting the nerve signals in the
fingertips, allowing the hand to sense tiny irregularities
below the normal threshold of touch. Kane went to the
nearest wall and rested the gloved palm lightly against it,
sweeping his hand back and forth. He moved slowly around
the room until he felt what he was searching for, the nearly
seamless break in the wall. He traced the outline of a low
door, swept his fingers across at waist level and fingered a
small circle on the wall. He stepped back. "It's activated
electronically on a closed circuit," he mused. "No use
beaming frequencies at it, because it's sure to be shielded."
He turned to Pendrake. "If you were Fowler Giacomin,

where in this room would you hide the switch to this door?''

"I do not see any door, Elias."

"Take my word for it."

The alien considered for a moment. "Mr. Giacomin seems to stay close to his chair whenever we are in this room."

"No, he couldn't be that obvious, could he?" Kane went to the desk, felt underneath the center drawer until he found the button. "I don't believe it."

"Perhaps the security chief did not hide the button because he never expected an intruder, even of your talents, to be able to penetrate this far."

Kane shrugged and depressed the button, and the section of wall he had outlined swung open.

"Hello, Kane," Giacomin said. He was standing in the opened section of wall, and there was a 'ruptor in his hand. Kane straightened slowly. Pendrake sighed. "Actually," Giacomin said, "your pumpkin-colored friend is right about your talents—to a point. I *didn't* think anyone could penetrate my security system. If I hadn't happened to be in, shall we call it, my little annex, I wouldn't have picked up your voices on the speakers I'm sure you must agree are necessary in an arrangement like this." Giacomin flicked the 'ruptor up to indicate an audio hook-up on his side of the wall.

"I had a feeling you'd be working late tonight," Kane said.

"I do what I can. But I'm being rude. Won't you come in?" Giacomin emphasized the invitation by centering the 'ruptor on Kane's stomach.

"Do me a favor," Kane said without moving. "Drop the gracious villain act. If I get even a second, I'll take you out. If you go on acting like you're enjoying this, I'll make it last."

Giacomin's patronizing smile slipped and slid until his face was stark, and Kane imagined that he was looking now at the true Giacomin, a vulture's head forever craned over horrors too dark to contemplate.

"That's clear enough," Giacomin said tonelessly. "I would expect more understanding in a man of your experience, but no matter."

"You killed Elizabeth Tyson," Kane said. "Do you seriously expect me to *understand?*"

Giacomin's eyes widened in fear, then became impassive again. Kane watched the reaction, glaring with an anger that was only half faked. He did not know, not yet, but it might have been this man. Still Giacomin's confusion had seemed real.

"Is that what you think?" the security chief said. "That I am the traitor? You couldn't be more wrong. Now, if you would just shrug out of that natty tool vest you're wearing and drop it to the floor." Kane complied. "Good. Now come inside." Giacomin backed well out of reach as Kane and Pendrake stepped into the annex. The short hallway, chiseled through the granite, turned right almost at once, terminating in a steel door. "Pull it open," Giacomin said. "It's unlocked."

Kane did as he was told, trying to gauge the distance of the security chief behind him. It was no good. Giacomin was staying well away, but not so far that his aim would be impaired. He was an old-time professional, who'd reached the top by never taking unnecessary chances. Maybe the careless moment, the fractional lapse of attention, the fleeting gap in Giacomin's defenses, wasn't going to come. Maybe the man would kill him. The image of himself falling under Giacomin's 'ruptor, of the world going gray and draining out, made Kane's jaws clench. He could die, yes. Part of him could let go almost gratefully—he'd known that from the moment on top of the palace when he'd found himself poised over the top of the guardrail. But not before he *knew*.

Kane entered the room and stopped, stared at the slouched form in the forcechair until Giacomin prodded him forward

again with the 'ruptor. Richard DuMorgan did not look up.
His jaw bristled with stubble and his forehead beneath the
wet strands of hair was a waxy white. Giacomin circled
around and released DuMorgan from the chair's restraining
field. The viceroy leaned forward and sprawled down,
knees and elbows flopping, and Kane noted that there had
been a thread of control in the way he'd done it.

"Into the chair, Elias."

"One moment." Pendrake's voice was intense, almost
harsh, but Giacomin did not look away from Kane. "Do
you intend to kill these men?" Pendrake asked. "Do not
try to deceive me, Fowler Giacomin."

"And don't try to bluff me, *alien*," the security chief
sneered. "You may be clever, sensitive to emotion, but I
know what a Cephantine can and cannot do."

"Do you intend to kill these men?"

"Not unless, someday, they ask me to."

Kane laughed sourly. "There you have it, Pendrake. He
knows you won't interfere unless it's to save our lives, and
he knows that even then you'd be careful not to hurt him.
And while you are being careful, the odds are that he
could gun you down. But if you do nothing, we may
someday beg this man to kill us. It's a nice dilemma for a
pacifist, isn't it? I think you'd better wait."

"Good advice," Giacomin said. "Now, get in the chair."

Kane sat in the dampness left by DuMorgan's back and
thighs. Giacomin flipped on the field of the chair and
switched his attention to Pendrake, keeping the 'ruptor
aimed at Kane's head as he moved around behind the
chair. "Just stay where you are," Giacomin said to Pendrake
in a soothing voice. "No one's about to die unless *you* do
something foolish."

Kane stiffened as something cool hissed into his wrists
where they were pinned to the arms of the chair. He could
feel the drug spreading into his muscles, chilling the
capillaries, taking him over cell by cell. Which of the
drugs was it, this coldness? What would it make him do?

"Why?" he said.

"Don't worry, Elias. It's just to lower your defenses. In about twenty minutes it'll start to take effect. I have some questions for you, and I'd prefer you in an open and pliant state of mind."

Kane resisted the panic, the urge to lunge and strain against the grip of the field. "What questions? What do you think I know that could be of value to you?"

"I won't know that until I ask, will I?" Giacomin said reasonably. "I'm in the intelligence business, Elias. I haven't stayed in it by letting opportunities pass. Besides, you've been conducting a very important investigation, and I'd be willing to wager that you've not shared all your findings with me."

Beyond Giacomin's ankle Kane saw Richard DuMorgan pushing himself with shaky care onto his side. The viceroy was staring feverishly at Giacomin's ankles. Kane tried to hold the security chief with his eyes, willing the other man not to look away, not to look down.

"Besides," Giacomin continued. "You're all going to be with me for some time and we have to talk about *something*. It would be cruel of me to let you hope you'll be rescued. Only a few of my people know this cell exists, and so you're really quite alone. If you cooperate, I will make things easier. You've had Amerdath's ear. No doubt you have used the advantage to work against me, to suggest that I be replaced. I'd be especially interested in hearing about that."

DuMorgan reached for the security chief's ankle. Kane tried desperately to think of something to say. "You're being paranoid, Giacomin. Amerdath has no plans to replace you."

"Good, good. If you repeat that in twenty minutes, I'll be even more pleased . . ."

The viceroy's hand closed around Giacomin's ankle. Giacomin pulled free easily and kicked DuMorgan onto his

244 Steven Spruill

face. He walked past Pendrake to the door, keeping the 'ruptor aimed at Kane's chest. "I'll be back shortly. Don't go away."

The door, one foot of steel, swung shut with an understated click.

CHAPTER 29

"Don't say it," Kane muttered as Pendrake released the field on the chair. The alien gave him a resigned look before bending over the viceroy. Kane got up and tested his legs. There seemed to be little effect yet from the injection, except a sensation that a cold glass tube was stuck in his throat. He knelt on the other side of DuMorgan and helped Pendrake sit him up.

"We meet again," the viceroy said. His voice was surprisingly strong, but ragged, as though he'd been shouting. "Sorry about missing that hyena. I thought if I could snag his ankles I could bring him down."

"Never mind," Kane said.

"How do you feel, Viceroy?" Pendrake asked.

"Embarrassed at being caught, mostly. When Giacomin closed in I was five minutes from boarding a tidy little private yacht fitted for deep space."

"But your physical condition?"

"I'll be all right. No broken bones. Our host isn't a slap-around type. His main hobby is pharmacology, and it's been a while since he injected me . . . I think. Trouble

245

is, he's been pretty absentminded about meals. I could go for a bite of what fell under the table at Amerdath's banquet. Here, pull me up.''

Kane and Pendrake lifted the viceroy and eased him loose. DuMorgan looked gaunt and feverish. He wobbled a few steps then grew steadier as he tapped hidden reserves. Kane looked around as the viceroy walked off his stiffness. The cell was approximately three meters long and four wide. The walls were granite, tapering into a tent-shaped ceiling only a few centimeters above Pendrake's head. There was no second door, nothing to soften the harsh embrace of rock. The only hope of escape was the one door, and Kane knew it was a vain hope. Still he nudged Pendrake and nodded toward the entrance.

''It is very thick steel, Elias, but I shall try.'' The alien folded his arms across his chest and lowered his head in meditation. DuMorgan stopped pacing and looked like he wanted to say something to Pendrake. Kane watched his face, realized that the viceroy was struggling with himself. DuMorgan turned to Kane.

''How long do you think we've got?''

Kane shrugged. ''Giacomin said the injection will take effect in about twenty minutes. He'll be back before then. Pendrake will be ready as he can get in a few minutes.''

''But if he can break the door out, which I don't think is possible even for a Cephantine in the *Tropos* trance, we'd be walking right into Giacomin's 'ruptor.''

''Not necessarily. He's probably going back over our entry route to make sure we don't have a backup. Besides, you didn't think Pendrake could break out of a forcechair either.''

''A point,'' conceded DuMorgan. ''By the way, *do* you have a backup?''

''What do you think?''

''Damn.'' DuMorgan slapped a fist into his palm, then sagged into the forcechair, glowering at Kane. ''What the hell are you doing here, anyway?''

"Looking for you, and you're welcome."

"So you were beginning to suspect how your side plays."

"Not my side. Giacomin's. Let me make something clear, DuMorgan. As far as I'm concerned, you're still a suspect in the attempts on Amerdath's life. Right now I hope it was *you* that got Clemis to take that shot in the garden, because I don't think we're going to get out of here . . ."

"And if you have to die, you want to know that the person who caused the death of Elizabeth Tyson is going out too. I understand. Now let me tell you something. I'll not repeat it. Neither I nor the colonists have been gunning for the Imperator. Giacomin would risk anything to prove it, but it's not true."

"Damn it, Viceroy, you and that bunch of underground commandos have been up to *something*. If you're not trying to assassinate Amerdath, what *have* you been plotting?"

DuMorgan looked at him steadily. "That's not something I can tell you. Not even now, with our heads on the block. Not while I know you're on the same side as Fowler Giacomin. I wish I could understand you, Elias. Giacomin's coming back here in just a few minutes to let the air out of you, and you're still falling for his 'mad dog colonists' propaganda."

"Is it just propaganda? Do you deny that you're building up for a clash between Earth and the colonies?"

DuMorgan hesitated. "No, I don't. As a matter of fact, I think it's almost inevitable now, thanks in large part to the ravings of Giacomin. For years he's been undermining us in the topmost circles of the Imperial power structure. Sure, we've got grievances with the Empire, and they might have been solved by diplomacy, but not when the Imperator and his top generals and admirals are told almost daily by their spymaster that the colonies are preparing for revolution. War is going to come, Elias, and if we live through this, you're going to be on the wrong side. All we

want is the freedom, the independence to pursue the interests of humanity in space at our own profit. But Imperial
taxes are strangling us. Fat entrepreneurs on Earth are
living off the sweat of colonist backs and keeping the
system in place with embargoes of high-tech goods and
materials.''

"Like dreadnaughts?"

"We need many other things, Elias. Things not so
controversial, but the Empire . . ."

"I won't talk embargo with you, DuMorgan. Right now
I want to know how, with all you've just said about war,
you can keep insisting that you've not been trying to kill
Amerdath. A strong Imperator is the biggest single obsta-
cle to colonist independence. If you're going to fight us,
you'd want Amerdath out at the start . . ."

"And see Briana take the throne? Another thing, Kane:
Despite what you seem to think, I'm an honorable man. If
I go against Gregory Amerdath it will be man to man, ship
to ship. I'd not dirty my lungs with the same air breathed
by a praetorian who'd think of killing his Imperator."

DuMorgan's face slipped out of focus then solidified
again. Kane fingered his eyelids and tried to swallow the
cold tube, which had thickened in his throat. The injection
was spreading through him, working its way into the
brain. "So you think Giacomin is behind the assassi-
nations?"

DuMorgan was watching Pendrake. "As a matter of
fact, I don't," he said almost absently. "In his own way,
Giacomin sees himself as completely loyal. After all, it's a
pretty good bet he'll not last an hour longer than Amerdath,
unless he's got a very fast ship hidden away somewhere.
No, he truly thinks it's the colonists."

"You sound sure of yourself."

"I just spent a day in this room with him. I know what
he asked me when there was no one else around to watch
the show. Poor Fowler. First Clemis and now me, refusing
to give his tape recorder a nice tidy confession." Du-

Morgan's expression became bleak. "Except that I *did* confess. He's got drugs that make you eager to say anything, anything to get him to let up. I confessed and I confessed, and each time the voice stress monitor showed I was lying, just as it would if he tried to play the tape for anyone else. But Giacomin's still sure I'm guilty. He's sure the lie spikes are there because I'm covering up for some of my associates." DuMorgan gave a bitter laugh. "I can't even confess."

Kane felt dizzy. The ground was too far down, his feet shrunken astigmatically into toy shoes at the margin of his vision. He tried to think. DuMorgan's words had the sound of truth, but if DuMorgan was innocent, if Giacomin was innocent, then who was guilty? The faces of his suspects swam on the backs of his eyelids—Briana, Lucian, Alvar Sabin, Martha Reik, Manoster, Giacomin, the viceroy, the empress. They merged into a composite face that taunted him.

"Elias!"

Kane shook his head drunkenly. Pendrake's face firmed up in front of him, a bizarre orange mask of concern. "I'm all right," Kane said, but he was not all right. His voice bounced back at him from the bottom of an empty drum. The cold tube slid up and down in his throat and the shapes and lines of the room were limned in prismatic brilliance. He wanted to close his eyes, shut out the sensations that were flooding in too fast, too sharp. He tried to concentrate on Pendrake as the alien moved toward the door of the cell. Kane wiped a flood of sweat from his forehead. Before Pendrake could hurl himself at the door, the viceroy gripped his wrist, pointed at a side wall of the cell. DuMorgan pantomimed kicking the wall, and Pendrake looked at him skeptically. Kane tried to make sense out of it. Why was DuMorgan suddenly afraid to speak? Why did he want Pendrake to hurl himself against solid granite— unless the granite was not solid. But it must be solid. There were sensors throughout the mesa. Giacomin's men could not have drilled a tunnel close to the cell without setting the alarms clamoring.

DuMorgan turned to Kane, his expression urgent. He pointed silently to the wall again, and Kane realized that he was afraid the cell was bugged.

"Do it," Kane said.

The alien pivoted on one leg and smashed the foot of the other into the granite with a karate-style kick. The wall blew into the tunnel with a rattle of falling rock. And then Kane remembered the fragment of conversation at the banquet between Amerdath and the Moitan ambassador. Amerdath had asked Manoster how his people blasted their underwater mines without suffering from water-magnified concussions. The alien had replied that concussion was not a problem. Now the cryptic remark came clear: The Moitan had developed a silent mining technique. And DuMorgan's men had somehow gotten hold of it and used it to tunnel up under the palace without triggering alarms.

"Quickly, let us go." Pendrake's voice sounded muted. The bright coronas around things had faded almost to gray. Kane felt his senses shrinking, leaving his body numb and uncoordinated. His mind was sharp, but the drug had flash-blinded his powers of perception. He could barely hear. His peripheral vision was gone, and the hole in the wall now looked far away. If Giacomin came back now, he would find his prisoner desperate for stimulation. Kane knew he would beg for Giacomin not to leave him, that he would tell the security chief anything to keep from being left alone, amputated from all sensation . . .

"Elias, can you hear me?"

"Pendrake?" Kane groped for the alien. His fingers closed on the thick arm as though through many layers of glove.

"Keep your grip," Pendrake said, "and follow. I will help you."

"Don't leave me. . . ."

"I will not, Elias. We must go quickly now. Lift your feet over these rocks in the entry . . . that is good . . ."

Kane made it through the hole clinging to Pendrake's arm. The alien started into the blackness of the tunnel but DuMorgan stopped them. "We can't just take off," the viceroy said. "Giacomin will get a light and follow us, and he's got the 'ruptor." DuMorgan bent over and picked up something that had been lying at the terminus of the tunnel. Kane strained to see. His vision blurred and swam as though he was looking up from the bottom of a well. The thing in DuMorgan's hands looked almost like a 'ruptor, but it was shorter and much fatter through the cylindrical chamber back of the barrel, where a 'ruptor's charge would be stored.

"What is that, Viceroy?" Pendrake asked.

"The Moitan call it a *ykestran*. We haven't had much time for creativity since we got ahold of these things, so we just call them tunnelers."

Kane strained to catch the dialogue between Pendrake and DuMorgan. Their voices seemed muffled, nearly swamped in echoes, whether from the injection or the tunnel behind them he could not tell. But he caught the word Moitan, and knew that his guess had been correct.

"We left these at the end of the tunnels," DuMorgan went on, "for when it was time to cut through."

"What do you intend to do with it?" Pendrake asked.

"When Giacomin comes back through that door . . ." DuMorgan cut the sentence short and edged away from Pendrake. Kane kept his grip on the alien's arm and was tugged along as Pendrake closed with the viceroy.

"You must not harm him," Pendrake said.

DuMorgan planted a hand on the alien's chest. "Stay away from me, Pendrake. It's got to be done."

"I cannot permit it."

Kane tried to say that DuMorgan was right, but the muddled feedback of his voice confused him before he could get the sentence out. Pendrake and the viceroy stared at each other, small gray faces on a distant screen.

"He'll follow us and kill us."

"You do not know that."

"Damn it, Cephantine, can you hate violence more than you hate evil?"

"Violence *is* evil," Pendrake said.

DuMorgan glanced through into the cell.

"Give me the tunneler, Viceroy," Pendrake said.

DuMorgan kept his grip on the device, glared at Pendrake. The alien reached out.

"Wait. All right. I won't kill him. I'll set the tunneler on low power. It'll heat the 'ruptor to the melting point as soon as it hits it and Giacomin won't be able to hold it."

"But if it will do that to metal, surely it will destroy the man."

"No. The beam works differently than normal heat. The denser a material is the faster the beam heats it. Giacomin's mostly water. It won't harm him at all. There's no time to explain."

Even through the fog of the drug, Kane could hear DuMorgan's desperation.

"Forgive me, Viceroy, but I must be certain you are not deceiving me. If what you say is true then you could turn the device on me and I would not be injured?"

"That's right."

"Then please do so."

DuMorgan stared at the alien. "Suppose I'm lying. What's to stop me from just blowing you away?"

"I do not believe you would do that, Viceroy."

DuMorgan smiled. He did something to the tunneler and turned it toward Pendrake. Kane tried to reach past the alien, to deflect the barrel of the tool. His shoulder prickled and he saw his fingers groping short of the mark. The end of the tunnel lit briefly with crimson light and the bridge of Kane's nose itched.

"Very well," Pendrake said. "But do not try to change the setting, Viceroy. I will be watching."

DuMorgan grunted. "I'd never try to fool you." He turned the weapon through the gap in the wall, aiming it toward the door of the cell. Realizing that DuMorgan had turned the beam on both of them, that the test was already over, Kane let his arm drop. The next moment moved almost too quickly for him to follow. The cell door swung open. The red light spilled from the tunneler and Giacomin screamed, flung the 'ruptor away from him and bent over his scorched hands. There was a drawn-out image of the weapon tumbling through the air, bending as though made of rubber, and sticking to the floor of the cell without bouncing. Then DuMorgan had the security chief locked into the forcechair and they were retreating into the blackness of the tunnel.

"I can't see," Kane said. He thought he had merely spoken it, but Pendrake's voice came urgent in his ear.

"Do not shout, Elias. Do not talk unless you must. The tunnel is dark, but the viceroy knows the way by feel. Here, put your other hand on the wall. See? It is smooth. The floor is also perfectly smooth. You will not stumble."

Kane felt the barest pressure along his fingertips. The sensation faded, the way a toothpick laid across the arm will soon drop below the threshold of awareness. He concentrated on the motions of walking.

"Good, Elias. You are doing well."

Kane bit down on his tongue, welcoming the threads of pain, forcing himself to remain silent while another part of him cried out for contact. He was in total darkness. He could feel nothing except wooden joltings in his hips that might have been phantom pains, twinges like the Imperator would still get from his missing body. It went on like that, on and on, interminably. Robbed of outside referents, Kane felt cut off from time, marooned in an empty endless void. He was alert and his head felt clear—too clear, the comforting murmur of muscle and flesh, of sight, sound, touch and smell gone silent. He began to feel that he did not exist, that only this place existed. He was inanimate, part of the fused tunnel wall, the permanent darkness. He would be here forever, awake but unsuspected, encased in stone beneath a world vibrating with warmth and light and sound. He willed the hand on the wall to come back, to press itself against his chest. He felt nothing. A mouth yawned open in his mind, an unvoiced scream that went on and on. Finally even the imaginary scream dwindled to nothing, a chimera of sound that his mind could not sustain. And then, in the frozen void of a consciousness emptied of all distraction, Kane knew who was trying to kill Gregory Amerdath.

CHAPTER 30

Kane knew who was trying to murder Amerdath. The knowledge thrust into him like a surgeon's fingers, cutting, breaking and, perversely, making him whole. First he felt the floor rocking from heel to toe with each step, and then he became aware of the perfect curving smoothness of the surface. He realized that one hand was clenching his shirt, knuckles grinding against his sternum. His elbow opened stiffly as he let his hand drop. He tested his vocal cords with a cough, felt vast relief as the sound of it, the feel of it came through cleanly.

"Elias?" It was DuMorgan's voice ahead of him in the darkness. Kane cut off his reply, realizing that he and Pendrake were only a few steps from being the viceroy's prisoners. Only colonists would be waiting at the end of the tunnel. Kane had no idea how long he'd stumbled through the blackness, but there couldn't be much time left. When the moment came to act, it would be best for DuMorgan to think him helpless. He continued to shuffle along the smooth floor, striving to make the same clumsy scraping sounds he'd first begun hearing a few minutes

before. The subtler cues of balance began to return and
Kane realized that they were walking down a steady spiraling decline. They passed side tunnels, identifiable by drafts
and changes in the timbre of their footsteps, and Kane felt
amazement at the viceroy's sense of direction. DuMorgan
must have negotiated these tunnels many times in pitch
blackness. Clearly, the colonist commandos were planning
an assault on the palace. Mere espionage could be carried
out without the tunnels, and such a network represented an
immense undertaking by any conceivable method, however new. The difficulty would be more than doubled by
the need for absolute secrecy. The Imperator and his admirals and generals believed themselves invulnerable from
military attack. They sat secure on their mountain of granite,
unaware that it was as porous as an anthill.

Kane wondered when DuMorgan had intended to order
the attack. If the viceroy had told the truth about being
minutes from boarding an escape ship when he was captured,
his plan must have been to postpone any attack against the
palace until things calmed down. That had to be the case if
DuMorgan had planned to lead the attack, and Kane did
not doubt what the viceroy had said about fighting
Amerdath's legions face to face. But when DuMorgan had
been captured, all bets must have been called off. The
viceroy's second-in-command—perhaps the big man, Dalt—
was now in charge. The situation was volatile, with the
colonists forced to improvise. When, after DuMorgan was
captured, no word of it reached the press, the colonist
spies in Amerdath's court would soon know that the Imperator had not been told about the viceroy's capture. The
colonists would know that Giacomin was sweating their
leader in some private cell, and that their plans would soon
be exposed. If Giacomin had not been obsessed with wring-
ing a confession for the assassination attempts out of
DuMorgan, he would probably have dug out the information that the palace was sitting on top of a maze of tunnels.
In any case, the colonists were probably massing right now

for the attack that had obviously been planned from the moment the tunnels had been started. When DuMorgan completed his escape, he could lead that attack—if it had not already begun. Against all political considerations, Kane felt a surge of admiration for the scarred and dashing colonial leader. He shrank from what he must do. But before either he or DuMorgan could do anything, they had to get out of the tunnels.

Though the influence of Giacomin's drug had dwindled, the tunnel was still totally dark. Kane could not suppress the struggle of his eyes to see. His lids spread and strained and the darkness chewed through to his brain. He thought about the Imperator. The knowledge of who wanted Amerdath dead was like a ball of clay, stuck in his hand, that he knew he must squeeze and press for a long time, perhaps for the rest of his life. The clay would create its own compulsion, taking shape after shape, but never the one that would allow him to let go, to set it down and say *it's finished.*

Pendrake stopped abruptly, and Kane had to hold himself off the alien's back. Then he saw the light too. It was faint, just enough to cut the dark forms of the alien and DuMorgan out of the deeper blackness. The light grew, spilling from a side tunnel about forty meters ahead of them. The tread of feet became audible. Kane released Pendrake's arm and stepped past him. The blade of his hand connected solidly with DuMorgan's neck at the base of his skull, and the breath the viceroy had drawn to shout escaped in a soft whuff. DuMorgan toppled forward and Kane caught him around the waist before he could clatter to the floor of the tunnel. The light was brighter now. The footsteps were distinct, the sounds of at least a score of men trotting. Kane looked for a side tunnel, but there was none. There was no niche, no outcropping in the fused walls to hide behind. Pendrake took DuMorgan from him, slung the viceroy over one shoulder and padded silently back up the way they had come. Kane followed, racing the

light that lapped their feet as the approaching party neared
the tunnel intersection. He glanced back over his shoulder,
tugged the alien's belt, and dropped, flattening himself
into the curving floor. Pendrake stretched out beyond him,
shielding the viceroy's prone form. The sound of running
feet spilled up the corridor and Kane lifted his head just
long enough to verify that the runners had not turned up
toward them. He pressed his face back into the floor, but
the sight of the passing men faded slowly on his retinas.
They had loped along with the loose, easy grace of panthers,
a disciplined group of commandos in peak physical
condition. Kane knew that if one of them got a good look
up the cross-tunnel, it was all over—there was too much
light and, even prostrate, their bodies would make three
lumps against the smooth rock. The light faded and the
footsteps receded, and Kane realized that he'd held his
breath. He let it out and gulped air from the blackness in
front of his face. If the commandos had not been running,
they could have gotten the good look, and at least it would
not be so suffocatingly dark again.

Pendrake got up, bumping against him. "Was it necessary to strike the viceroy so hard?" the alien whispered.
"He is still unconscious."

"I didn't like it any more than you did," Kane said.
"But those were his men."

"I am not sure that is true, Elias. They seemed to have
dark uniforms, like the praetorians."

Kane recalled the image of the running men and realized
it was true—the uniforms had been dark and tight, like the
Imperial guard. But it was impossible. The only Imperial
who knew about the tunnels was Giacomin, and he was
sitting in a forcechair, locked inside his own secret cell.
"Forget it. They were the viceroy's men, and we've got
no time to argue. We've got to get out of here. How long
have we been walking?"

"Approximately half an hour, I believe."

"Then we must be almost to the foot of the mesa. The

question is, do we go back up the way we came or try to get out the bottom?''

"I do not believe we can go back, Elias. There were several turns, and I am not sure I can remember them all. We could easily become lost."

"We'll have to gamble," Kane said, "that those men came from somewhere close by. Can you carry the viceroy?"

"I can carry him, Elias." The alien's voice was still reproving.

Kane ignored the disapproving tone. "Okay. Keep a hand on my shoulder." He felt his way back down the corridor they'd been traveling, keeping his hand on the wall to his right. When he reached the cross-tunnel, he turned into it in the direction from which the commandos had come. He leaned back as he walked, further back than the decline required. Knees, groin and face whined silent warnings along the nerve paths, the fear of an unexpected blow dragging him back like a harness. Behind him the viceroy began to grunt with the rhythm of Pendrake's steps, and Kane wished he'd waited for DuMorgan to come to instead of striking out on his own. And then there was light again, a thin blade of it, and Kane realized he was looking at the bottom of a door. He approached cautiously. The door was steel, set into a chipped frame of granite. There was no handle visible in the meager light that bled up from the sill. The door was locked. It could be opened only by a recorded palm pressed against its central plate.

"Viceroy," Kane whispered. "DuMorgan, snap out of it."

Pendrake lowered the stunned man to the floor. Du-Morgan's head lolled and his eyes remained shut, the lids inert. "You struck him quite hard, Elias. He was weak from hunger and abuse. . . ."

"I did what I had to do," Kane snapped. "One shout out of him and we'd have had an honor guard of rebels to take us where no one would ever find us. Then they'd have gone back to what they're doing now, which is why we've got to get through this door. Stand the viceroy up. I need his palm.''

Pendrake lifted DuMorgan and Kane pressed the viceroy's hand against the palmplate. The door rolled back, revealing a cellar stairway. The stairs led up into the living room of a house where a ceiling light burned. The living room was sparsely furnished—a sagging couch, two armchairs and a nicked wooden table. Kane dipped a finger into a half-full cup on the table. The coffee was still warm. They were in a staging area from which the commandos had just departed. There was no sign of a rear guard. The kitchen of the house was deserted too. Kane felt little relief that they were alone in the house. An empty staging area meant that the big push was already on. DuMorgan's second-in-command must have decided that, with the viceroy in Giacomin's cell, it was dangerous to wait any longer. It was an initiative DuMorgan would approve. Kane wondered how many other houses like this had spewed men into the tunnels beneath the palace. He searched the house quickly. There was no phone.

"Let's go," he said.

"May we not leave the viceroy here?" Pendrake asked.

"No. He's my prisoner."

"Surely, Elias, you can forget the enmity . . ."

"It's not a question of enmity," Kane said. "An attack is being launched against the palace right now by DuMorgan's men. We've captured DuMorgan, and it's my duty to see he doesn't get back with his men."

"But he will only slow us down. Is it not our first duty to warn the palace?"

"Are you too tired to carry him a bit farther?"

"No, Elias."

"All right, we'll leave him in the first vend-motel we can find. A vend-motel will have a phone. Carrying him there won't take any longer than leaving him here. Now let's go."

A side door led into a yard smelling of new-mown grass. Nearby street lights bathed neatly manicured lawns in a soft glow. Crickets chirped in a hedge beside the house's flagstone walk, a soothing sound from a separate reality. Kane looked up at the mesa that towered in the midst of the city, at the dazzling crown of the palace. Beneath that crown, desperate men were crawling up through smooth granite tunnels to gut an empire, while other people dozed away a summer evening on their back porch swings.

When they'd gotten several houses away on a deserted sidewalk, Kane motioned Pendrake to stop. "Put DuMorgan down," he said, "and we'll support him between us. If we run into anyone, we're just walking our drunk friend home." Pendrake eased the still unconscious viceroy down, pulling one arm over his shoulder while Kane took the other. DuMorgan's feet moved sluggishly, and his head bobbed as they hurried him through the warm, jasmine-scented darkness into the lights of Chronos' commercial district. By the time they'd found a vend-motel and gotten him into the last unit, DuMorgan was beginning to groan and mumble. They deposited him on the bed and Kane retrieved his credit card from the slot on the door, and slid the bolt. He went to the room's phone and dialed Alvar Sabin's private number. The vid-screen lit with static and then a printed message: *Phone temporarily out of service. Please try again later.*

"Damn!" Kane said.

"Perhaps another unit will have a working phone," Pendrake said.

"No. That burst of static means the whole system's down. The colonists must be jamming it so when they hit the palace no one can call out for reinforcements." Kane cursed again, the unconscious man on the bed, the nightmare that trapped him like a rising sea through which he must run. "Get some sheets from the bathroom and tie

DuMorgan up," he snapped. "I'm going to commandeer the nearest aircar. Meet me out front right away."

The Imperator was in a drawing room of his private quarters. The Empress Eunice sat in a shadowed corner. She eyed Kane and Pendrake with stony detachment as they came in, as though she associated them with everything that had befallen her husband. Beside Amerdath's life-support cart, Martha Reik was preparing to ease a trickle of sleep medication into the artificial circulatory system. Chuddath and the overhead blue eye of the compusayer watched Reik and everything else, a tandem of flesh and machine, of alien and of human once removed. The tranquillity of a night-silvered desert shone in through the perfect artifice of a holowall. Reik straightened and looked quizzically at Kane.

"Elias?" Amerdath queried.

"Sir, what I've come to say will raise a lot of questions, but there isn't time for them. Please believe that."

Amerdath's expression did not change. "What is it you want?"

"I want everyone out of this room immediately. Get up at least five levels. The middle floors of the palace would be best."

"But this suite has the most protection of any . . ."

"*Please*. While we're moving, have your compusayer turn out Sabin and the praetorian guard, every man. Have them deployed on the ground level of the palace ready for attack by armed commandos from below."

Amerdath stared at him. Seconds passed; Reik remained poised over the circulatory tubes, her fingers stilled. The Ornyl bodyguard tucked his vocal arms beneath the muscular fighting ones as he edged closer to Amerdath.

"Morulius!" the Imperator snapped.

"Yes, sir?" said a cultured voice from the ceiling.

"Do as Mr. Kane has asked. Use my image and voice

in your call to Commander Sabin in accordance with the code *Simulacrum.*''

"Code number, sir?"

"You know damned well there's no code number," Amerdath said with an incongruous lack of expression.

"Verified. I will comply at once."

Martha Reik activated the suspensors on the life-support cart and pushed it toward the private elevator of the suite. The Ornyl warrior loped ahead of her on his giant insect legs as the compusayer opened the doors of the lift. Pendrake offered his arm to the empress. She took it with stiff dignity and followed the others at an unhurried pace.

"There is a malfunction," the compusayer reported in its maddeningly calm voice. "Power to the elevator has just been cut off through sabotage in maintenance section 32A. I have locked the saboteur into the section and tranquilized him and am switching to auxiliary power."

"Have you reached Sabin?" Amerdath asked.

"I'm talking to him now, sir. I have also summoned all praetorian patrols in our vicinity."

There was a disciplined clatter of boots, and the door to the suite slid open, admitting about twenty of the black-suited palace guard, 'ruptors unslung and at the ready.

"Auxiliary power has also been cut off at the top of the shaft, sir," the compusayer said. Its next few words were drowned out by a keening noise from Chuddath. The warrior shoved Reik to the side and took charge of the life-support cart, pushing it back into the suite and bulling through the praetorians toward the door. There was an orange flash and an explosive whump in the corridor outside the suite. Something black and red windmilled through the door, narrowly missing the Imperator. Kane winced as the thing splattered against the holowall and slid down to the edge of the desert scene. It was a praetorian pulped into a mass of flesh and bone by the explosion. Chuddath reversed the cart as the praetorians already inside the door turned in the direction of the blast.

". . . in sector 1B," the compusayer intoned. "The guard is mobilizing. Main units should arrive in four point five minutes if there are no further explosions . . ."

"Never mind that," the Imperator said. "Can you drop a shield?"

"If you will move to the designated area, sir, I do not think that function is impaired."

Chuddath pushed the cart back to its original location and stepped back as a clear cylinder thumped down from the ceiling to enclose Amerdath. The Ornyl braced his back against the shield and faced the door. Smoke poured in from the hallway and sirens began to wail. Kane looked around for Reik, saw her attempting to coax the Empress Eunice back out of the elevator. The older woman was balking, trying to pry the physician's fingers from her arm. Kane started in her direction and then the ceiling tilted down, rushed under his feet as a hot breeze fanned his face. The sound of the explosion carried him like a wave, the seconds ticking by with nightmare slowness. The ceiling skidded to a halt. He stared up at it between upraised feet. The aftershock of something breaking his fall at the shoulders and knees welled up in bruised muscle. The ringing faded into shouts and screams and he pushed himself up from the flattened armchair, shaking his head drunkenly. The explosion had opened another hole, this one in the floor of the suite, about ten meters from him. Through the smoke he could see Amerdath's protective cylinder beyond the breach, still intact. Praetorians ringed the cylinder and fought on either side of the alien warrior for whom they ordinarily showed such contempt.

The colonist commandos *had* dressed in black, Kane saw, just as he and Pendrake remembered from their glimpse in the tunnel. Their uniforms were like those of the praetorian guard. He felt a distant admiration for the strategy as he ran to a fallen guard and pulled the man's 'ruptor from limp fingers. The colonists would have drilled themselves in instant recognition of some unobtrusive feature of their own uniforms, some small but clearly visible way in which it differed from the praetorian dress. The guard, having no such preparation, would be confused, would hesitate just that extra, fatal second before firing.

The blue bolt of a 'ruptor crackled past Kane's face, singeing his cheek and sending him into a dive. He brought the 'ruptor around to fire as he fell, but he glimpsed only black uniforms among black, and his finger froze on the trigger until the blast came again. Then he saw the man who was shooting at him and fired back, rolled, and fired again, and the difference registered. Kane stared, as the man toppled forward, at the crest of ceremonial decorations pinned high to the chest. Such medals were worn by praetorian officers on ceremonial occasions but never on regular duty or in battle. The colonists were recognizing each other easily, while the praetorians, in the heat of the fighting, were failing to make the crucial judgment.

"Medals," Kane shouted. "They're wearing medals." The din was too great and he knew he was not being heard. A panel slid aside behind the cylinder that protected Amerdath and fresh praetorians poured into the room, then slowed in confusion. Kane ran crouching to the side of the barrier and shouted up into the compusayer pick-up. "Morulius, Morulius, acknowledge."

"There is no need to shout, Mr. Kane."

"Broadcast at maximum volume: colonists are wearing ceremonial medals. Maximum volume and keep repeating."

"Acknowledged."

The compusayer began braying the message. Kane glimpsed the Imperator, alone and still inside the cylinder, before someone crashed into him, knocking him to his hands and knees and jarring the 'ruptor loose. He scrabbled for the 'ruptor, but someone tripped over it first, kicked it away. A weight descended, elbows and knees jamming, hands groping for his throat. Kane gouged at the eyes and then, as the man reared back, snapped a collarbone with the edge of his hand. Shoving the convulsed

form away, Kane got his feet under him again. To his right
he saw Chuddath, still backed against the cylinder, arms
churning at a speed the eye could not frame. Before he
could turn away, Kane saw the heads of two men torn off.
He bent over, gagging, but nothing came up. He straightened to see Pendrake wading through a crowd of combatants,
a wounded praetorian slung over one shoulder and a squirming bloodied colonist on the other. Kane saw Martha Reik
helping the alien ease the injured men into a cleared square
of floor in the corner before the fighting closed again in
front of them. The compusayer was still blaring its message, and a ragged order of battle was beginning to take
shape as praetorians continued to pour into the Imperator's
quarters. Kane saw Alvar Sabin behind a knot of his men,
red-faced and shouting orders that were drowned out in the
clamor of the compusayer.

Kane shouted at Morulius to stop broadcasting, and the
machine cut off in mid-sentence. Sabin got his men into a
phalanx that began to shove the bulk of the attackers back
and out of the room. Colonists began to retreat into the
breached floor beside Amerdath's shield. Praetorians charged
down into the tunnel after them, and the hiss of sidearms
threw up waves of acrid heat-distorted air. As the main
body of attackers was forced back through the door of the
suite, colonists beyond them could no longer move up. A
stream of covering fire began to converge through the
doorway. Sabin screamed at his men to pull up and return
fire. 'Ruptor beams buzzed through the room, the field of
fire narrowing as the colonists continued to pull back. The
space around the Imperator's shield was cleared now.
Kane stared through at Amerdath's profile, chilled by the
man's remote expression. It was as though the outcome
did not matter to Amerdath, or perhaps even that he was
disappointed. At what? The tide of the battle? Kane knew
it was something else, and the chill deepened. He turned
away as Amerdath's head began, clairvoyantly, to rotate
toward him atop the life-support cart.

Time and details blurred. Kane jumped down into the tunnel under the Imperator's quarters and found himself in a hell of blue light and screaming men. He grabbed another 'ruptor and ran up and down beneath the Imperator's quarters, pulling wounded back to the breach and handing them up to Pendrake and Reik. Once he collided with a colonist who'd doubled back in confusion, and grappled with the man, smelling his sweat, feeling his fear in the spasms of muscle driving mindlessly for escape. He let the man go. When he was too exhausted to push bodies from the tunnel, Pendrake dragged him up by the wrists and he wandered through the smoking ruin of Amerdath's quarters. He was standing a few feet from Amerdath's shield when Alvar Sabin came to make his report. Sabin was flanked by two majors and Kane thought how absurd the formality seemed in the midst of such chaos. The commander's white-blond hair was stuck to his head with sweat and there were smudges of ash on his cheek and jaw. His uniform was torn and his shoulders sagged with weariness, but there was a maniacal grin on his face.

"They're beaten, sir. It's all over but the mopping up." Amerdath said nothing and Sabin's grin faded. "We're chasing them down the tunnels now, sir. We'll get all but the few cowards who were first to run."

"Very good, Alvar. Carry on."

Sabin saluted and moved off. Kane stumbled over to Amerdath's shield and sagged against it. Chuddath was just beyond the clear curvature, standing motionless now, the fighting arms still extended. With peripheral vision Kane caught the twitch of movement on the floor. He turned and shouted as the wounded colonist brought his weapon to bear on the Ornyl warrior, but he was too late. The blade of energy sheared into the alien, and one of the great fighting arms fell away from the insect-man's body. Kane lunged, kicked the 'ruptor away from the commando. The man collapsed again onto his face. Kane fell across him on hands and knees and stared at the blood-soaked carpet, fighting back nausea. He felt a massive hand on his shoulder and looked up. The Ornyl was stooping over him. A sticky greenish fluid congealed on the stump of the missing arm. The alien's vocal arms extended and moved easily over the abdominal chitin.

"I thank you . . . Elias Kane. Do . . . not be disturbed. This will . . . be my fourth arm."

Then Kane did throw up.

CHAPTER 31

Kane waited a day before telling Amerdath. He knew that the next attempt to kill the Imperator of the Terran Empire could come at any time, and yet he waited. He thought about it on the night of the battle, after he'd returned to his room and flopped on his bed, exhausted but unable to sleep. When at last he did doze off, it was with the light over his bed burning into his face. Perhaps sometime he would sleep again in the dark, but not soon. Not soon.

He got up at noon and let Pendrake haggle him into eating. He picked through two stacks of toast, chewing and swallowing mechanically, and left the rest of the breakfast untouched. Pendrake went with him to the garden where Beth was killed.

"You know who killed her," the alien said after walking with him, up and back between the glittering hedges and lush fragrant trellises. "You know who is trying to kill the Imperator."

"I know," Kane admitted. He stopped at the spot where Beth fell. Pendrake said nothing while he stooped and dug his fingers into the warm brown earth. He stood again and looked at the soiled hand for a long time before yielding to the urge of conditioning, the civilized and unthinking need to brush the dirt off. He walked to the edge of the garden and sat on a stone bench. Pendrake settled beside him and looked up at the sky.

"You do not wish to tell me?"

"My friend, I don't wish to tell anyone."

"If you do not tell the Imperator, will there be further assassination attempts?"

"I think so."

"Then you must tell him, Elias."

"You don't understand."

Pendrake continued to stare up at the arid blue of the sky. For a long time he gazed up, as though teasing some pattern from the void. Then he looked at Kane, and there was compassion in the dark alien eyes. "I think perhaps I do understand."

Kane called Martha Reik on his way to the executive offices and asked her to meet him there. One of Morulius' ceiling eyes scanned him and Pendrake and passed them through to a brace of praetorian captains, who immediately escorted them into Amerdath's presence. The Imperator was eating an apple held for him with incongruous daintiness by the single huge hand of the Ornyl bodyguard. A cart laden with lunch meats, coffee and rolls sat in front of Amerdath's life-support cart. He finished chewing and made a little subvocal sound, and Chuddath withdrew the half-finished apple and moved around to his customary place behind the Imperator.

"Elias, Pendrake, I've been calling around for you."

"We were in the garden, sir."

Amerdath's eyes steadied on Kane's. "I see. Well, I thought you might be interested in a report on the colonist attack—something we weren't aware of last night."

"The colonists hit Giacomin's section at the same time they were attacking you," Kane said.

"Then you already knew?"

"I'd guessed it. And Giacomin is dead?"

"He and all his subchiefs," Amerdath said, his face contemplative. "What else would you guess?"

"That the data banks of the Special Branch computers were wiped clean."

Amerdath's eyes narrowed. "Very good, Elias. There's nothing left, including the extensive matrix pertaining to known and suspected colonist subversives and their activities. The commandos even got the back-up computers hidden in a secret subbasement level. Giacomin's successor will have to start from scratch. I thought you ought to know that, since I'm offering you the position."

Kane bit back the instant refusal, not wanting it to become an issue that would delay what he had come to say. "I'm honored that you'd consider me, sir."

Amerdath snorted. "You don't fool me for a second. It's a damn shame, too, because I need you, Elias. Now more than ever. I can't mourn Giacomin personally, and I think you understand why as well as anyone. But he was a relentless and ingenious enemy of my enemies."

"And of some of your friends, too, sir."

"Perhaps." Amerdath sighed. "We didn't find Du-Morgan, you know."

Kane felt a relief so vast that it shocked him. It had been his duty to report leaving DuMorgan tied up in the vend-motel room. After the battle, he had told the story of Giacomin's unreported capture and interrogation of the viceroy and then he had closed his mind to it. DuMorgan had planned an attack on the palace and that made him an enemy of the Empire, and there was no other course. But the thought of the viceroy escaping made Kane want to cheer. The disloyalty of the impulse and all of its implications he would consider later. He had not caused the death of a proud and honorable man, and that was all that mattered now.

"Perhaps you should add a boy scout course on knots to your more academic credits," Amerdath said dryly.

Kane glanced at Pendrake who, after all, had been the one to tie DuMorgan. The alien's face would look calm and impassive to anyone else, but Kane saw the slight wrinkling of the simian upper lip, the trace of a smile around the eyes. "Perhaps so, sir."

"Well, no matter. He was a loyal viceroy in better days, and I would not have relished dealing with him. His conspiracy here is ended, the rebels crushed, thanks to you. We'll fill the bottom level of the palace with beta-steel and leave the tunnels to remind us of our complacency. If you hadn't given us the head start on mobilizing the guard, I wouldn't have had twenty good praetorians to hold off the first rush, and they'd have nailed me for sure. It's a relief to know that the guard is loyal; that it was the colonists all along who were trying to kill me."

Kane felt the moment arrive and yet he hesitated. "Yes, sir, the guard is loyal and always was—everyone but Clemis. But it was not the colonists who were trying to kill you."

Amerdath gazed at him without any visible reaction. "Don't be ridiculous. Of course it was the colonists. You were there last night."

"Yes, I was there, helping fight off a diversionary feint on you while a select cadre of commandos killed their real enemy and wiped out his private empire."

"Giacomin? You think their whole purpose was to destroy Giacomin and the Special Branch?"

"That and rescue Richard DuMorgan, who they thought was still in Giacomin's prison. Think about it, sir. Before Giacomin set DuMorgan up to capture Pendrake and me, you were sure the viceroy was loyal—and you were right. DuMorgan *was* loyal to you. Perhaps he still could be. But he knew that Giacomin would never rest until he had succeeded in poisoning your mind against the colonies. He knew in a way that you could not just how paranoid and xenophobic Giacomin's self-appointed mission was, and how dangerous to any future hope of peace between Earth and the colonies.''

"But, damn it, Elias, there *was* a colonist conspiracy. They took you captive. They melted tunnels into the granite beneath this palace. They attacked last night.''

"Only because Giacomin's warmongering became a self-fulfilling prophecy. DuMorgan had to mount a major effort to stop him. He had to do more than kill Giacomin, he had to destroy his files.''

"But doesn't that prove that the computers had damaging evidence of colonist plots?''

Kane shook his head. "Computers can only work with the information they're given. Giacomin and his henchmen fed the Special Branch computers—every suspicion, every innuendo, everything that looked or smelled wrong to them. But they were already sure that a plot existed. They saw what they wanted to see, and they filed it away. If the colonists limited themselves to assassinating Giacomin, his successor would only inherit the computers and find the black and white 'proof' of a colonist conspiracy, not the shades of paranoia and bias. No, DuMorgan knew he had to cauterize it all. That's why he made the tunnels and mounted a major attack on the palace—to wipe the slate clean.''

"I still don't see the advantage of it. What I might think was in those destroyed computers could be even worse than what he wiped out.''

"It was a gamble," Kane admitted. "But DuMorgan saw which way things were going. There were a lot of innocent names in those computers. I think Richard DuMorgan cares a very great deal for his people, sir.''

Amerdath's eyes focused beyond Kane. "I wonder if it's too late," he said softly.

"Your wondering that is a start, but I'm afraid DuMorgan does think it's too late. He'll have to be convinced, and I don't know if that's possible.''

The twin doors to the executive chambers opened and one of the captains ushered Martha Reik in. Amerdath made a failed effort to smile in greeting.

"Thanks for coming," Kane murmured. She nodded. He could smell her perfume, a scent like vanilla, more distracting than it should have been.

"All right, Elias," Amerdath said. "Let's just suppose it wasn't DuMorgan and the colonist underground who've been trying to retire me. Then who the hell was it?"

"The one person I could never suspect," Kane answered, "and yet the only person it could be." He looked beyond Amerdath into the faceted eyes of the Ornyl warrior.

CHAPTER 32

The bodyguard did not move. Amerdath's mouth fell open and he stared at Kane. "Are you out of your mind? Chuddath is linked to me by the S'edhite bond. He is incapable of the slightest disloyalty to me."

Kane turned to Reik. "Martha, I want to ask you for a medical opinion."

She glanced at Chuddath, then back at Kane. "I'm no expert on Ornyl physiology."

"I'm not asking that. I want you to summarize your evaluation of the Imperator's adjustment to losing his body."

"Really, Elias . . ."

"No, no," Amerdath broke in. "It's all right, Martha. By all means go ahead."

"Well . . ." Reik began. "He's obviously made an incredible recovery . . ."

"You use the word recovery," Kane said. "Does that mean you consider him to be back to normal?"

"How do you define 'normal'? Of course he's not leading the same life he would if he had not been . . . injured."

"I was hoping you could define 'normal,' " Kane said. "How would a man normally react to what happened to the Imperator?"

"The shock might well kill him at the start," Reik replied without hesitation. "If not, then there would be a rapid physical recovery, since there remains essentially no injured tissue to burden the system and . . . ah, much less system to be burdened."

"How about emotionally?"

Reik studied him before answering. "There would be a profound depression, perhaps a chronic depression for many months or years."

"Have you observed such a depression in the Imperator?"

"No . . . I haven't observed any depression."

"Then there has been no depression?"

"I didn't say that. I said I've *observed* no depression."

"Oh." Kane glanced at Amerdath. "Does that mean the Imperator might be having a depression that you are not able to observe?"

"It's possible."

"He could be hiding it, then."

"He might be unaware of it," Reik said, looking steadily at Kane.

Amerdath grunted. "I don't see what you're driving at, Elias. I'm not depressed. . . ."

"Not that you're aware, sir."

"What kind of rubbish is that?"

Kane walked closer to Amerdath, forming and re-forming the words in his mind. "Sir, I was given a drug by Fowler Giacomin just before we escaped into the tunnel system. The drug cut me off from my senses, from touch, heat, cold; from the sensations of my arms and legs. I couldn't feel my body. It was as though I had no body. It only lasted for about half an hour, but I screamed inside myself. I screamed and went on screaming." Kane looked into Amerdath's eyes and saw the fear yawning deep behind the pupils. "I was where you are, sir. For just a half hour,

I was there. And I can tell you that if I had to go back, if I had to stay in that place for the rest of my life . . ."

"What . . . are . . . you . . . ?"

"Chuddath *is* loyal to you," Kane said. "Completely and unquestioningly loyal. That's why he tried to kill you. Twice he tried. He saw it in your mind every time you linked—a part of your mind that even you would not acknowledge. The never-ending command: *Kill me, kill me, kill me*. . . ."

The warrior leaped around the cart and even though Kane had been expecting it, the lashing arm nearly took his head with the first stroke. He rolled on the floor, his hair pushed up where the armored wrist had grazed it. A gray-green foot smashed down next to his face and he rolled the other way. Reik screamed something at Amerdath. Kane caught a dizzying glimpse of Pendrake jumping over him and then the floor shook as both aliens crashed against it. Kane scrambled up in time to see Pendrake absorb a tremendous blow across an upraised forearm. The Ornyl straddled the other alien and hammered at the face and chest with his single arm. Pendrake tried to shield himself but made no attempt to strike back. Kane ran to the Imperator, shouted into the dazed face until Amerdath blinked and looked down with dreamlike slowness at the struggling aliens.

"Stop," he murmured at last.

Chuddath's arm froze at the top of a swing. He raised his head to the Imperator and Kane could feel the plea locked behind the expressionless insect face.

"Get off him." Amerdath's voice was slow and befuddled. "Stand in front of me."

The bodyguard obeyed and Pendrake got up, rubbing his arms and flexing his hands. "Are you all right?" Kane asked.

"Perfectly, Elias. I only hope the Ornyl did not injure his remaining arm."

The warrior keened his rage and frustration and Kane

choked back a hysterical urge to laugh. He turned back to the Imperator. Amerdath was gazing at his bodyguard, at the hideous creature that was closer to him than any human could ever be.

"Is what Kane says true? Is that what you've been seeing in my mind—the command to finish me?"

The Ornyl stood rigid. The vocal arms jerked. "No, Imperator."

"He's still being loyal," Kane said. "He knows you don't want to hear him say yes."

"Damn it, I want the truth," Amerdath shouted. "I've *got* to have it."

Chuddath's arms made several passes before a barely audible moan emerged. "Imperator . . . knows the truth."

Amerdath's eyes pinched shut then, and tears began to seep between the quivering lashes. Reik went to him and reached up, smoothing the white hair again and again while Amerdath wept. "Go ahead," she said softly. "Don't stop. Let it out."

At last Amerdath's face firmed and he opened eyes now puffy and rimmed in red. "Do you know, Martha, that's the first time anyone's physically touched me since I lost my body? I mean really *touched* me."

She looked down at the life-support equipment and then raised fists to cover her own eyes.

"I should have known," Amerdath said. "I wouldn't let myself know. Oh, I thought about killing myself, but I can't, you see. What would I do? Take poison? Shoot myself? I can't even hold my breath and pass out. I'm *helpless*. Too helpless even to die. I knew all this. What I wouldn't face is that I was determined to die anyway. I put it all on Chuddath—I'm sorry, old friend. I'm sorry. God forgive me for asking this, but if you really saw that I wanted to die, why didn't you just wait until we were alone and blast me?"

"That's horrible," Reik exclaimed. "You would not

have wanted Chuddath put to death for your murder. If he
had done that . . ."

"You don't understand," Amerdath said. "Of course I
wouldn't have wanted it, but that's beside the point. If I
asked it, Chuddath would turn the blaster on his own brain
without hesitating. If he truly saw that I longed to die, he
could have killed me straight out. The consequences to
him would not concern him. His loyalty, as you put it,
Elias, would come first over everything else."

"But that loyalty is the very reason . . ."

"I am here," Chuddath said, interrupting Kane. "I will
speak . . . for myself. Imperator wished . . . to die. But
Imperator is . . . a proud man. A true king." The warrior
was silent a moment. Kane gazed at him, feeling for the
first time a true and deep sympathy for the grotesque alien.
"If I had openly killed . . . Imperator, Kane and . . .
others who know the . . . S'edhite bond would have
understood. Imperator could not . . . bear the humiliation
of . . . being remembered as a suicide." Chuddath lifted
his remaining fighting arm fractionally and then let it fall
again, as though he had wished to place a comforting hand
on the shoulder Amerdath no longer had. "You did not
wish either . . . to dishonor your family. You did not
wish . . . even after death . . . to seem weak. All this I
saw too . . . when we were linked."

A fresh gloss came to Amerdath's eyes, but he clenched
his jaws, and the tears did not spill. Reik turned to Kane.
"Then Clemis *was* telling the truth. He was just a crazy
religious fanatic who acted alone."

"That's right. We were on the verge of believing that
when the second attempt—the Imperator's first unconscious attempt at suicide, arranged through Chuddath—came
to convince us all that there *was* a conspiracy.'

"It even convinced me," Amerdath said. "That's how
thoroughly I was denying it."

"There were signs of the truth," Kane said, "but none
of us wanted to see them. The second attempt came right

after the failure to attach the artificial body. Chuddath forced the page to write the note. He killed him with a chop to the neck and hung him with the atomizer belt on. Before this he had sprayed the tubing of Amerdath's life-support system with diluted cattaric acid, doing it in a way the compusayer couldn't detect—easy, since there would be nothing suspicious in Chuddath's moving very close to Amerdath.''

Pendrake frowned. "Excuse me, Elias, but Chuddath is large—a distinctive-looking alien. Would not someone around the page's quarters remember seeing him? And yet you had all of the inhabitants questioned and no one reported seeing the Ornyl.''

Chuddath made a derisive sound.

"You're not giving him enough credit," Kane agreed. "Chuddath is not just a big, distinctive-looking alien, he's an expert in all aspects of warfare—and he has all the skills of the insect. He could take an aircar to the roof of the building and get out only when he was sure no one was around. His senses are vastly superior to ours in the ability to detect anyone nearby. He would make no sound going down the hallway or coming out again.''

"It's true," Amerdath said. "He could do it easily."

Kane turned back to the Imperator. "Your depression worsened when you saw you couldn't have the artificial body. It worsened again when you saw that you could not bring yourself to take Clemis' body either. The third attempt came right after that. Chuddath spliced the extra power source into the queson generator while he was helping the praetorians guard it.'' Kane paused and the silence grew heavy. "I could have seen it earlier," he said, "but the fact is, none of us wanted to understand. You regarded yourself as weak and helpless, and compensated with rigid control, acting out the old role of command that we all demanded of you.''

"Well, it's finished now," Amerdath said. His voice was low, and too breathy, as though the vocal cords could no longer summon themselves to the proper tension. "There'll be no more hiding."

"Good," Reik said. "You can learn to deal with it . . ."

"No, Martha. I *can't* learn to deal with it. Thinking that I could is what brought all of this about. I was a strong man, but there are things I cannot do."

"But there are ways you haven't tried. Psycho-therapy . . ."

"Not for this, Martha. The problem doesn't originate in my unconscious, even if it did try to hide there. The problem is that I had arms and legs and a heart. I had a stomach and I had gonads, and I was a human being. That's what I signed up for when I was born. Someone else, someone stronger than me—or weaker, maybe—might be able to deal with this. I can't. I want to die. Do you understand me, Elias?"

Kane thought about the half hour in the tunnel, the drug-induced panic that he would never again be able to *feel*. "Yes, sir. I do."

"Good. Will you clear this room please and see that no one disturbs Chuddath and me for the next five minutes?"

"No, sir, I won't."

There was a room in the palace that was built like a vault. It contained its own fully independent life-support systems—circulated air, power, water, food stores and everything else necessary to withstand a prolonged siege. Its purpose was to provide a place of safety for the royal family in the event of a palace revolt. There were several such safe-rooms at strategic locations throughout the palace. The great door of each towered ten meters high. The facing of the door was a bronze bas-relief, intricately molded, impressive. It would say to anyone wishing to break it down, *Beyond this door waits the Imperator of the Terran Empire*. The door would open only to a member of the royal family or to the Ornyl bodyguard, Chuddath.

Amerdath sat atop the life-support cart in the center of

the vault room. A cone of soft light shone down on him from the ceiling of the vault, giving his hair the luxuriant sheen of silver. There was no sign that only a day earlier millions of microscopically small slivers had passed through that hair without ruffling it, embedding themselves in carefully selected matrices of brain tissue. A lifetime of memories had been brought to the edge of the present, firmed up, prepared to happen at Amerdath's whim. In the same way that thought can be directed, Amerdath had learned to direct his memories, to draw them into the solid three-dimensional instant of the eternal present. He would live them all again. He would walk and love and run and hurt, and he would escape into the sleep of the body, and awaken mornings with a pleasantly stiff back. He would fight the unification wars again, and pin the Legion of Mars on a loyal Richard DuMorgan, and it would be the first time each time. Life would not go on for Gregory Amerdath, but he would cheat death. Perhaps for a thousand years he would cheat it, while perfectly pure and nutrified blood circled endlessly through the flesh that was left to him.

Outside the great door to the vault stood Alvar Sabin, the Princess Briana, Kane and Martha Reik. Not wanting his presence to antagonize the Ornyl in the other alien's hour of grief, Pendrake had declined to be present. Lucian and the Empress Eunice were not in attendance either, and their reasons remained private.

Reik raised a hand to catch the Imperator's attention. "I'll check the life-support systems daily," she said.

"I know, Martha."

"The outside telltales will alert us right away if anything needs attention. . . ."

Amerdath smiled with weary patience. "I'm not worried."

"Well, damn it, I'm worried."

"That's why you're the Imperial physician. Daughter?"

Briana stepped forward. She was wearing the uniform of

a praetorian guard, bare of any symbol except the tree emblem of the Amerdath line at her belt. "Yes, Father?"

"You are Imperator now. I ask you to remember only one thing. The colonies are already frightened of you. You have nothing to prove to them. Bend every effort to peace."

Briana returned his stern look. "As you said, Father. I am Imperator now."

Amerdath scowled and then smoothed his face with an effort. "I suppose that is the only good answer an Imperator could give," he said.

"May *you* have peace, Father."

"I'll have it, and you must guard it well . . . Imperator. Do not awaken me, not ever, unless it is to give me back the body."

Briana inclined her head and stepped back again, and Kane was amazed to see a tear wobble down the perfect curve of her cheek, a pioneer finding no path already broken. Chuddath swung the great brass door shut with a clang of finality, turned and braced his back against it. He made no further movement, and could almost have been a part of the carved door, a jade sentinel who would rage to life if anyone came too close. The lost fighting arm had begun to regenerate—a misshapen nub on which the buds of finger and thumb were beginning to be visible. Sabin and Briana walked off together, the Imperator in the lead and the old soldier striding with an air of long-suffering dignity behind her.

Reik stared at the vault door for a long time and then moved against Kane with a suddenness made clumsy by urgency. "I need someone to hold on to right now," she said.

Kane hung an arm across her shoulders and pulled her closer, walking her away from the vault. "So do I," he said.

Behind them the Ornyl warrior began the long vigil over his dreaming lord.

Steven Spruill has a B.A. in biology and a Ph.D. in clinical psychology. He is a full-time author. His previous novels include *Keepers of the Gate*, *The Janus Equation*, *Hellstone*, and the first Elias Kane adventure, *The Psychopath Plague*.

GORDON R. DICKSON

CONAN

"Nobody alive writes Conan better than Robert Jordan" —L. Sprague de Camp

FRED SABERHAGEN

62515

HARRY HARRISON

☐	48505-0	A Transatlantic Tunnel, Hurrah!	$2.50
☐	48540-9	The Jupiter Plague	$2.95
☐	48565-4	Planet of the Damned	$2.95
☐	48557-3	Planet of No Return	$2.75
☐	48031-8	The QE2 Is Missing	$2.95
☐	48554-9	A Rebel in Time	$3.50